"And it has to do with México Irredenta, General Robles." Oliver sighed mentally.

"Very much so," said Robles. Again the general was looking up the street past Oliver. He frowned at whatever he was looking at. Smiling, politely puzzled, Oliver leaned toward the balustrade, turning to follow the direction of Robles's eyes.

And then—in the corner of Oliver's right eye— the general slammed his beer on the tabletop, the goblet shattering before Oliver's face, bursting like shrapnel, shards of glass glistening in the air. The general lurched backward, then slumped toward the table, coughing, banging his head into the glassy mess on the plastic tabletop.

Also by John Horton
Published by Ivy Books:

THE HOTEL AT TARASCO
A BLACK LEGEND

THE RETURN OF INOCENCIO BROWN

John Horton

IVY BOOKS • NEW YORK

Ivy Books
Published by Ballantine Books
Copyright © 1991 by John Horton

Library of Congress Catalog Card Number: 91-91841

ISBN 0-8041-0563-4

Manufactured in the United States of America

First Edition: June 1991

To the anonymous members of
that international legion
who, like Inocencio Brown,
were the shock troops
of the operations of the CIA

To actuality the novel owes nothing, although to reality it gives total allegiance. . . .

—LIONEL TRILLING, "A Novel of the Thirties"

Chapter 1

The CIA officer's mood was as low and gray as the sky when he braked his car to a stop at the VIP parking lot in front of CIA Headquarters. It was raining hard and the traffic had been terrible coming back into Virginia from Washington. From the looks of the people in the other cars they would have been out exchanging their Christmas presents for larger sizes. Some would have been at Boxing Day parties, as he was supposed to be, too. He bet he was the only one on the road doing any work that day. Trust the National Security Council to pop a long-drawn-out emergency interagency meeting the day after Christmas. Lucky it hadn't dragged on into the night! Trust it to rain. Lucky it wasn't snow with the lousy Washington drivers! As it was, the late-afternoon columns of constipated traffic barely crept across the Theodore Roosevelt Bridge. He'd timed it. He had to sit for one stretch of twelve minutes without even moving, windshield wipers thumping, in plain sight of the cars swishing along the gleaming dark macadam just past the ramp to George Washington Memorial Parkway. God! He could walk it!

A quarter mile ahead in the gray murk the lights of a police car flashed red on the wet roofs of a hundred shining cars. He beat his hands on the steering wheel when he thought about the overweight intellectual type who had held him up in the hall when he burst out of the meeting on Syria. He was in one hell of a hurry to get back and get a cable out to Beirut. He was half running down the high echoing hall of the Old Executive Office Building when this self-important idiot in the thick glasses materialized right there in front of him. If he was going back to

1

Langley, would he mind very much sending a most urgent inquiry from the Latin American element of NSC to the CIA station in Mexico? Yeah, yeah. Actually he minded the hell out of it. Where is it? Turned out the fathead hadn't even taken the trouble to put his most urgent inquiry down on a piece of paper. So he lost more time standing there in the high-ceilinged hall, scrawling the message down on the back of his own goddamn manila envelope. Jesus!

Now he put a smile on his face as he rolled down the window to talk to the ex-marine in the black slicker, the black cap cover, the black boots, sloshing toward him through the puddles and the rain from the shelter of his kiosk. "Merry Christmas, gunny. I swear to God my regular space is a good fifteen miles from the building. Anyway, it's after five, isn't it."

"Strictly against regs!" barked the parking-lot supervisor. He winked and grinned. "Right over there, sir. Anywhere. Merry Christmas!"

"Semper fi!"

Even that close to the building he got good and wet running through the rain. He took off his topcoat and shook it as soon as he got inside, swiped the rain from his forehead, the sound of his quick footsteps clattering off the walls of the deserted foyer. His socks were soaked.

He was putting the wet topcoat on a hanger in his own office while he dialed the watch office number, cradling the phone under his chin. "Hi. Get this down to Mexico, will you?" He read off the short message. "No, I don't," he said. "No. Listen. This goofball at the NSC dictated it at me as I was leaving a meeting over there. Said it was urgent. That's the one. Well, if you want, you can call him. No. How would I know his number? Well, don't send it then. It's no skin off—Yeah? Well, that's too bad. Stick around. I've got a long one coming myself." He hung up and went out to the table by the secretary's vacant desk to find the coffeepot cold and empty. "Aw, Jesus," he said.

The watch office supervisor looked at the draft of the cable to Mexico. "Pretty thin stuff to be so urgent," she said.

The man in shirtsleeves shrugged and took a sip of coffee. "That's all he gave me. You know, NSC equals urgent. Oh, and the Mexico desk doesn't answer."

She shrugged, too, and tossed the cable into her out basket. "This can go routine."

The following afternoon, the drinkers at the next table at the University Club on the Paseo de la Reforma in Mexico City were laughing, topping the leather dice cups with their palms, making the dice rattle hollow in the cups. In the restrained orange light of the chandelier hanging above the formal clubroom, Jack Winters leaned across the table toward Ted Oliver. Winters was trying to make himself heard, frowning at the crescendo of shouting as the dice rolled to see who would pay for the last round of drinks. Winters made a face as a wild die shot through the air to bounce on the floor and flicker past his chair, clicking to a stop at the wall. He leaned forward, his faded blue eyes disapproving. An athletic-looking young North American in dark suit and bow tie skidded after the die, as though chasing a Ping Pong ball. Winters asked Oliver to repeat himself. "I couldn't hear a word you said."

"The word was *no*. No can do."

Winters sat back in his chair, shaking his large bald head from side to side, the corners of his mouth pulled down, his heavy thighs spread apart. With both hands he took his dark gray waistcoat by its points and yanked it down over his stomach. He picked up his empty glass, rattled the ice in it, sipped the dregs, handed it to the waiter, pointing at Oliver's glass as he did. Oliver nodded to the waiter.

There was a burst of elated cackling from the next table. "Please!" thundered Winters. "Gentlemen!"

"Sorry, Jack," their nearest neighbor called over his shoulder, including Oliver in his smile. "Hold it down, fellas," he said. The other four kept up their hooting, paying no more attention to him than they did to Winters.

"Louts!" Winters mouthed to Oliver in a low tone. He might as well have said it aloud. "Why not, for Pete's sake, Ted? This is critical."

"Well, a couple of reasons. I can't go running in to the ambassador and get him to put his prestige on the line in some kind of Chamber of Commerce squabble—"

"Well, of course, if you were to put it to him like that—"

"What's more, the ambassador is orderly. Wouldn't expect that from me. He'd want that from his commercial counselor. I guess I could talk to *him* about it. But he's awfully touchy about—"

Winters had drawn his large face into a heavily wrinkled scowl. He leaned back in his chair and spread the lapels of his jacket to tuck his thumbs into waistcoat pockets. "I've talked to him. Finicky little fellow, isn't he? It's guerrilla warfare in the Chamber, I tell you, Ted. Quite beyond your commercial counselor's comprehension." Winters showed disgust by flapping his large hands like flippers.

"And touchy about his prerogatives, I was saying. About his turf, as you would say."

"No, I would not!" said Winters.

Oliver grinned. "Jack, the Chamber is his pidgin, not mine. And look." Oliver gave his head a quick shake. "The ambassador's got one hell of a lot more to worry about in Mexico than playing nursemaid to the American business community, getting in the middle of some spat, catching it from both sides. You know."

They were silent as the waiter came to put drinks before them, setting a fresh dish of peanuts on the dark varnished tabletop. The dice players had left their table and were guffawing toward the cloakroom, their voices ringing in the high ceiling above them. Winters was watching them through hooded eyes he then directed at Oliver. "Didn't expect *you* to take the bureaucratic tack."

Oliver bared his teeth in a false grin and raised his scotch to Winters.

Winters's cheeks puffed with a short laugh despite himself. "Rather counting on you, Ted. Told them I thought I could find one sensible person in the embassy. Someone who'd understand the threat this presents to everything we stand for. The ambassador would listen to you. Oh, I didn't say who. Don't worry."

He sighed. "Hate to go back to them with nothing." Winters turned his body stiffly to look around the room that had lapsed into its dim air of end-of-nineteenth-century elegance, a last lush souvenir of the Porfirato. Winters's large head, the neck of the same diameter, the shoulders that strained the dark gray cloth of his suit, worked as a fused unit. "Thank God that bunch has gone. Those vulgar conglomerates pay no attention who they send down here." He picked up his drink. "Something more in your line, then. You've heard of this bunch that calls itself México Redenta? Nutty left, lunatic fringe sort of thing?"

Oliver leaned to clutch peanuts from the dish. He was some ten years younger than Winters and looked the younger for being slimmer. "Sounds religious the way you put it." He sat back in his chair, chewing, dusting his hands, rubbing one hand across the balding top of his scalp, across the thicker graying blond hair further back on his head. "If it's the outfit I'm thinking about, it's Irredenta, actually. México Irredenta. What about it?"

"Oh, well, Redenta, Irredenta, either way, crackpots, as I understand it." Winters made a slurping sound with his drink. "Political crackpots—huh. Excuse me! Out of channels. Take it to your political counselor."

Oliver laughed. "Go on, Jack."

"Not much more to it. Fellow I know lives down near San Miguel—old friend—Carlos Robles—retired general. Ever run into him? No? You'd like him. Very pro-American. Thinks we should be alerted. Says it's the nasty sort of thing we should know about. Ah!" Winters held up a hand. "Now I'm with you. Irredenta! Irredentism—is that what's rearing its ugly head? I can't remember quite what irredentism was all about."

"Was all about is right. Past tense. The Germans with Danzig, the Polish Corridor, all that. Bolivian claims on Chile. Peru and Ecuador. Guatemala and Belize. Venezuela and Guyana. Everyone's got a grudge. Italia Irredenta, a hundred or so years ago. Some piece of the world the Italians were after—the Tyrol, wasn't it?"

"Perhaps. Forgotten my history. I thought it was Corsica."

Oliver moved to sit up straighter in his chair. "Well, Jack, what now—Mexican irredentism? They want Arizona back? Texas? Did your general elaborate?"

Winters shook his head. "That's all, but I'm sure he would. I say let 'em have Texas, if they want it. I'll set it up so you can run over there and talk to him, if you like."

Oliver hesitated. He didn't like. He had come reluctantly to the University Club, an Anglo-Saxon center of Mexico City, when Jack Winters called him. Oliver's secretary, Mrs. Pott, had seen Winters at church—another center of Anglo-Saxon culture—on Sunday and she reported that Winters was upset by a decision of the nominating committee of the American Chamber of Commerce in Mexico City, that he told her he would be calling Oliver about it.

Oliver, thus warned, had time to consider his reply. When Winters did call, he had gone right to the ambassador to say that he expected to be approached by an influential member of the North American community and to be asked for help with the trouble in the American Chamber. "If he does, I'll just tell him that I can't get involved. Much less involve you. You're the one he'd be after."

"Quite right, Ted," the ambassador had said. "Do I need to know who the influential member is?"

Oliver made a face. "No, sir, I don't think so. Just that if he's worked up, it means all the old hands, all the solid types, are worried too."

"I've heard talk of this, of course. But something tells me I don't want to get involved. What do you think?"

"Quite right."

Thus, Oliver, by speaking to the ambassador before seeing Jack Winters, felt he had done as much as he could, if not quite what Winters wanted. He had been preparing to congratulate himself on having refused Winters without offending him. By that accomplishment, however, he had maneuvered himself into the position, apparently, of either going to see Winters's friend from San Miguel de Allende or of refusing Winters yet again. Unthinkable: Winters was a pillar of the North American business community in Mexico and it would not do to show a second idle ear to what he thought to be important.

The well-connected Winters had done Oliver several small but useful favors, arranged things that Oliver could have taken care of himself only with a good deal of trouble. In return Winters had the prestige of a direct line into the embassy, the illusion of some undefined influence in Washington, and the satisfaction of doing something for his country. Actually none of this was much more than a prop to Winters's sense of position, as he himself knew, but he knew as well that it was a relationship that no amount of money could buy. As for Oliver, he knew that one does not carelessly insult such a figure as Winters and he did not do so now.

"Sounds interesting, Jack. I'm sort of pushed at the moment. Maybe I could send someone—?"

Winters's large smooth face wrinkled up in a scowl. "Rather not, frankly, Ted. Carlos's an old friend of mine. Retired general, you know. Told him you're a straight shooter." He winced and looked sheepish as he found himself admitting that he had already spoken to Robles about Oliver without his permission. But Winters recovered immediately. "Told him you'd go at it fair and square. Carlos implied he's onto something odd. Doesn't feel he can trust his own people, you know, Ted. Thinks a lot of your outfit. God knows why." He gave a gruff laugh.

Oliver did not show his annoyance. "Sure, of course. I appreciate it. I'll work something out."

Chapter 2

Oliver stood alone on the sidewalk in front of the University Club to take in a rare breath of clean Mexico City air. With Mexican families out of the city on vacation, few cars were on the streets. The light of the low sun was amber on the high buildings along the Paseo de la Reforma, glowing a rich citron from the occasional reflecting window. The strange tranquillity kept him standing to look along the avenue. A lone orange Volkswagen spotted Oliver's solitary figure in front of the club from half a kilometer away, speeding up to roar confidently into the lateral. When the taxi driver turned his head to peer through the car window, Oliver waved him off, starting off briskly to walk back to the office. There were few people on the street, and the emptiness gave a pleasantly old-fashioned air to the city. Were it not for the high buildings that had replaced the fine mansions—the University Club was a rare survivor—and eclipsed the low houses of the last century, he might have been walking on the grand avenue through the city of the revolution some seventy years earlier. In deference to that conceit, he whistled a cheerful bar of the dancing tune "Adelita"—her eyes as green as the sea—the song Pancho Villa's people sang as they rode through the dry expanses of Mexico from one wild skirmish to the next, leaving their blood and that of the Federales to soak together into the ground.

In the office Mrs. Pott, plumply neat in her gray-brown dress, was retying a lavender scarf around her neck. She stood at her desk by the door as Oliver entered. "I waited but I do have to leave—choir practice. It's very quiet."

"Sure, Mrs. Pott. Go ahead. Thing is, the town's so nice these days with no one on the streets, I walked."

"What a pity it can't stay like that. Mr. Lankester is here. How is Mr. Winters?"

Charles Lankester appeared immediately, a chubby figure in a blue blazer, to stand framed in the doorway of his office.

"Hi, Chas. Winters? Indignant, just as you reported," answered Oliver. "Why don't they make him a bishop?" he asked her. "He'd look good in black gaiters and knee pants."

"He *is* senior warden," said Lankester.

"But he couldn't be a bishop," said Mrs. Pott. "A layman can't just jump to bishop."

"You make it sound like a chess game, Mrs. Pott."

"Oh, Mr. Oliver." She giggled. "Try to explain it to him, Mr. Lankester. I must run."

"Anyway, Jack Winters's jumping days are over," said Oliver to her back as she went out the door. "A prisoner of gravity."

"You were joking with Mrs. Pott, weren't you?" asked Lankester, following Oliver into Oliver's office. "Although I agree that Mr. Winters would make a good bishop, in appearance, anyway. Here's a cable. Things are very quiet, aren't they?"

"Yeah, everybody in Washington's off somewhere too. All quiet on the Potomac. So much for Pearl Harbor. Wait till Easter. Mexico City's even deader then."

"Just this one cable." Lankester was ruddy, prematurely gray-haired, as neat as Mrs. Pott. There was a subdued club patch on the left pocket of his blazer, the costume, Oliver supposed, a concession to the holiday period. Lankester was the second officer in less than six months' time to be assigned to Mexico City as Oliver's deputy chief of station. The other one didn't last long. Again and as usual Oliver wondered whether the station would ever get back to normal or get ahead to normal, having then to wonder whose definition of normal would apply.

For a time there had been only Oliver and Mrs. Pott, then the others. They were soon swept away and now they had Charles Lankester and Pedro Sanders, and Oliver was still struggling with CIA headquarters to get the station back up to strength. First, the excuse had been the trouble with the Soviets, the KGB. The counterintelligence people in CIA headquarters had paralyzed the station by climbing, as deliberate as two-toed sloths, out on one of their intellectual limbs. Oliver had been able—with a lot of luck and a moment of frozen violence—to destroy their argument, sawing the limb off with them on it.

No rational obstacle stood in the way of rebuilding the station, but the political world is not required to be rational. What stood in the way now were the expensive prejudices of the director of the CIA, a wide spectrum of private irritations that had reddened into chronic annoyance with Mexico. Mexico did not comport herself as she should. If she wasn't misbehaving by exporting heroin and cocaine, it was the debt question, and if not the debt, then it was illegal immigration, and if it wasn't immigration, it was Mexican foreign policy. Sometimes it was all of them at once, with a footnote on petroleum and another on Central America. It was amateurish, unprofessional of the director to let his biases get in the way—but then he wasn't a professional—and to express his rancor in the staffing of his own CIA station in Mexico. There was still another reason. The director disliked Oliver as intensely as he did Mexico, by now hardly distinguishing the one from the other, narrowing his eyes at the man through the same cloud of spite through which he glared at the nation.

From a job on the staff of the National Security Council, Lankester had been taken to the CIA by the director as his personal assistant. After some months of earnest Lankester's work, the director had granted his fervent wish to become an operations officer, assigning him as deputy to the Mexico City station. Whatever was sardonic in the director's motives for this—Oliver privately suspected them—the assignment was wildly unsuitable.

Oliver found no obvious defect in Lankester's character. The obvious was Lankester's complete lack of experience in intelligence operations. Worse: Lankester did not seem to grasp the worth of such experience. His work in Washington had given him an acute appreciation of important issues of foreign policy. That fitted him excellently for writing position papers in Washington but did nothing to prepare him for operational work in Mexico. He was beginning to ask questions—a hopeful note, Oliver told himself, trying not to notice that they were not always good questions.

Whether Lankester would ever get the experience he needed was questionable: he had an exasperating inability to learn to speak Spanish. He could not get his mouth around another tongue, unable to persuade either hemisphere of his brain to produce anything but a shy muttering. But he took daily lessons and Oliver tried not to notice that nothing seemed to improve.

On arrival in Mexico Lankester had several times spoken highly of the director to Oliver, extolling his brilliance, his precision of thought, his unusually decisive worldview. Set apart by his seriousness, according to Lankester—who admitted that the director was a clever politician—but one with convictions, rare in Washington, unique in an administration obsessed with opinion polls and driven by partisan advantage. Oliver thought Lankester knew well enough how much the director disliked Oliver, although he doubted his new deputy knew where it started, well before Lankester's time. Therefore, Oliver found a lack of tact in the man's constant praise of a person one of whose chief characteristics—in Oliver's view—was his detestation of Oliver.

The sight of Lankester had triggered a repeated firing of these impulses along a worn path of synapses in Oliver's brain. Oliver took a deep breath. Lankester cleared his throat. Oliver held the breath. He had been staring at Lankester's waistcoat, rudely preoccupied, while Lankester stood patiently in front of Oliver's desk, holding the cable out to him. Oliver let out his breath. "Yeah, the cable," he said. "Thanks."

Oliver sat down. Lankester remained standing. Oliver read the cable. "Hah!" He looked up. "It's funny, Chas. Winters just got through talking about this. This México Irredenta business, I mean. A friend of his in San Miguel—" His voice tapered off and he frowned as he reread the cable.

"Really? Quite a coincidence."

"Well, I wonder."

"What do you mean?"

Lankester's spontaneous questions must lead to a random jotting of notes on a number of different clean slates. "What do I mean about what?" asked Oliver.

"Why do you say it wouldn't be a coincidence?"

"Nothing, really," said Oliver slowly. "Just that a coincidence isn't necessarily casual. Not always what it seems to be, anyway—maybe not a coincidence at all."

Lankester stared at the chief of station. "Oh," and he sat slowly down in a chair in front of Oliver's desk.

"But I'm not saying it isn't a coincidence, either," added Oliver slowly, staring again at the message.

"Oh," said Lankester, again.

The outer door to the suite of offices banged open and Pedro Sanders came to stand, grinning, in the doorway of Oliver's office. Where Lankester was plump Sanders was thin, a follower of the jogging fashion, almost gaunt from his serious insistence on his daily run. Sanders was taller and younger than Lankester, much younger than Oliver. To Lankester he said, "Hi, Charlie," without looking at him, keeping his eyes on Oliver. Lankester got up and started for the door.

"Stick around, Chas. This cable—" Oliver tapped the paper with his free hand. To Sanders he said, "That's a clip-on tie."

"No, sir!" Sanders's hands went up to tighten the bow tie. "Christmas present. Tied it myself." He grinned, blinking at Oliver.

"Distinctive, at any rate. You look like one of the waiters. What were you doing jackassing around with that bunch of halfwits at the club a while ago?" Oliver asked him.

"I gave one of the half-wits a lift home and he agreed to front for the safe house—the apartment on Amberes."

"Oh, well, that's good. This ring—"

"So I've done half the assignments you gave me," said Sanders. "Set up your safe house. He travels a lot and we'll fix it to look like a sublease. So all I have to do now is find your imaginary, nonexistent Cuban."

"You may get a few more assignments before you're finished here, Pete. Would have been nice if you'd found your imaginary, nonexistent Cuban first, then done the safe house. First things first, Pete. This ring any bells?'' Oliver held out the cable to Sanders, who took it and read it aloud.

'' 'NSC officer'—hey, NSC! Big deal—'disappointed lack of embassy reporting on México Irredenta, ultranationalist movement and apparent nucleus new political party. Requests station fill this inexplicable vacuum, furnish urgently needed coverage. Need fullest information on leadership, objectives, overall organization, strength, influence, etcetera. Advise soonest.' ''

"Good old overalls," said Oliver.

"Good old etcetera." Sanders handed the cable back to Oliver. "We supposed to drop everything and fill his inexplicable vacuum? Sounds like someone who doesn't understand how a thermos bottle works."

Lankester, who had sat back down, was clearing his throat, but Oliver spoke first. "Well, you have heard of México Irredenta, haven't you?"

Sanders closed his eyes and shook his head slowly from side to side. "Didn't come all the way down here to fool around with a lot of scruffy Mexican politics," he said, swaying. His eyes came open and he leaned against the wall. "Does it matter if I've heard of it? But in a word, nope. Nope," he said again. He closed his eyes.

"Just happens at the same time you were horsing around with the football fans down there, Jack Winters was asking what I know about the Irredenta outfit. Chas and I were saying it's funny the way it comes up the same day. So I'm off to see some friend of Jack's in San Miguel who says they're a nasty bunch, wants to alert us. Some retired-general friend of his. Just as well, what with this cable. It's got it all wrong, of course."

"How all wrong?" asked Lankester.

"The cable, laying these intelligence requirements on the station like this."

"Not going through channels, you mean."

"Well, more than that. This NSC person ought to be over at State banging on their desk, not on ours, if he's so interested in the Irredenta outfit. You don't tie up a CIA station doing State's work, embassy reporting."

"But if they don't," said Lankester, "then don't we have to?"

"That's how we get off target, that sort of thing. That's the history of the agency, always filling someone or other's inexplicable vacuum, getting our people tied up in Vietnam—" Oliver shrugged. "Well, to hell with it, I'll go see Jack's general. As a favor to Jack, though, not to do the embassy's business for it."

"Mayn't I go in your place?" said Lankester immediately.

"How you coming with your Spanish?" interjected Sanders.

Oliver ignored Sanders's remark, although he also supposed that the general would not speak English. "Wish you might. Thing is, Winters wants me to go."

"Winters wants you to go," repeated Sanders. "Where's Winters get off telling you to go? Some people think Winters is a pompous ass."

"That crowd you were with would think so. They might learn a few things from him instead of yahooing around like that. How come he can tell me? Winters is a friend of the station's. A good friend. That's why."

"Friend of the station. Is that a form of asset, would you say?" asked Lankester, assuming that any term new to him might be another established phrase in intelligence jargon.

Sanders snorted.

Oliver was patient. "Asset. That can mean anything. Or just as likely, nothing. I knocked off using it once the newspapers picked it up."

"I like that—a friend of the station." Lankester got up. "Has a nice ring to it. I should be getting along. We have a dinner."

"See you, Chas," said Oliver. Sanders and Lankester nodded at each other.

When Lankester had left, Sanders sat down and said, "I'll go see your general in San Miguel."

"No. It's important to Jack that I myself go, drat it. Anyway, there's no need for Winters to know you're affiliated."

"No, I suppose not." Sanders raised his arms above his head, laughed, and said, " 'Mayn't'!" Then: " 'Chas'!"

"Okay, that's his choice to make, isn't it, Pete? How'd you like it I start calling you Pericón?"

Sanders was quiet for a moment as Oliver looked at the cable once more. "Okay," said Sanders. "Chas it is. But what good's a Ph.D. in systems analysis if you can't speak Spanish?"   .

"All right, Pete, he's working on it. He's really boning up on Mexican history. He can read Spanish well enough. Some people have a block."

Another snort from Sanders: "Some people could speak Spanish before they joined the agency."

"Some people had Spanish-speaking mothers too."

Sanders grinned. "You really stick up for him, I'll say that much."

Oliver leaned back in his chair. "And you really let it eat on you."

"Not really," said Sanders, with a one-sided grin. "But— systems analysis? C'mon, boss."

"Look at it this way, Pete. The Chinese studied the Confucian analects. The English read Cicero. So we do systems analysis. Whatever the hell that is," Oliver added.

Sanders snickered. "You see?"

"Okay, Pete. I've got a couple of kids up there I want to see before bedtime and I gotta catch Jack Winters first."

Sanders stood up and gave a half salute, half wave to Oliver, grinning still as he said good night. The answering smile on Oliver's face faded as he heard the office door close behind Sanders. Just three evenings past, on Christmas Eve, the Olivers had the Lankesters and the Sanderses in for drinks. Mrs. Pott, busy with the choir, could not come. As he spread pâté on a piece of dark bread Sanders had spoken of his brother in Chicago, going to make a couple of hundred thou that year, the brother had told Sanders. "Says I ought to be back there where the action is. Or end up the way our father did. Dad was always kicking himself," Sanders had said, shaking his head. "Always talking about the chances he'd missed, always the regrets. I don't want to end up like that, wait till it's too late to make my move, spend the rest of my life regretting it."

"Well," said Oliver, careful, "I guess it comes down to what you want to do with your life,'' allowing himself the sententious remark to encourage Sanders to say more.

But young Mrs. Sanders had stuck her pretty chin into the talk just then and said she thought her brother-in-law was right. ''Some people think this sort of thing doesn't really matter anymore,'' Susie had said. Oliver was able to keep his face politely neutral, encouraging her to go on, waiting to hear her say Pete was wasting his talents on CIA work. But Oliver's wife, Marge, her eyes quick on Oliver, had changed the subject.

Despite the efforts of CIA management to dispel the notion, young officers had the idea that the CIA elite was made up of those operations officers who specialized in working on the Soviet Union. Thus it was that Pedro Sanders had studied Russian, grabbed at the chance to be assigned to the station in Mexico City, arriving just after the station had dealt a crippling blow to the KGB residency in Mexico. Rather than rejoicing at this accomplishment, Sanders took it as a personal affront, annoying to Oliver yet understandable in a young officer eager to get to work on his chosen subject only to find it had been abolished.

Sanders referred scathingly to ''the fat Soviet target'' he had been promised in Washington by Slasher O'Rourke, the chief of the South American Division. O'Rourke had told Sanders he could make a name for himself in Mexico, Sanders had reported to Oliver—write his own ticket if he did well. Sanders had added, ''Huh! With what's happened, it's like sending a skier to Tahiti. Nothing much doing around here anymore.''

Along with that was Sanders's jealousy of what Oliver had done, Sanders's suggesting that the station's victory was more a result of luck than of skill. As much as this opinion in a fresh young officer nettled Oliver, it would be beneath him, as chief of station, to show his annoyance at Sanders's belittling Oliver's personal achievement. For that matter, it was true that more than one dash of luck had gone into the coup that had demolished the KGB residency in Mexico.

But isn't that always the case? thought Oliver. We pretend that an intelligence operation can be broken down into component parts, rationalized, approached logically, according to form. We teach it that way in the training courses. It's like teaching military science as though logic were the sum of it, saying nothing of luck, of imagination, of inspiration—nothing of art. In the case studies, we like to look at the victories, try to isolate the gene of success when we should be looking as closely for the virus that causes failure. It's a mistake to ignore the power of luck, as when victors congratulate themselves, leaving the losers to blame bad luck for their defeat, to grouse against fortune—all these things Sanders had yet to learn. Maybe he never would, Oliver grumbled to himself, thus relieving his feelings.

Shortly after that exchange on Christmas Eve the Sanderses had gone for dinner with another young couple from the embassy. After seeing them out the door, Oliver turned to insist that the Lankesters stay on. Oliver grinned and shook his head at Lankester. Mrs. Lankester was on a stool by the fire. Oliver's wife, Marge, sat on the sofa; two sleepy children, one on either side of her, were staring with glazed eyes at the Christmas tree.

"There's a lot of that now," said Lankester, who was mixing a whiskey for his wife and a seltzer water for himself. "That impatience. They expect to be put in charge right away." Reasonably charitable of Lankester, thought Oliver, considering Sanders's manner toward him.

"They're all impatient. They don't know what they don't know." That was Lankester's wife. "They can't wait. The wives too. They're just as bad."

"Well, maybe not everyone," said Lankester. "But they don't appreciate what's involved. A young person like Sanders doesn't see the need for apprenticeship. They want to be in charge right away." While Oliver tended to agree with that, the remark sounded strange coming from Lankester, who was serving his own apprenticeship as a relatively senior officer. And his superior rank gave him nominal authority over Sanders, who actually had more experience in the work.

"Let her go back and live in Lake Forest, then, if that's the life they want, like you said, Ted," said Mrs. Lankester.

Marge was diplomatic. "I think we all start that way, the way Chas said, don't you?" She looked at Oliver and raised her eyebrows.

"No," said Oliver, unwilling to confess to youthful arrogance, smiling to admit to her his evasion. "Thing is, you can't wheedle people into staying on, give them guarantees, pussyfoot around to please them. You put it in front of them and they decide. You're right," he said to Mrs. Lankester. "If they don't like what they see, then back to the country club."

"I must admit," said Lankester then, with a twisted smile, "I think you are a mite too easy on Sanders. After all, you handed him that Cuban illegal on a silver platter."

Oliver had changed the subject then, not liking shoptalk before wives. And now, sitting in the dark in his office, he found himself unhappy with Lankester and Sanders both.

The Cuban matter was simple enough in outline. A defector from the Dirección General de Inteligencia—one of the Cuban intelligence services—had spoken of an important Cuban illegal working in Mexico. The defector could not say who the illegal— a Cuban intelligence officer living under a false identity—was or where he was working. All the defector did know came from the bragging of a hard-shelled colleague over a shared bottle of scotch—not rum, for the DGI had its privileges—in La Habana late one night some years before. "It's very long range, I can tell you that—insurance against the very worst the yanquis can do," said the colleague. "Bold. A revolutionary concept that will reveal—by no means incidentally—the sham of that so-called Mexican revolution of 1911. The Cuban revolution is destined to survive no matter what happens here in Cuba—that surprise you? Let the counterrevolution do its worst!" Fascinating! Pushed to elaborate, the colleague had changed his knowing expression to a wary one. Clambering to his feet with some difficulty, he had leaned heavily on the table, shaken his head, stubbornly refused to say more, probably wishing he had said nothing at all, and insisted he was able to find his own way home.

Oliver had assigned the defector's lead to the Cuban illegal, such as the lead was, to Sanders—his way of trying to make up for the loss of the fat Soviet target. You'd have thought, Oliver was saying again to himself, going over it all again in his head, sitting in the empty offices as the amber day thickened to blue dark, that Sanders would be at least mildly excited to be put on the scent of such exciting prey. Rather than showing gratitude, Sanders had reacted with sour amusement and impatience. It was Oliver's way of needling him, claimed Sanders, literally needling him—taking him to a haystack and telling him there was a needle to be found somewhere in it. "There's nothing there!" Sanders had cackled in protest. "If that's what they call counterintelligence, count me out."

In the dark Oliver sighed, not knowing that he did, as he contemplated Lankester and Sanders, his operations staff. If Sanders accurately, but annoyingly, saw the difficulty of tracing a Cuban illegal with no leads at all, Lankester seemed as innocently unaware of the difficulties in solving such a case.

Oliver shook his head and remembered then the promises to his children. Letting out his breath in another long sigh, he leaned to flick on a desk light, to pick up the phone, and was mildly refreshed by hearing Winters's voice on the line. Oliver was annoyed when Winters confirmed that he had already given Oliver's name to the general, and when he hung up he sighed again.

Oliver then got up to find in the files a long list of entries under the name of Robles. A Colonel Carlos Robles was listed as a social contact of Lester Lazaire. Oliver frowned at that: Lazaire, one of the old hands, a chief of the Mexico City station some years before. A later entry noted the promotion of Carlos Robles to general, describing him as "hunting buddy of Lazaire, a comer in the army."

Oliver remembered that Lester Lazaire spent his winters in San Miguel de Allende. He was frowning again as he closed the files and locked the office.

Chapter 3

Oliver was able to squeeze the Toyota into a parking space, headed to the road that goes out of Guanajuato to the fast highway to Mexico. He had not expected Guanajuato to be so crowded. The Sunday-evening retreat of the vacationers to the capital would mean a clogged highway. Oliver was hoping to break away from the general early enough to keep his promise to take Marge and the children for a twilight walk in the hushed streets of Mexico City's center, closed off for the Christmas season. Instead of an easy trip back, the cars would be jammed together as though fleeing a doomed city, tailgaters looming in the rearview mirror, flashing their lights, shoving past him over hills and through blind curves.

Winters's friend, the retired general, had arbitrarily picked Sunday to meet. Thoughtless of him: "Must be a bachelor," Oliver had told Marge. And why did they have to meet in the hilly silver-mining town of Guanajuato, rather than in San Miguel itself, a good hour closer to Mexico City?

As he shut the car door Oliver took a pair of heavy, clear-lensed, black-rimmed glasses from his pocket and slipped them on. Hardly a disguise, but distinguishing, the detail that people remember, like Sanders's bow tie, and the plain lenses were quite free of distortion.

The glasses were feeble protection. By giving Oliver's name to Robles, Winters had prevented Oliver's using an alias, as he had noted to Winters on the phone the other evening. His complaint was dismissed.

"What the hell, Ted! You're not dealing with the Mafia. What

20

kind of people you hang around with, anyway? You and Carlos—you'll get on like a house afire. Give the old boy an *abrazo*
for me.''

So, at the restaurant the general would know Oliver, the obvious North American, by the glasses, by the gray herringbone
jacket, and also by his true name. Oliver supposed he was being
overcautious. Robles was known to Winters, and Oliver had to
give in to Jack Winters's judgment, silence the chiding alarm of
experience in the back of his head.

The street was moving with Sunday visitors and Oliver walked
slowly past the steps leading up to the Alhóndiga. He had driven
fast once the sun had cleared the misty roads of the morning.
He was early enough to let time run. Just ahead of him a small
boy with shining black bangs and bright brown eyes sat singing
on his father's shoulders. He clasped his father's head, absently
twisting one ear, the father holding him by the ankles, singing
with him, leading Oliver to take a breath of loneliness. Oliver
had not seen Guanajuato for years. Marge and the children had
never been there. He had come alone because of his rule of not
mixing family and work, not expecting to feel the holiday lift in
the streets. There was really no good reason beyond professional
habit for his having come off alone. Marge could have taken the
two children off to lunch somewhere while Oliver saw General
Robles. Oliver shouldered his lonely way through the clots of
family groups at the entrance of the nineteenth-century market
building, its gunmetal frame a light and rusty artifice among the
heavier stone buildings, its shell rattling and shaking with the
shuffling feet and the talk inside.

Beyond the market Avenida Juárez wound along more quietly. The two- and three-storied buildings of pastel stucco were
those of a provincial Spanish town, tall windows edged with
stone, wrought-iron balconies, dark passages giving glimpses of
green atria cool away from the sun in the street. The Paseo de
la Reforma in Mexico City would have shown that same face
had not the developers traded the old charm in on their sky-
scrapers. Past another turn the stone-paved street widened, fa-
cades of low stone buildings on either side, their balconies
underlined by shadows from the high sun. Here the avenue was

bisected by a line of heavy round concrete planters to give those on foot their share of the street. Red géraniums bloomed in some pots, cactus in others. At the top of the street was the green garden of the Parque de la Paz, the stone towers of the yellow ocher basilica—Our Lady of Guanajuato—high above the plaza.

Avenida Juárez sloped narrow down from the basilica to the Jardín de la Unión, crammed into a tight triangle by the street and shaded by the buildings that crowded up to the walks on either side. The concert bandsmen in powder-blue uniforms were at rest, talking to each other beneath the metal roof of the bandstand, nearly hidden by the shiny leaves of the circling trees, the *laurel de india*, a copse of them with white-painted trunks sheltering the bandstand from the sun.

The street was so narrow here that Oliver had to back away from the building next to him to read the name of the restaurant above the door. As he turned to go in the door he sensed that a slightly built man, also in jacket and tie, was standing by him, smiling up at him with bright blue eyes. His nearly bald head was sunburned, freckled and spotted, some long strands of reddish gray hair coaxed across from one side to the other. Oliver tentatively returned the smile.

"How is Jack Winters?" asked General Robles in Spanish. He pointed to the door of the restaurant and urged Oliver ahead of him to the stairs.

As they went to the upper floor of the restaurant the general was at Oliver's side, slightly behind him, Oliver's elbow in his hand, steering Oliver up the stairs to a narrow balcony looking down on the roof of the bandstand nearly hidden in the dark green of the leaves in the Jardín de la Unión. Here the general let go Oliver's arm.

Below the freckled scalp were gold-rimmed glasses, a reassuringly direct look from the blue eyes, a reddish mustache, a brown tweed suit, more the cliché of a professor of history than a Mexican general. Not at all what Oliver had been expecting. He felt a prick of shame for the caricature of the Mexican general that had been lurking, unseen, in the primitive backwater of his mind, to hop out now like a troll: squat, bandy-legged, a cartoonist's great nose, cap pulled down on a low forehead, the head sunk without a neck between broad shoulders. The actual general, with no such awkward features, was being greeted with deference by a white-aproned waiter. "A beer?" They turned to look at Oliver. Oliver agreed, standing at the balustrade, soft jumbled talk welling up from some twenty feet below, where the street was half in the blinding sun and half in purple shadow.

Across from them sat a three-story building with elaborate wrought ironwork on the windows at the same level at which Oliver stood. More balconies on more houses ran uphill on the street that dwindled from sight to the left. Above the tiled roofs the stucco walls of the smaller tower of the basilica were lemon yellow in the sun. As clouds blew over Guanajuato's sharp-sided valley the tower tracked them like the mast of a ship.

The noise of the town was many-toned, like the rushing of water through a rapids, the lilt of light Mexican voices an octave above the other sounds. On Oliver's face the sun reflected hot from across the way to the shaded balcony. Garlic and coriander flowed sharp on an updraft from the kitchen below. The colors in the street, the sun's heat on his skin, the sharp odors, stayed long with Oliver, hardly fading, recalling—with a stab that could take his breath away—what later so pained him to remember.

He had gone so far as to promise himself he would come back some Sunday to this very place with Marge when he felt a nudge from behind. The general was tucking a white envelope into his hand. The general's motions were small, quick, less nervous than eager, the lively, good-humored gestures of an officer cheerfully in charge, enjoying the role of host. "Take this with you. A background—you'll see—to the portraits I shall be sketching over our lunch. It all has to do with this so-called México Irredenta." His mustache danced and twitched as his lips formed each syllable precisely, shedding an amused contempt on the last two words, as though giving them a flick with his riding crop. He finished with a quick smile, another brisk and confident nod.

When Oliver began to fumble with the flap of the unsealed envelope, standing there, the general waggled a finger at him. "No, no. Later. After I explain." Again he took Oliver by the upper arm to steer him to a chair at the round table that sat on the narrow balcony, half in the doorway half on the balcony. The general squeezed around the other doorpost to sit opposite Oliver at the small table.

"I follow what I believe to be the approved practice in writing of matters requiring unusual discretion. That is, on the paper a general discussion without names for you to read later. Here, over lunch, I shall identify the dramatis personae. After describing the principal characters, as though composing the program notes for a play, I shall explain specifically what it is that puzzles me and why. And finally, Señor Oliver, I shall explain how you can help me if you will have the goodness to put at my disposal a small part of your vast resources to answer what may seem to be"—here the general paused, took a breath, his head on one side—"no more than a misapprehension of reality by a retired person who spends entirely too much time by himself. The odds are in favor of that, I force myself to admit. Yet"—he raised an imperious finger—"if there is one chance in a thousand that what I suspect is right—well, then. We shall see."

There seemed to be no fitting answer to this introduction. Unlike the general Oliver had not rehearsed his opening remarks. An advantage of being a North American, a dour Anglo, Oliver thought as he stuffed the envelope into the side pocket of his jacket, was that the general did not expect his own eloquence to be matched by Oliver. So Oliver only smiled back at the general and waited for his next words.

They were both quiet then as they watched the waiter place on the table two goblets, misted with cold, and two bottles of Corona, freezing vapor curling from the clear reused glass of bottles worn as soft, as cloudy, as shards of glass in the sand. The waiter leaned stiffly, pouring the beer into the goblets with exaggerated care. When he had filled them, he set them down by the goblets, stood back, looked from one to the other, and clicked his heels, smiling, before turning away.

The band in the park below them, beneath the shiny leaves of the thick-growing laurels, had begun an elaborately misleading introduction to a waltz that began to imply and then confessed itself to be "Over the Waves." Oliver laughed with pleasure at the way the musical ambiguity had been resolved. "Sobre las

Olas,'' said the general, smiling back at Oliver, understanding his amusement, turning then in his chair to look over his right shoulder down at the park. The general's face was freckled, too, and that, with his light way of moving, of speaking, made him look younger than his some seventy-five years. "They used to trim those trees in the French fashion,'' the general was saying, "shape them''—sketching a cup shape with one small hand— "and you could see the orchestra from here. Canada,'' he said then, unexpectedly, turning his face again to Oliver. "Canada,'' he repeated as though the word flowed logically from the discussion of the pruning of the trees. "What I need is your help in Canada.'' He picked up his goblet and held it toward Oliver.

Oliver raised his own, politely half smiling at the general, unready to take his cue, to ask the expected question about the unexpected mention of Canada. Oliver found that he was surpassingly content at just that moment and hanging on to it jealously, unwilling for it to be dissolved by the demands of responsibility. Oliver had embarked in an ungrateful temper on the visit to the general, grudging a trip that had turned out to be entertaining rather than a chore. Would that all the work were like this!

The cramped corner of the Jardín de la Unión was the stage, the waltz an overture to the general's program notes. Oliver was in no hurry for the curtain to go up. The music—"Over the Waves''—was the ideal selection for the performance. Oliver could not have chosen better himself. He contemplated for a few more carefree seconds the goblet of beer—the concept of cold, a physics lesson attractively illustrated—until saying "Canada,'' and he heard himself saying it, dragged him back to business.

"Yes, an investigation in Canada. If you will do me that favor. You must not think it idle of me to ask. That might be your first impression, I know. One reaches a certain age and—'' He smiled, perceiving what was in Oliver's mind.

"And it has to do with México Irredenta, General.'' Oliver sighed, mentally, and put his beer down so as to overlap the one wet circle on the tabletop, make a crescent of it.

The general was flexing his own fingers about the stem of his goblet as though to drive the arthritis out of them. He nodded and looked past Oliver's left shoulder, up the street toward the basilica, out of Oliver's sight behind the doorpost against which he sat. "Very much so," he said, looking Oliver in the eye as though to underline the reference to Méxica Irredenta. His fingers were moving to grasp the goblet by its bowl; there were freckles—liver spots—on the back of the hand. General Robles's blue eyes left Oliver's just as Oliver looked up at him. Again he was looking up the street past Oliver. He would be looking at the potted red geraniums on the balconies out of Oliver's sight behind his left shoulder. The general frowned at whatever he was looking at. Smiling, politely puzzled, Oliver was leaning toward the balustrade, his eyes still on Robles, turning to follow the direction of his eyes.

And then—in the corner of Oliver's right eye—the general slammed his beer on the tabletop, the goblet shattering before Oliver's face, bursting like shrapnel, shards of glass glistening in the air. Oliver was blinking, gasping, splashes of beer on his false eyeglasses, the general lurching backward, then slumping toward the table, vilely drunk, coughing, banging his head into the glassy mess on the plastic tabletop.

A bottle of Corona whirled flat on the tabletop, beer gushing from its top. The second bottle bounced with a loud ringing to smash foaming on the balcony floor. The general was jerking, twisting in his chair as though trying to raise his head, to struggle to his feet.

The echo of the shots was clapping between the buildings, up the narrow way, racketing down toward the Teatro Juárez. Stone splintered on the wall behind Oliver's head, flecks pecking at his left cheek and ear. It seemed terribly important to Oliver just then not to spill his own beer. He let go cleanly the stem of the goblet still cold in his fingers to push from the table and fall away from the balustrade onto the tile floor, where under the table the general's brown oxfords were kicking at him. Oliver's eyeglasses skittered across the floor toward the wrinkled leather of the waiter's shoes, dry and scuffed blue with wear.

Screams and hoarse shouts from the street snapped that span of seconds on the cold tiles. From the bandstand the notes of

"Over the Waves" still swooped through the balcony onto the painted ceiling, flowing down the walls to writhe like smoke on the cold floor.

Oliver put his arms beneath him and crouched to frogwalk away from the balcony, straightening to see the waiter great-eyed before him. He stopped for the waiter to pass him, glide on past in a slow waltz time. Then more staring eyes were gathered before him, people knotted together like terrified dancers.

"The general," said Oliver, pointing, not looking, holding the hand with the napkin behind him. He wiped at his face as they flowed on past him, seeming to move with the long steps of skaters, large-eyed, turning, closing behind him, Oliver knowing, as one knows in a dream, his own steps in an ancient reel.

He turned to see them gather silently at the edge of the balcony. The general was going quiet on the tabletop, blood dripping from his fingertips as one loose arm stopped its swinging, the other hand a tight claw whose fingers began to unfold by Oliver's unspilled beer.

Oliver took quick, deep breaths, shook himself, snatched his glasses from the floor, wiped them with the napkin, put them on, and without looking back, walked quickly down the stairs to the ground floor, stopping at the corner of the building, wary of what might be waiting for him up the street to the left.

A pushing crowd was swaying in the street at the corner of the restaurant. Someone was running at the loose far side of the crowd—a white-haired grandmother in gray rebozo and long russet skirt twisting away from terror, towing two stumbling children, their heads swiveled backward like owls, mouths open in protest, large eyes turned toward the crowd.

A thin-faced man with dark curly hair and sunglasses was pointing up at the balcony, the other hand shielding his eyes, talking to the openmouthed crowd, their faces turning from him to look to where he pointed now, back toward the geraniums on the balcony farther up the street. Oliver could see no clear escape behind him, so he put his head down and hurried across the street to the sidewalk leading up the slope on the left side of the park. The band had stopped playing. Some of the musicians were standing, holding their instruments, peering under the branches, around the white trunks, toward the street. The conductor had his blue uniform cap off to wipe his brow with a red handkerchief. He put his cap back on and began tapping his baton on the music stand. The musicians seemed not to hear him but Oliver could hear the tick-tick, tick-tick-ticking, until he went around the corner of a building at the upper corner of the park.

He paused to look into the shade of a narrow street that would take him a crooked way down to Avenida Juárez. He was sure he did not want to go near there. He kept on up the slope until he reached another street that led behind the basilica and the Parque de la Paz. He paused again at that corner, stopping to lean against a wall, looking back from where he had come.

Whoever had shot the general could not have seen Oliver. He had been hidden, more than half-hidden, maybe his left shoulder and arm visible, his back to the doorpost, half in the door to the balcony. One round, though, at least one, had hit the wall just above his left ear. It had to have been like that, the general sitting across from him looking up the other way toward the basilica. Oliver had been careless walking to the restaurant, wishing now he had been more conscious of the people around him on his way through the streets. He regretted that lapse but immediately questioned himself: Wary of what? Looking for whom? Whom might he have picked from the crowd? For that matter, would anyone have known to pick Oliver himself out of the crowd? They might have gotten a look at him only when he and the general met—if then—the short moment they stood together before going into the restaurant. Oliver took off his jacket, mildly surprised to find the napkin balled up in his hand. He took off his tie, rolled up his shirtsleeves, put the eyeglasses in a jacket pocket.

People were drifting past him toward the park, yet unaware of how midday had been blown apart below. The brasses echoed, the band brisk now with the Zacatecas march. A child and then a young woman looked hard at Oliver. I'm a foreigner, different, that's all—wishing he did not appear outlandish. From his ear where it stung he brought back a smear of blood on his fingers, a fine network of blood on his palm when he put his hand to his cheek. He saw the hand was trembling. That dull thudding was not the bass drum but his own heart thumping in his ears.

He turned to walk up a street where every corner leaned toward him, an ambush site. He put the napkin to his ear. There was not much blood, a scratch, a few pocks on his cheek, crumbs of stone gritty in his hair. He could shake the tension from his muscles by walking fast.

. Ahead he saw the baroque facade of the church of La Compañía. He walked up to it, turned left to pass the high stone walls of the university on that higher road, glimpsing at the small intersections the sun on the light gray paving of Avenida Juárez below. He walked rapidly toward his car, from time to time dabbing the napkin at his temple and his cheek.

Chapter 4

"I tried to reach you last night," Oliver said to Jack Winters.

It had been a bad night. Marge had seen right off that something was seriously wrong. Oliver had been curt with her. "There was a bad accident. Yes, that's all. Look, I'd rather not go into it."

He groaned in his sleep, waking himself up, carefully lifting the blanket to slide out of the bed and turn on a light and sit in the living room. When Marge came out he said, "Nothing. I can't sleep, that's all. Go back to bed."

He went to the kitchen and heated a glass of milk. He crouched in a chair in a wool bathrobe, not reading the magazine in his lap, sipping the milk and staring at the ashes cooling in the fireplace. Marge had found him sleeping there when the first gray light was coming through the windows. She brought a blanket to put around him, turned off the reading lamp, went to the children's room to be sure they were covered, stood in their door to wonder—not for the first time—whether it might not be better living in a quiet American town with a husband who did something normal every day. She had gone to sit in the dusk of the cold kitchen until the coffee was ready.

"I tried to reach you but I decided it could wait," Oliver was saying to Winters. The early Mexico City sun was weak on the beige glass curtains that lined the ceiling-to-floor windows of Jack Winters's office three flights above the Reforma. The old air inside smelled of carpet, cigars, and leather. Winters sprawled in the black leather chair behind the mahogany table that served as his desk. He waved a large hand through the air, letting it swoop to the floor. "I feel a spiritual heaviness," he said in a low voice. Almost immediately he straightened to bring the hand down hard on the edge of the table. "Why, Ted?" His voice was too loud in the room. "That's what we always ask, isn't it?" In a lower tone he said, "Never an answer, is there? Never anything to be done."

Oliver had been holding the curtain to one side to look down at the thin morning traffic roaring by on the Reforma through the mist of its own fumes. "Somehow it was worse because it was so unexpected. When you're expecting trouble it's bad enough but you're somewhat prepared." Oliver walked back to Winters's desk to stand on the reddish-purple Turkish rug in front of it, to a smell of furniture polish. "Probably bothers you I didn't stick around."

"Well." Winters did not look at him. "I would have thought you'd want to make sure—you know—there was nothing to be done."

Oliver nodded. "He was gone, Jack. Right away."

"But I don't understand. You just up and left?" Winters looked at Oliver now. "Just damn well got up and walked the hell out of there?" Oliver went slowly back to the window without replying. "Cripes," continued Winters, "you're a material witness. That's the least of it. Maybe they'll think you set him up, ever think of that?" He was still staring at Oliver. "I must say, you're pretty damn cool about the whole thing."

"Not really. It didn't hit me really hard until I was in the car, on the road coming back here." Oliver blew out a breath. "I couldn't get mixed up with the police there. It'd be all over the place. The embassy—you know."

"I know but—"

Oliver interrupted. "Use your phone?"

Winters nodded and pushed the instrument across the table. "Help yourself."

When Oliver had finished a terse exchange on the telephone, Winters stared at the phone: "So, that's it. Screw the locals. Go right to the top. You call Diego, who just happens to be minister of government, senior minister of the Mexican government.

These connections do pay off, don't they? That's how you get off the hook.'' Winters pushed closer to the table, leaned to take a cigar from a silver box on the far side of the table, turned the cigar in his fingers, frowned at it, put it back in the box, slamming the lid shut. "Diego—hell, I first ran into Diego back when he was a young officer in the presidential guard."

"Still pretty young." Oliver walked back to the window, pulling aside the dusty curtains to look out, not actually looking at anything.

"What's he like now? They can get pretty puffed up with their perks."

"Diego's all right. He does take himself seriously," said Oliver. "I suppose he always has."

"It's all in the upbringing. Not like today."

With that remark, Winters reminded Oliver that he himself had no children. What Oliver said was, "Diego's so overwhelmed with work I don't think he has time to strut around much. Works his ass off."

Winters sighed. "Where'd we ever get the idea Mexicans were lazy?" He cleared his throat. "See here, Ted. I guess I ought to apologize. The hell! Who am I to—I could have gone over there with you, you know. I got you into this mess."

"Well, Jack. That's all right. What difference would that have made?"

Winters seemed to be thinking about that but what he said was, "How'd Marge take it?"

"I didn't go into it. She knows something happened, that's all. Thing is, Jack, with Diego—I'll have to say something about you."

Winters moved in his chair, made a quick gesture with both hands: "I can see that."

"Just between me and Diego. Just as this was between you and me." Oliver let out his breath. "And the ambassador. I can keep you out of that."

"I understand how you want to get shet of it. I understand that. Look—I don't give a damn about this Irredenta business. I'd like to know who would have done that to poor Carlos. A decent guy. No, more than that.'' Winters shook his head impatiently.

"I know. I saw it in him. I have an idea what you mean."

Winters slammed the table again. "Why? Who would do such a thing?"

Oliver turned at the door. "Okay, Jack. We'll find out."

As Oliver turned to leave Winters called out to him: "Wait, Ted. I suppose it must have occurred to you—I mean, how can you be sure they weren't gunning for you?"

Oliver knew that Diego, behind his dignity, was surprised and exerting trained nerves to conceal it. Not the flicker of an eyelid. Diego sat erect in the straight-backed leather chair, correct in the pin-striped suit he wore like a uniform. The rhythm of the tapping of the miniature scimitar against the palm of his other hand did seem to slow a bit. "You don't wear eyeglasses," was what Diego said. Despite the stiffness with which an observer would have noted their regarding each other, Diego was using the familiar speech of friends.

A high carved mahogany door at one corner of the office swung quietly open. One of Diego's people carrying a silver tray in large hands was shuffling in with small steps. The man set the tray on the table in front of the cold fireplace behind Oliver. He straightened and looked toward Diego. Diego nodded at him and the man set a cautious stream of black coffee to gurgling in the two demitasse cups and put the pot down. He looked again toward Diego, who nodded at him curtly. The man gave Oliver a small smile as he turned to tiptoe out and Oliver blinked back at him. When the door had swung shut, Diego threw the letter opener onto the top of his mahogany table with a clatter, a table like the one in Winters's office. The last time Oliver had sat in front of Diego the desk had been the Victorian one with the dark, bowed legs and the veined marble top. Oliver must remember to tell Winters that if large mahogany desks are a sign of self-importance, Diego was no more puffed up than Winters himself. If he took satisfaction from his stature—Diego was hardly less powerful than the president himself—Diego, senior minister of the government of Mexico, rarely let it show.

They rose to stand by the coffee table of polished dark wood with a black marble top. Diego put his arm out straight toward a gilded and tapestried chair. Oliver sat down in it. Diego sat across from him and put his arm out again to invite Oliver to have coffee. As Oliver leaned to pick up the cup he responded to Diego's comment. "You're right, I don't. But I wore glasses yesterday." The people in the restaurant would have described him thus.

Diego did not touch his cup. He awaited Oliver's explanation, sitting back in his chair, crossing his legs, narrow black shoes bright, shot his cuffs with the gold links, and waited, head on one side, a finger stroking one side of his narrow black mustache. Oliver turned to let his eyes go up to meet the gaze of Benito Juárez, whose portrait hung above Diego's desk. At other crucial times—and what had happened the day before had a crucial look to it—Oliver had looked for omens in the great patriot's stare. Juárez had never smiled on Oliver: his expression ranged from neutral to downright unfriendly. Juárez's look today was neutral, so far—"Oh, you're back again"—waiting to hear what Oliver had to say for himself. Oliver looked back at Diego, neutral in his expression, like Juárez, if more cordial, but alert, on the lookout for gringo mischief. Oliver marked in Diego's face again the features of his friend, Diego's father. "Please pass my respects to your father," he said. Diego nodded, a polite smile passing over his features. He kept on stroking his mustache.

Oliver sat confidently enough in Diego's office, never allowing himself to wander outside the bounds of their peculiar relationship. Diego's father and Oliver were close friends—had been from the time they met at the hotel in Tarasco where Diego's father had lived for a nearly half a century since leaving Spain. But when Diego received Oliver in his office, it was as minister of government, responsible to the president of Mexico for both political and security matters. So Diego had to look at Oliver, representative of the Central Intelligence Agency, with an official eye. And Diego was a wakeful sentry, watching constantly for any sign of a threat to Mexico's independence from the north. Love of *patria* burned hot beneath his suavity. It could flare as passionately in Diego as in the young cadets who had hurled themselves from the ramparts of Chapultepec rather than be taken by the North American invaders a century and a half ago.

Oliver knew that clever hands saw to it that every attack on the CIA—from the Mexican press, the world press, from the North American press itself—appeared on Diego's desk. In front of Diego was the actual Oliver whom he might be inclined to trust. In the back of Diego's head were the whispers of warning against such complacency.

"Obviously," said Oliver, with that in mind, "my first thought was to inform you of this. But I don't know that I can help. I saw no one. It was like this." He put a hand on the tabletop to illustrate, moving the tray to one side and drawing a finger across the green and white veins in the black marble. "I was sitting here, more or less with my back to the wall, away from the balustrade. The shots came from behind, back here." He put the other hand behind the first one. "Now look, Diego— this is important. There are vertical iron balusters on the balcony that support the rail of the balustrade—you follow me?"

Diego nodded. "Important in what way?"

"They could not have fired from the level of the street. At that acute angle to the balcony, the balusters would have been so closely spaced as to act as a shield. Bullets would ricochet from them. You couldn't be sure of hitting anyone sitting on the balcony behind them—more or less protected by them. You see?"

Diego nodded again. "Go on."

"I believe they fired from one of the buildings up the street, higher up. A clear shot. And General Robles was looking up that way, his expression was just changing, surprised— something he saw. At this level," gesturing, "not down below in the street."

"What you say is correct. They entered a private house, locked the *portero* in a closet, going then to the upper floor, stepped out on the balcony for a moment, fired." Diego snapped his fingers. "There were two of them. They overturned a pot of geraniums but left no other trace, not even a cartridge."

"Oh." Diego had lost no time in getting himself informed.

"The *portero* is incoherent. No one has come forward. The authorities in Guanajuato are quite without a hypothesis. The general was a respected figure, above reproach." Diego played with his mustache, his head on one side, looking at Oliver. "I would like to hear your hypothesis."

"One moment, Diego." Oliver shook his head. "You can't lay on a job like that. You don't spot your target on a balcony, rush to a nearby building, hammer on the door, jump the *portero*, run upstairs, open fire, all in, what? Three or four, maybe five minutes?"

"General Robles is from an old family, landowners, of the state of Guanajuato, their land lying between the cities of Guanajuato and San Miguel. His father and his grandfather before him sat on that same balcony in that same chair, kept for him when he asked for it. That was well-known. And his murderers seem to have known that, too, no?" Diego picked up his coffee cup then put it back down on the saucer without drinking from it.

"Oh. And so we infer they might also have known he had a date with, well, someone, and that he'd be there."

"What was your business with him?"

Oliver did not seem to have heard the question. "I only just met him, we had hardly spoken, but I was much taken with him, his manner—courtly, old-fashioned."

"He was all of that. An old army family. An excellent reputation in the army. If he had any fault, it was like his father's, too blunt an honesty. There were those who resented that in him. The family was prominent in the revolution. His father achieved a species of prominence later by supporting General Almazán against our governing party in the election of 1940. That *almazanista* taint did not help General Robles's later career in the army. So be it. Like his forebears he was respected for his independence of mind and his generous spirit. The last of the line. A sad business."

"But at his age—was he a threat that someone would eliminate him?"

Diego shrugged. "What was your business with him?"

"He wanted to talk to me about México Irredenta. The political party."

Diego raised his eyebrows. "I know what México Irredenta is. Why would General Robles want to talk to you about that?"

There you have it—Oliver sighed inwardly. México Irredenta—any aspect of politics, of internal Mexican affairs—was out of bounds for Oliver. "All right, Diego, I don't know why—"

More proof that Diego was overworked: his usual good manners were showing the wear. He was blinking with irritation now. "You don't know! What did he say to you?"

"Hardly anything. We had just sat down, he was just getting around to explaining—"

"You must have some idea. Why would he talk to you? Explain your connection with him."

Here Oliver explained that Jack Winters had asked him, as a favor, to see his old friend General Robles.

"Ah, Winters, a prominent member of the American business community." Diego had stopped stroking his mustache and his fingers were tapping rapidly on one thigh.

"Now, Diego, one problem with my occupation is that people assume that everyone I know, to whom I talk, with whom I am seen, is affiliated with my work. Winters, for example, is simply an acquaintance of mine, a friend who—"

"You accuse me of naïveté. I made no such assumption. On the other hand, you should not complain if you are misunderstood. The nature of your profession stimulates speculation in others."

Oliver looked up at the face of Juárez. The portrait wore an intolerant expression: two against one and it's their country too. "We seem to be leaving the subject of the death of General Robles, Diego."

"Your 'acquaintance' Jack Winters—I know Jack Winters—asked you 'as a favor' to see his 'old friend' Carlos Robles, who, for reasons you say you are unable to define, wanted to talk to you about a lunatic political faction of no significance whatsoever in Mexican life." Diego had his hands clasped across his waistcoat and was twirling the thumbs in small but intense circles.

Oliver moved his head slightly to show he was not going to quibble with the description although tempted to do so: of no significance? Hardly, with the attention it's getting.

"A little group, a sect. Not a party, as you call it," Diego continued. "Headed by a malcontent. A malcontent whose ambition outruns his talent. What is your interest in this? Does Winters, prominent in your North American business group, find something of interest in this insignificant cabal? Very dangerous, such an idea. I cannot imagine Carlos Robles lending himself to such a scheme."

"Diego, really, I must ask you to consider that I came here this morning as soon as I could to report to you. I have nothing to conceal. I agree. You say it may be insignificant—"

"Insignificant!" Diego grasped the arms of the chair. "Hardly insignificant when a man of honor, General Robles, an officer, of a noted family—"

As Diego was speaking Oliver put down the cup he had been holding and rose from his chair. "Good day, Diego. I'll ask you to excuse me. Let me know when you find it convenient to discuss it." Oliver walked across the room to the door.

"Come back!" Oliver had one hand on the knob of the high mahogany door. Diego's mouth was working, his mustache moving from side to side under his narrow aquiline nose. He was not looking at Oliver but he waved one hand at him. "Sit down, sit down."

In the twitching about Diego's eyes the state of his nerves below the surface showed themselves. When Oliver had sat down again and picked up his cup, Diego began talking, not as smoothly as usual but in control of himself. "In recent years, we must remind ourselves, General Robles, a lonely widower, had immersed himself in the study of our history. He became known, in a limited circle, for the pieces he wrote on obscure bits of history, the odd forgotten episode of the revolution. Military history, this regiment or that battalion, a campaign in the north against the Indians. But México Irredenta?" Diego shook his head and lifted both hands, letting them fall in his lap. "My point is this: General Robles was getting along in years. We know from our own parents—my father"—here Diego's expression softened—"the signs of age. Forgetfulness, the pre-occupation with ideas of no importance to the active person busy with actual affairs." Frowning, he picked up the coffee cup. It rattled on the saucer and he put it back on the table. "But, it must be added, one does not kill for that!"

It had been on Oliver's lips to tell Diego of the coincidental inquiry from the National Security Council about México Irredenta. Diego would read dire motives into that casual cable. Leave it for later, he decided, rather than stir Diego's suspicions. Whatever the reason for the cable, the death of General Robles had given México Irredenta an importance beyond bureaucratic curiosity. Oliver had little sympathy with Diego's suggestion that the general was in his dotage. Until he knew better, the urgent question was the motive for the murder of the general. Furthermore, Oliver had to consider his own position, the embarrassment that would result were it to become known that he had been with Robles at his death.

Diego, recovered, raised the matter before Oliver could. "There are several points here. You have burdened me with knowledge. What am I to tell the authorities in the state of Guanajuato? They would be only too eager to talk to you." When Oliver started to speak Diego silenced him with a hand. "I shall tell them nothing of you. Not at the moment. But unless they come up with the assassins or you can supply some information that would lead to that—" He raised his eyebrows and continued. "The authorities will be looking for you, you realize. Secondly, his death has been greeted with great indignation in Guanajuato circles. Others—other than the authorities—will be pressing the search for you."

Oliver shifted in his chair. All of that had occurred to him but he didn't like hearing it. "Third," said Diego, holding up three fingers, "the assassins may be looking for you as well. They may consider that you may have earned the same attention they gave the general. Or they may think you can identify them. For that matter, can they identify you?

"And, finally, are we right in so easily assuming that those bullets were meant for General Robles alone?" Diego put his fingertips together and looked at Oliver over them. "Was that their intention or, from that distance, did they miscalculate and were those bullets meant for you?''

As if agreeing with that thought, the face of Benito Juárez seemed to show that he also thought it unfortunate that General Robles had been the victim rather than Oliver.

Chapter 5

While Oliver told them of the killing in Guanajuato, Sanders for once listened quietly. Lankester paced slowly along the edge of the carpet, head down, his eyes on his shoes, plump in his well-tailored gray flannel suit, not looking at Oliver, but stopping from time to time to study the wall, pausing to look out a window, a thoughtful frown on his face.

"Why Canada?" he asked as soon as Oliver had finished.

"I wish we knew, Chas."

"Isn't it more probable that you misunderstood him?"

"It's not a question of probabilities. I heard him say it. Clearly. More than once."

Then Oliver reviewed his talks with Winters and Diego.

Lankester sat down during that, keeping the same frown on his face. When Oliver finished, Lankester asked immediately, "Wouldn't it have been better to allow Diego to tell the Guanajuato authorities about you?"

"Better how?"

"Better all 'round. Make a clean breast of it so we have nothing to hide and Diego's not under that pressure. Consequently, all the better for our liaison relationship. Avoid this atmosphere of suspicion. Doesn't that make sense?"

Oliver regarded Lankester for a long moment before replying. "What atmosphere of suspicion?"

"What you described. Diego suspects you're holding something back."

"Look, Chas. Diego and I—we know each other. I've cleared today's hurdle. You're the one who knows I'm holding something back, namely, the cable from headquarters and the mention of Canada. I couldn't afford to mention the cable, the state he was in. He would have read it all wrong, thought it was more evidence of meddling. And his getting so worked up drove the Canada matter right out of my head. Anyway, Diego was okay when it came to the real test. He doesn't want to see me put up against a wall in Guanajuato any more than I do."

Lankester shrugged his shoulders and resumed pacing. "Just a suggestion, in the interest of things going more smoothly."

"Well, I also have this strong personal interest in not having Robles's friends or Robles's enemies—either party—banging around Mexico City looking for me."

Lankester paused in his pacing. "Of course, that's your decision. But you have let it become—you are treating it as a personal matter, aren't you? I have the impression the whole incident hasn't bothered you much, that is, you don't take it as seriously as Diego must." Oliver looked from Lankester to Sanders, trying to decide how to reply to that when Lankester went on to ask, "Have you reported this to headquarters?"

"Yeah, last night, when I got back. It's there. Just look in the cable file. Why?"

"What did they say?"

Oliver shrugged. "Nothing, as yet."

"I was wondering what guidance they might offer."

"Guidance. Screen invitations to lunch? Stay off balconies in Guanajuato?"

"Well, not that, obviously. More politically sensitive than that—how to deal with Diego on this."

"That'll be the day—they start telling me how to handle Diego."

"This could be serious, it seems to me, not to be taken too lightly."

"Jesus!" Oliver's mouth was half-open as he regarded Lankester. He started to say something else, closed his mouth, then said, "Chas, as far as guidance is concerned, something like this, you're on your own." Lankester did not reply to this and Oliver noticed, not for the first time, the way Lankester had of raising his eyebrows about halfway, of knitting his brow. It

was less a worried than a pained look, a look of disapproval—
not just disagreement, disapproval. Can't give in to that, Oliver
scolded himself, let a sensitivity to mannerisms, no matter how
superior or annoying, cloud his mind. Here they were alone
together—the four of them. Think of them as sailing in a boat
together—the need for tolerance was that strong, the importance
of consciously refusing to be irritated. No call for charity with
soft-voiced, soft-hearted, soft-featured Mrs. Pott. It was the
other two. Oliver took a deep breath and prayed to be granted
patience.

Sanders, who had been sitting on one arm of the blue couch,
his eyes going from one to the other as they talked, slipped down
onto the couch and asked, "How about that envelope?"

Oliver got up from his desk and went to sit next to him on the
couch. Lankester sat in the chair on the other side of the coffee
table.

"Well," said Oliver, "let's see what you two make of it."
He began reading aloud from the papers in the envelope General
Robles had passed him, translating as he went: " 'I write this
as I shall speak to you with utmost trust in your discretion and
faith in your integrity. I say this because your question will be,
naturally, why do I turn to you, a foreigner, to you, an official
of a foreign intelligence organization? I do not know you, but
the friend we have in common assures me that you are serious
and straightforward. And I believe your organization to be above
politics, devoted to pursuing truth without favor, no matter how
difficult or unwelcome the discovery may be.' "

"Wow!" said Sanders, looking over at the neat handwriting
on the paper Oliver held. "How about that!"

"Exactly," said Oliver. "Nice opening. Something we could
well chisel on a piece of limestone in the main hall back home.
You know, the old guy really meant it—not the usual greasy
windup with the old pitch for dough sliding into *para* seven."

"Of course, we don't know that. His true motives would have
been revealed later on in the conversation had you been able to
complete it," said Lankester.

Oliver started to speak but did not trust himself to avoid being
testy with Lankester. Aside from being annoyed by with his re-

marks, Oliver needed to caution Lankester about making sweeping statements without evidence. Sanders showed no such compunction: "You trying to tell us there's no Santa Claus, Chas?"

"All right, you two, listen, will you? 'With a contrasting estimate of our own Mexican authorities, I do not bring this to them, fearing they would deal with this politically, subjectively, either suspect my motives or ignore what I say—do whatever they find convenient at the moment.' "

"You gave this to Diego," said Lankester.

"Heck, no, Chas, not with those remarks. Maybe later on when we know more, get some idea—" Oliver waved an impatient hand. "Listen. Then he says we must agree on what action I might take on the basis of what he tells me, what he would have told me there at the table, I think he means, rather than what he wrote here. 'You will be aware of the struggle between church and state that broke out'—I guess that means—'in the decade of the twenties when President Plutarco Calles chose to enforce the, uh, anticlerical, uh, provisions of the Constitution of 1917. The reaction of the faithful and of the church hierarchy itself, which responded by suspending the practice of religion throughout Mexico, was, uh, earthshaking. Yet for many of the ordinary people, who retained their pre-Colombian superstitions and the worship of idols, the removal of the sacraments was not—was less a—hardship than the bishops had thought it would be. But there was nevertheless, uh, fierce resentment of the government's action.

" 'For example, the superstitions of the campesinos in the western states of Jalisco, Michoacán, and Colima, were exploited by the more sophisticated opponents of the Mexican revolution—' "

"They kill him for giving you that?" asked Sanders, sliding lower on the couch.

"Okay, okay. I can skip some of this. He goes on to talk about the Cristeros—"

"The faithful who rebelled against the government to defend the faith," interjected Lankester.

"He goes over all that," said Oliver. "All of this way back, you know—their blowing up the Guadalajara train and the government's reaction or overreaction. Concentration camps. Government troops destroying about half of Jalisco. Priests hanging from the telegraph wires. Refers to the assassination of President Obregón just after his election. That was in, let's see—"

"Nineteen twenty-eight," said Lankester.

"Talk about ancient history!" exclaimed Sanders.

"And then, okay. He picks up here with Sinarquismo in the 1930s. The conservative opposition to Cárdenas. Effect of the civil war in Spain. Support for the Loyalists on the one hand versus the influence of the Church and the Spanish Falange. The government's tolerance of German mischief making in Mexico, turning a blind eye to Abwehr operations in Mexico—"

"The Germans bought Mexican oil for a time, a form of bribery," said Lankester.

"Yeah, right. All that was during something known as World War Two, Pete."

"Seems to me I heard that mentioned somewhere once," said Sanders.

"What's more, Pete, in 1917 you had the Zimmerman telegram with the Germans offering Mexico Texas, New Mexico, and Arizona, if they would declare war on us."

"Today's history lesson," said Sanders.

"Well," resumed Oliver, "he goes over all this background as a context so we'll know what's going on."

"But what do we know?" asked Lankester.

Oliver held up a hand. "Let him finish. Here. 'Among the loosely connected organizations of a reactionary, xenophobic category at that time was one known as México Irredenta—' "

"At last!" That was Sanders.

" '—its program explained by the name, the return of the territories lost to the United States subsequent to the Treaty of Guadalupe Hidalgo in the year 1848. Any rational observer would pronounce such a notion as absurd, forgetting that politics are as often fueled by emotion, by exaggerated nationalistic anger, as by cold intellect. This group had a following sinister and bitter enough—although small—to lead the government of the time to try to suppress it, scatter its followers. But it can no more be stamped out than can a deadly virus.' "

"This all going to be on the exam, prof?" asked Sanders.

"All right, I'm nearly there. 'There are those who will scoff at my warning of a reversion to the power of fascism of half a century ago. The abuse of the term by the collectivist competitors of fascism—the communists—has rendered the term almost meaningless with the result that we have grown callous to the mention of it.' " Oliver took a breath and read on.

" 'I warn you. Yes, the young firebrand of those days may be an aging madman. But surely you will not scoff at the power of the demagogue. He—I warn you again—is a species of genius whose field of operations is the manipulation of bitterness and hatred. Therefore, your people, for whom I have, like most thoughtful Mexicans, both affection and respect, must examine what I have told you of the persons involved against this background. See them set in a matrix of evil—another word contemporary man has forgotten. Comprehend how they take advantage of the latent, smoldering resentment over our lost territories that today form your southwest. These sentiments are by no means merely historical, nor are they confined to the cabal that I shall have described to you. And together with contemporary grievances against the ruling party by an influential minority of the upper classes—who may draw a religious cloak about their selfishness—not to mention the play of so-called liberation theology among the easily swayed members of the ill educated—the latent volatility of the Mexican masses—you see here the very fundament of the clever if quite dishonest appeal of the so-called movement for México Irredenta.' "

"This all strikes me as highly unlikely," said Lankester.

" 'What concerns me most is—' " Oliver continued reading, "and here he says *'impostura'* that I take it means 'an imposture'—we don't use that word in English, do we?—'that I suspect an imposture, the launching of a grand deception, a political swindle, a grave interference in Mexican political life that could unleash the dogs of jealousy and suspicion. The imposture would be unnecessary, would make no sense, unless, as I will have explained it to you, my thesis of the reason for it is true.' "

"But does he give the reason?" asked Lankester.

"No, Chas, he doesn't. Listen."

" 'I fear first for Mexico but I fear also for the relations that bind our two peoples together in what must be friendship if we are to live as neighbors in peace. And—' " Here Oliver paused.

"And?" repeated Sanders.

"Get the last part of this sentence, you two: 'from what I will have told you, you will quickly gain an appreciation of the threat of the so-called movement for México Irredenta and that which renders its leadership so dangerously *verisímil*.' "There. What does he mean by that, *'verisímil'*? Verisimilitude?"

"Credible," Sanders offered.

"Verisimilitude? Plausible," said Lankester.

"Yeah," Sanders agreed. "Plausible—that's more like it."

"Lemme see something." Oliver walked to the stand where sat a fat *Webster's Unabridged*, flopped it open, wet a finger, and began to turn the pages. "Verify. Verify. Here. 'Verisimilitude. The appearance of truth.' " He closed the dictionary and sat down.

"Could you run through that last part again, boss?" asked Sanders.

Oliver did so.

"All that buildup—who's he talking about?" asked Sanders.

"Well, hell, Pete. That must have been what he was going to tell me."

"We don't know that," said Lankester. "Doesn't Diego imply that he was senile?"

"Not that, exactly. Old. You can be old without being senile. Anyway, Chas, we have to work a lot of the time on the basis of things we don't know or, anyway, can't be certain about," said Oliver.

"We should not have to, in my opinion," said Lankester. "I don't think we should put any credence in this very strange account. We should not invest agency resources in anything as vague and inconsequential as this."

"Look, Chas, it's not a matter of choice. It's not as though we deliberately went out of our way to get involved in a vague and inconsequential matter. In this business you have to take things the way they get served up to you. And they don't come all wrapped up in neat packages.''

"It's so inefficient.''

"Well, now, Chas, if it's efficiency you're looking for,'' said Oliver, walking over to his desk and tossing the papers on the top, "then—''

"—you chose the wrong career,'' Sanders finished for him.

Oliver thought about the observation. He would like to give Sanders credit for realizing how inefficient a process it is to grub for secrets that others have taken great pains to conceal. Some people never did accept that. On the other hand, Sanders might just have been making a cute remark.

"Well,'' Sanders went on, uncrossing his legs and leaning back, yawning and stretching. "Maybe Chas is right. Does it really matter now, with him dead? Too bad, I'd like to have known more about the young firebrand who is now an aging madman.''

Lankester laughed. "Exactly my point. Maybe the lesson is not to overreact to a request from a 'friend of the station' like Winters.''

Oliver felt like a lecturer in a basic course in intelligence operations. "Chas, the day we stop reacting, examining every lead that comes our way, we better close down the shop.''

Lankester smiled. "That seems to be your modus operandi.''

The smile could be as tiresome as the raised eyebrows.

"Don't forget we got a query from headquarters on this,'' said Oliver.

"True enough. I was in danger of forgetting that. We do have the obligation of replying to the NSC request, don't we? There is that point, at least.''

"See here, Chas,'' said Oliver. "We're in the field, not in Washington. Here, we have to put more weight on whatever it was that led Robles to approach us than on the NSC query with its etceteras. Talk about vague!''

"You can be sure the NSC knows more than the message itself reflected,'' said Lankester.

"Woulda been nice, in that case, if they'd filled in some of the blanks for us," Oliver could not help adding.

"Is that what they do at the NSC—crossword puzzles?" asked Sanders.

Oliver laughed, Lankester frowned, and Mrs. Pott stuck her head around the door. "I'm sorry but I have the most persistent person, Mr. Oliver. On the phone. A woman, an American. I asked for her number to call back, but she won't give her name. She says it's important to see you." She shook her head. "I'm sorry but—"

"No, no. That's all right." Oliver could not prevent Mrs. Pott's trying to protect him. Were Sanders's Cuban illegal to call in to surrender himself, Mrs. Pott was capable of telling him to call back the next day. Oliver took the phone at his secretary's desk. In a moment he was back. "Okay, Pete, get across, fast, to the hotel coffee shop and sit back, away from the windows." He gestured.

Sanders jumped to his feet. "What happened?"

"Nothing! I don't like getting called out like this. After yesterday—you know. Get a look at her. See if anyone came with her. I mean, not sitting with her. She's in a window booth. Gray jacket and black sweater. Drinking coffee. With a book. Go on. Hurry up. Get there before I do and watch me leave."

"Drinking coffee with a book." Sanders ran out the door.

Lankester stood up. "What's this all about?"

Oliver shook his head, pulling on his jacket as he hurried out the door after Sanders.

Oliver spotted her right away. He strolled slowly across the coffee shop an aisle away from where she sat with her eyes on the book in front of her. Despite the bustle in the coffee shop, waitresses moving about, voices rising from the tables and the booths, Oliver sensed her eyes to be straying from the page to track his progress through the edge of her vision. There was an alertness about her, a self-conscious stiffness in the way she held herself as she read or pretended to read. Without looking directly at him, she showed that she sensed he was there—business fitting the stage more than a coffee shop. Her eyes drifted to the floor of the aisle as Oliver came closer and she put a smile on her face when he stopped at the booth.

Hair dyed blond, showing mousy at the roots, the hair thick, full, drawn into a ponytail, a black ribbon tying it. Head narrow under the sleekness of the hair. Suit jacket a light gray plaid over a black sweater, gold chain around the neck. Full round brow, skin clear, lightly tanned, smears something on it at night. Pretty, undistinguished American female face of North European stock, bluish under the eyes, not fading but the first freshness gone—hard to tell: maybe thirty. Two vertical lines forming between the blue eyes, the first hint of a web at the outside corners of the eyes, an arc at either corner of the rouged lips. Small-boned, figure attractive enough, what could be seen of it, somewhat overweight—pleasingly plump, say.

She looked up at Oliver, blinking at him, squinting slightly: add contact lenses. The smile fading—hard to keep smiling indefinitely—then coming and going on either corner of the red lips, a smile not always reaching her eyes, coming and going again, never quite disappearing.

With a half bow Oliver asked, "Are you looking for me?"

She raised eyebrows darker than her hair. "Oh, hi," she said in a cracked voice. She giggled, cleared her throat. "You Mr. Oliver?"

Oliver sat down as he nodded assent, turning to wave for a waitress. "I didn't get your name, Miss—"

"Debbie."

"What's your last name, Debbie?"

"Just Debbie, what my friends call me."

"More coffee?" he asked. Oliver looked past the waitress, so that his eyes took in one sleeve of a brown tweed jacket at the far side of the central counter, Sanders being enveloped and made otherwise invisible by the copy of *Excelsior* he had grabbed on leaving the office. Sanders would hardly be able to see anything unless he poked a hole in the newspaper.

Oliver felt her eyes on him. When he turned back to her she was looking down at her book as she closed it. "Had my caffeine fix," she said. "Can't drink it the way I used to, know what I mean?'' She laughed. Her speech had a flatness to it that defied his analysis: an accent suppressed.

Oliver asked the waitress for coffee. "José Vasconcelos," he said, craning his neck to look at the spine of the book. "You read Spanish."

"Oh, sure. It's his biography? I mean, autobiography? Fabulous. I haven't finished it yet.'' She gave Oliver a smile, blinked, and smiled even more intensely, showing even white teeth, crinkling her eyes.

"I have to admit," said Oliver, smiling himself, trying to put her—or was it himself?—at ease, "he put me to sleep. Not before I got the drift. Rather hard on us, isn't he?"

"Us? You mean—?"

"Us. North Americans. You and me."

"Oh?" She put her head on one side. "That get you uptight?" She frowned. "Don't you think we should listen to what other people say about us?"

Oh, Lord, thought Oliver, deciding he should move the conversation along. "Well, I guess that's right," was what he said, encouragingly. He took a sip of coffee and put the cup down. "Well, you said you wanted to see me, Debbie. Here I am. What can I do for you?"

Her eyes flickered and blinked rapidly as she smiled again. "I wanted to talk to someone from the embassy?" She gave a small laugh. "A citizen, like you said. Really I'm more like a citizen of the world? Like someday it won't be 'us' against 'them'?"

"Well, that would be nice," said Oliver. If she was going to turn out to be nothing but a nut, there remained the task of classifying her in that genus by species and variety and putting her full name in the file, if he could get a full name from this member of the no-surname generation. "What's your last name, Debbie?"

Her hand started toward her coffee cup and just as suddenly she withdrew it. "I'm like—wow!" She bent her arms at her side and twisted in the seat as though dancing. "Unbelievable! Here I am talking to this big high official from the embassy." She gave a loud laugh. "Wow, Mr. Oliver!"

"Look, call me Ted if that will lessen the tension any."

"Lessen the tension. I love it! I'm like—he's much too important to talk to little me." She squirmed with her torso in a charade of meekness. "You're great to see me, Ted, no kidding!"

Oliver could feel the stiffness of his facial muscles as he tried to keep smiling back at Debbie Full-name-unknown. "How'd you happen to call me, Debbie?"

She was nodding as he spoke. "Okay." She spoke quickly, eyes on his. "I guess you've heard of this organization called, um, México Irredenta."

Oliver, sitting with his elbows propped on the table, was able to maintain that stance long enough to absorb the blow with apparent calm. Mentally, he was skipping about, dancing from one foot to another, putting his guard up. He was preparing to reclassify her from the harmless-nut category into a poisonous genus. "Well, yes, I have," he said, frowning thoughtfully. "Why, it's one of the opposition factions, isn't it? Opposed to the government and the government party, to the Institutional Revolutionary Party, the PRI."

Her eyes were close on him, waiting for him to give something away. When he did not she moved back in her seat to lean against the corner of the booth and recross her legs, her eyes still on him. Oliver leaned back the same way, as though to mark the end of the first stage of their conversation, easing the tautness of his body, keeping his eyes on her, trying to keep his gaze casual, to keep from clearing his throat, to hold his body loose, to avoid the needless gesture—show no physical response to the shock he had felt at her question.

"Sure. The PRI line, the government line. What they tell the embassy. Hey! México Irredenta? That's just some little faction. Some unimportant little opposition faction. Sure. That's what they want you to think."

"As a matter of fact, I don't remember that I've heard it referred to in any particular way by the PRI."

"Maybe they don't want to talk about it? Did you ever think of that? They'll be talking about it soon enough. Wait and see."

"Well, I don't know. Tell me more."

"I'm really serious, Mr. Oliver."

"What's it all about? What does that mean, México Irredenta."

"Mexico Reborn? Like, the rebirth of Mexico, I guess you'd translate it, something like that?" She leaned forward to rest an elbow on the table and she flipped that hand to wave aside the petty question of translation. "There's this group of really incredibly dedicated people, they've rediscovered the real Mexican traditions? The ancient tradition sort of thing? Their really incredible native past sort of thing. And, um, along with that the very, very important traditions they got from Spain? Mexicans don't like to admit that? You know, it takes, like, courage to go up against what people think? What Vasconcelos said? The new politics? On the cutting edge, literally. Literally, ground breaking. Fabulous, the incredible difference it's going to make in Mexico. Stop the oppression of the campesinos? The oppression of women? And a really genuine concern for the environment? I mean, see for yourself. Look at the air pollution! What are they doing?" She laughed. "Look, Ted." Intimate smile. "You know it's not just some kinda little faction, like they try to say, don't you?" When her hand went to the coffee cup and then to her lap, Oliver did not need to look directly at it to see it was trembling.

I'm the one should be nervous: "What's your connection with México Irredenta, Debbie?"

"My connection with the Movement? That's what they call it, Ted. The Movement. In Spanish, of course. Oh, nothing special." She put her arms behind her head to adjust the bow on her ponytail, arching her back as she did so. Then she put her arms on the tabletop, resting her chin on one hand—several large rings, no wedding ring, bracelets. "All my friends are like, Debbie! What're you into now? Like they're all just so literally amazed the way I get involved, wherever I am—so very, very amazed. In Mexico you have your oppression by the ruling elite? Your United States intervention? Your embassy so very, very close to the PRI? To your Institutional Revolutionary party? Everybody sees that. The PRI *is* the government and the source of the oppression. So unbelievably corrupt. And your embassy so incredibly supportive? I mean, they're, um, not really your friends, you know.''

"You mean our friends, us Americans.''

She gave an impatient shake of the head. "The American government, I mean.''

"Debbie, this is interesting. We've got to talk more about this. Let me have your name and phone number, so we can—''

Her smile stopped where it was and she shook her head so that the ponytail fluttered behind her head. "Maybe you're one of those people who don't like to hear the truth, how all this looks to the Mexican people. The real people, not the elite the embassy sees all the time. So, okay, maybe you'll put me on your blacklist, that would be something to be proud—''

"Oh, come on, Debbie. What blacklist? I appreciate—''

"Why do you keep on asking and asking for my name, as if I did something wrong, unless you have a blacklist?''

Oliver shook his head. "No, Debbie, not for any such reason. The thing is you obviously know a lot about the Movement. And I appreciate your wanting the embassy to know more about it. What's your own connection with the Movement?''

She still had a sulky look. "Like I said, the embassy ought to know and you're making me feel I did something wrong, you know? All these questions.'' She smiled hard, then, waving one hand in front of his face. "Okay, Ted! You say you appreciate— tell me—what were you doing in Guanajuato yesterday?''

This time Oliver was ready. Debbie was after something more important than babbling on about the Movement. He allowed a moderate expression of mild surprise to come onto his face. "Guanajuato? Well, I certainly wasn't in Guanajuato yester- day. I don't know when I was last there. But it wasn't yesterday. What gave you—''

"Tell me, Ted. I want to know! Come on! You were, weren't you? It doesn't matter but I want to know.''

"Debbie.'' Oliver tried to look amused and exasperated at the same time. "You've got the wrong guy. Where'd you get— what is it you're after?''

She looked uncertain. "You weren't there yesterday?'' She

wiggled about in the seat. "Come on, Ted. You telling me you weren't there yesterday?"

"Right, Debbie. I don't get the point of your question. Is it connected somehow with the Movement?"

"No, no. Never mind, never mind. The Movement. Like I said, the embassy ought to check it out. It's coming on very strong."

"Well, you can help us with that, Debbie."

"Yeah, right." She nodded vigorously and began to slide along the seat toward the aisle. "I really gotta run along now, Ted." She picked up her purse. "Got the check there?"

"Never mind. I'll take care of that." Her feet were in the aisle. "But about the Movement—"

Black purse and book in her hand, she had one leg out of the booth. "Yeah, like I said, check it out. I really gotta go."

"Wait." Oliver was standing clumsily by the booth, so that she could not easily get to her feet. "How can I get in touch with you, Debbie?"

"Hey, pardon *me*, Ted, old boy." She half rose, pushing against him, so that he had to step back or be more than rude. "I'll call you."

Oliver watched her walk through the shop to the passage that led to the lobby of the Hotel María Isabel. Yes, maybe a little plump but a good figure. A nice pair of legs brought her on her devious assignment. When she went out of sight through the far door of the coffee shop, Oliver sat back down, twirled the half-empty cup on its saucer for a moment before signaling the waitress.

Chapter 6

"You, Pete, with the newspaper wrapped around your head there, what were you hiding from?" Oliver asked Sanders when they had both returned to the office. "Get a look at her?"

"Yeah," said Sanders. "When you left I went out the door to Río Danubio and up around the corner. I slowed down when I reached that angle of the storefronts there. Good thing I did. She was getting into a red Nissan parked in the lateral. Belongs to a guy named Chato Escobar. He's with the foreign office, External Relations. He's standing right on the other side of the car. He didn't see me. Neither did she. Her name's Debbie Kraus."

"If you don't mind my saying so, it would be completely impossible for you to have worked all that out in such a short time," said Lankester, frowning at Sanders and turning to regard Oliver with eyebrows raised.

"Well, I tell you what, Chas," said Sanders. "I just happen to know her. That's why I hid behind the newspaper. Keep her from seeing me. She teaches a class at the university, at UNAM. That's how Susie knows her. It's the same time as Susie's archaeology."

"Now there is a coincidence," said Lankester, turning to Oliver.

"I sure as hell hope so," said Oliver, looking at Sanders. "Is it?"

"What do you mean?"

"Well, to put it bluntly, has Susie, well, mentioned me, that is, did she suggest that Debbie Kraus call me?"

56

"Certainly not! No! She couldn't have."

"All right, Pete, I know," said Oliver, holding up both hands. "But we've got to work this out, understand? What do you mean she couldn't?"

"Okay. I mean, she wouldn't. Debbie's been there a few times when I get home. That's how I know Escobar—Debbie came home with Susie and he came by to pick her up. A couple of times. Stayed for a drink, at least twice, I guess. Drives that same Nissan 200X something—whatever. They've given Susie a lift home a couple of times."

"What's he like?"

"A pain in the ass. Sits there looking around the room, bored, not taking part in the conversation. Try to say something, to bring him out, he's not interested. I don't know whether he's stupid or just cagey. You get the impression he's not over-worked at External Relations."

"Doesn't go out of his way to be friendly?"

"Not with me. Turns on charm with women. What he considers to be charm."

"Speak English?"

"Yeah. We speak Spanish together, but he's translated for Susie a couple of times. Susie's Spanish isn't as good as Debbie's. He's good-looking, if you like the type. Blow-dried. Sharp clothes. Mustache. Susie says he has no manners. He's mainly interested in himself, doesn't treat Debbie very well, according to Susie."

Oliver got up from behind his desk and came to sit across the coffee table from Sanders. "What's the relationship?"

"They live together. At least, some of the time. He's married. I mean, not to her. She's divorced. From Texas. Worked in television in the states. Politically trendy—the Third World, Africa, the environment—wild stories about the agency. All according to formula. Give her the subject, she's got the current line."

"What kind of course she teach?"

"Communications something, or media something. Has to do with television production."

"She know about you?"

"No. I don't think she'd come out with the things she does about the agency. You can be quite sure Susie wouldn't ever say anything to her."

"I see," said Oliver.

"I can't say that I do. What do you mean?" asked Lankester.

"For Christ's sake, Chas. Want me to draw a picture?" asked Sanders. "Susie would jump off the top of the embassy before she'd let on I'm with the agency. Especially with someone like Debbie. I mean, not that she would to anyone."

Lankester was red. "That's too bad."

"Don't worry about it. Don't think I haven't been working on it," said Sanders. "God knows. Then someone like Debbie has to come along and work on Susie."

"How work on Susie? Debbie doesn't strike me as any intellectual giant. Could she influence Susie?"

"Oh, her political chatter, that's all."

"But Susie wouldn't be impressed by Debbie's ideas, would she? The way she talks."

"That goes with television, I think. She was in advertising, did television spots for car dealers. Worked up to doing political spots. That mentality."

"What mentality?" asked Lankester.

Sanders thought for a moment. "Well, the negative political ads, for example. She sees nothing wrong with that. She's fascinated by technique, the effect, whatever's clever. The manipulation doesn't bother her. We've talked about it. She laughs it off. That's the way the world is—that mentality. Substance is nothing, it's all form."

"But from what you say she has quite a grasp of politics," said Lankester.

"The words, yeah. The jargon. She thinks of herself as real political, but it's more gossip—no, not only that but—I just don't think she's given much thought to half the things she says."

"I had trouble understanding her, Pete, but she's not exactly dumb either."

"No, I didn't say that. She exists on some other level, that's all. I think her real interests, beyond television, advertising, the manipulation of campaigns, are clothes and restaurants—those are the things she talks about. Funny, she's not bad looking, physically quite attractive, but I find her boring. Irritating.''

"Hasn't she ever mentioned México Irredenta?''

"Never. Not a word.''

"She ask questions?'' asked Oliver. "Fill out somebody's questionnaire?''

"I don't think so. Talks too much for that. Damn! I'll ask Susie.''

"Okay. Not to worry. But look. Someone sent Debbie to see me. I can't conceive her doing this on her own. Can you?''

Sanders shrugged his shoulders.

"First thing, Pete, sit down and write everything you remember about her and Escobar. And, Pete—''

"I was going to do just that as soon as you finished,'' said Sanders, getting up, nettled at being told to do what he had already planned to do.

"Okay, Pete.'' Prima donnas! "Get what you can from Susie, but she shouldn't—I mean don't go into this about Debbie and me. Okay?''

That needless advice made Sanders scowl even more. He turned and left.

Oliver got out of his chair, walked back to his desk, sat down. "Well, crap!'' he said. "Goes to show you. At first I was sitting there thinking she was just some kind of a nut.''

"Pete knowing her. That's not at all good.''

"Well, we can't change that. Maybe it'll help with this Irredenta business. And I gotta get busy on my own contact report. Still not one word from home. You'd think—last time I got shot at the director perked up, showed some interest.''

"I remember that very well. I don't think you need feel it's a lack of concern. I'm sure they're working up some guidance.''

"We'll have to struggle along a bit longer without that. Question is: Who gave little Debbie my name?''

"Better we give some thought to the Sanders couple. They seem to be consorting—''

"I'm writing, okay?'' Sanders had come back in. "But how come she called you? I swear it wasn't Susie.''

"What's your guess, then? Had I ever heard of México Irredenta? Yes. So what? Was I in Guanajuato yesterday? No. Once she checked that item off her list, she stopped being seductive, if that's what it was, and couldn't wait to get the hell out of there. And right now where is she reporting in? To whoever sent her—to whomever sent her.'' Oliver found to his distress that he couldn't keep a smile on his face. The smile wasn't working out at all and he looked down to confirm that, indeed, his hands were, as he thought, shaking. The scene at the table in Guanajuato had burst open in his head without warning, leaving him suddenly short of breath. To prevent the other two from noticing, he jumped to his feet to begin pacing around the room. "Damn!" He forced the word out with an explosion of breath and slapped his hands together. "Why the interview? If they have my name, the stupid little show across the street was pointless.''

"Size you up?" asked Sanders.

"Has it occurred to you that Diego might have told them?" asked Lankester.

"No, it hasn't. He wouldn't without letting me know."

"How can you be so confident of that? Isn't it in his interest to do so?"

Oliver decided to drop the point rather than argue. The three of them were quiet for a moment.

"Robles had my name from Jack Winters," said Oliver. "If I'd used an alias, then we wouldn't—but I didn't and we are. So he told someone he was meeting me? Or—or what?" He sprawled on the couch.

"Maybe Robles wrote your name down somewhere and they found it and they're checking you out," said Sanders, who had taken up pacing back and forth as soon as Oliver stopped. "That is, they don't *know* you were with Robles. The police found it and they—whoever—found out from the police. You know, nothing that would prove that you were actually with him at the time. How about that?"

Oliver nodded. "Let's get to writing. Sometimes when you put it all down . . .''

Mrs. Pott introduced herself with a nervous giggle. "It's Washington. Mr. O'Rourke. On the phone, I mean."

The three men stared at Mrs. Pott and then at each other. Oliver moved to his desk to pick up the phone.

"Hello?"

"Just a moment, Mr. Oliver. I'll put him on."

"Ted?" shouted O'Rourke.

"Yeah, you reading your mail up there?"

"Listen, Ted, you're not the only client we got to look after, know what I mean?"

"Sorry to bother you, Slasher."

"Okay, smart guy. You got a visitor coming, reason I called."

"Oh, coming because of what happened?"

"Oh, that. Yeah, maybe related but essentially—no."

"Well, you cleared that up."

"Ted, you'll catch on once he gets there. He's got guidelines for you. You with me?"

"Guidelines."

"Yeah, maybe tied to the little problem you had Sunday. I mean the other guy had." A chuckle came over the phone. "You with me?"

"Um. We've had some interesting developments here since then, assuming you're interested."

"Listen, smart guy, I've been running my ass off up here on this thing. The visitor, the one who's coming, he'll fill you in. Just wait, understand? He'll explain everything. It's all laid on. Relax. Know what I mean?"

Oliver made a face and shook his head at Lankester and Sanders. "How about a name for the visitor?"

"No. He'll get in touch. Just hang in there."

"In the meantime?"

"There's no meantime, Ted."

"We're going to have to do some digging on that outfit."

"What outfit?"

"The one—hey, Slasher—what other outfit is there? One you cabled us about."

"That thing. That just slipped out. The holidays. Slipped through the net. Forget it, Ted. Never happened. You never got asked. Ted, take your guidance, repeat, take your guidance from the visitor, okay, Ted?"

"Forget cable, take guidance from visitor."

"Right, Ted. Never happened. Never was any half-assed query from some goofball on a nonexistent subject. We'll take care of that up here. Damp it down. Know what I mean?"

"Hmm."

"And burn it, Ted. I mean, get rid of it. All copies. Including commo. Deep-six it, literally. No record. Got me?"

"Forget the whole thing."

"Now you're talkin'. Forget the whole thing."

"Look, Slasher. How can—"

"Good talking to you, Ted. Keep up the good work down there."

O'Rourke hung up. Oliver laughed. "That was O'Rourke. On the little problem I had. Says just forget the whole thing."

"What can he mean by that?" asked Lankester.

"Some unnamed visitor is coming with the guidance you've been waiting for, Chas. So, as I said—" Mrs. Pott was back, pointing to the phone again. Oliver picked it up and listened for a minute and then made some comments. When he hung up he turned to Sanders. "Okay, Pete. You were right. The Guanajuato judge handling the investigation called Diego to say they found this name on Robles's memo pad and a phone number which led them to the embassy. Damn! You see where an alias—anyway, like a good boy, the judge calls Gobernación and asks whether he should call External Relations and Diego says oh, hell, don't do that, lemme check into it personally. He's going to call the judge back to say he found out I have something to do with scholarships, that sort of thing, and Robles was   trying to get some kind of grant for some deserving group in Guanajuato. All very dull and boring. I said fine and said— you heard me—to say I was real hazy about the whole thing and couldn't place Robles at first, finally recalled him. Mild shock, perfunctory regrets at the news. Had been getting around to asking him for a letter outlining his idea, sometime when I got around to it. Impression of bureaucratic indolence.'' Oliver frowned. ''Diego's not real happy about this, but then, to be quite frank about it, neither am I.''

The two phone calls had rid Oliver of his attack of nerves. ''Oh, yeah. Diego said Robles had been going around asking questions about México Irredenta. How about that? Maybe asking the wrong questions of the wrong people. Wonder what he was after? Something led him to Canada, didn't it?''

''Does that judge know more than he's saying?'' asked Lankester.

''Hell, how do I know? Diego's thrown him off my scent anyway.''

''I wonder if that's wise.''

Sanders raised his eyebrows a millimeter and got up to go back to his own room.

''Well, it's wise enough for the moment, Chas. What are you waving around there?''

Lankester had been clutching a wad of papers during the whole conversation. He looked at them now. ''Mrs. Pott has traced Irredenta, La Irredenta, México Irredenta, Méxica Irredenta, including Mexíca, the accent on the middle syllable as it is often written, with no results, including all embassy files. And Redenta. La Redenta. 'Mexico Redenta,' '' he added. ''She has made xeroxes of what she found. There is no classified material, just newspaper clippings. You'll want to read them but I don't think you'll find anything new. Then, concerning Robles himself. According to Mrs. Pott, who went to the defense attaché's office: various army postings, all in the gazette. There is a reference in an old *Who's Who* to the grandfather who was in the revolution with Venustiano Carranza.''

''Good old Venustiano,'' said Oliver. ''Case like this you might do better to run the file checks with someone like the military attaché yourself, rather than have Mrs. Pott do it.''

''I don't see why. Hardly seems a good use of my time,'' said Lankester.

''Well, Chas, I prefer to do the checks when we go to another

office. It hasn't done me any lasting harm.'' Oliver smiled to
take the edge off the remark. ''D'you know that 'La Cucaracha'
was the song Carranza's troops sang?''

Sanders, popping back in, heard that. ''Great place to pick up
folklore; I don't get it. O'Rourke told you to drop the whole
thing? How can you?''

''Good question, Pete. I'm not sure we will.''

''Well, we must, if they say so,'' declared Lankester.

''Look at it this way, Chas. Say we're tidy bureaucrats.
We get something in writing, we reply in writing. Something happens, we report it. In writing. On the other hand,
as you point out, orders are orders. Orders given, it should
be noted, by an off-the-record phone call.'' Without waiting
for an answer, he said to Sanders: ''You writing a contact
report?''

''Yes, sir, yes, sir.''

Sanders's problem, thought Oliver, is that he can't really
be sure about Susie. That's his problem. And mine, he
added. He heard Lankester saying something along the line
of not taking O'Rourke's phone call, his orders, lightly.

''Huh?'' said Oliver.

''—wager that he's operating on orders from the director.''

Before Mrs. Pott left that night Oliver told her to destroy
all the copies of the cable with the query from the National
Security Council. ''All but one,'' he said. ''And put that in
an envelope with my name on it in the file with my personal
papers.''

''I'll take care of it,'' she said. ''What happened in Guanajuato got me to thinking, Mr. Oliver.''

''About what?''

''About the time those awful people tried to shoot you at that
lovely spot where we went picnicking that time. Do you know?
That incident changed it completely for me. I have never been
able to bring myself to go out there again.''

Oliver had been feeling better until she said that. Now he

could only shake his head and force out a croak of a laugh. "And now they've ruined Guanajuato for you."

"That's not what I meant. I'm not thinking of myself. Really, I wonder whether you should not be asking whether you are safe in Mexico any longer, Mr. Oliver."

When he got home that night Marge had the paper folded to the story about the assassination of General Robles. "There," she said, handing it to him. "That was Guanajuato, wasn't it? That's your 'bad accident,' isn't it? How were you involved?"

Oliver looked at the article. "I wasn't involved. I just happened to be around when it happened. That's all."

"Funny the way you happen to be around."

"Well, it was unpleasant but it has nothing to do with us."

"Ted?"

"Really." He put his arms around her. "Just chance, one of those things." He could feel the shiver go through her. "It was a coincidence, that's all," he said, an inspired borrowing from Lankester. God knows it would be nice if it turned out that way! He gave her a squeeze.

She pulled away from him to examine his face.

"That's all there is to it." He smiled at her. "Where're the kids?"

After another second of looking into his eyes she said, "In bed. Do you know what time it is? I take it you're ready for dinner. I certainly am."

"What did Chas and Pete think of what happened in Guanajuato?" Marge asked at the table.

"Oh, I don't know. This pesto is perfect. They had nothing particularly useful to say." He put his fork down. "To be honest, they don't contribute one hell of a lot. You know who I miss? Old Harley Drew."

"Harley was fun. What made you think of him?"

"Oh, today I was talking and I used *who* instead of *whom* and I fell all over the place correcting myself. Habit—before Harley could jump on me. Reminded me how I miss him."

"As I remember, you and Harley were always arguing pointlessly about something or other."

"Oh, I don't know about that. It may have seemed pointless to you. As I remember, by the end of it we'd gotten somewhere. Reminds me, I owe Harley a letter."

Before going to bed, Oliver went to stand at the edge of the dark of the children's room just where Marge had stood the night before. He listened to Tom's noisy breathing. Nancy turned in her sleep. Oliver was examining the barrier he had built between them and his work, inspecting it for leaks, wondering whether repairs or maintenance might be needed. It had been so much simpler those days when he was alone with his work.

Chapter 7

The brown adobe wall on Calle Aldama in San Miguel de Allende was right on the street, ivy growing thick over shards of broken glass set in the cemented cap of the high wall. Oliver raised the forged-iron ring, a rusty outsized doughnut that hung heavy on the center of the door and tapped it against a pocked metal plate.

Immediately there was an answer in Spanish from the other side, a high voice that quavered over the top of the adobe wall: "Yes? Who is it?"

Oliver backed away from the heavy stone doorsill onto the cobblestones of the narrow street. "Hello! I'm looking for Señor Lazaire. I come from the American embassy in Mexico."

The door began to shake. "Oh, dear!" Oliver heard the woman say—that was in English.

So was the man's voice. "Now what?"

"There's someone—" The woman's voice went low and Oliver could not hear what she said.

"Well, let's open up, then!" That was the man. "Here." There was the sound of a bolt being drawn and the door swung back. The tall man frowning at Oliver through the doorway had a red face, wavy white hair, a white *guayabera* bulging at the waistline. The magazine he had been reading dangled from one hand while he held the door with the other. He must have been strikingly handsome once. He would have a distinguished look about him now were not the symmetrical structure of his face puffed over with mottled red flesh. His blue eyes were bloodshot in their pouches. Pink wattles hung soft below his chin.

The woman in a wide-brimmed straw gardening hat stood to one side in a striped cotton dress, the tines of the small weeder in her hand black with fresh earth. Under the brim of the hat soft brown eyes in a green-pale face went from the man to Oliver and back.

"Mr. Lazaire?"

The man nodded, looking Oliver up and down.

"I'm from the embassy in Mexico. I'd like to talk to you about something that's come up. We think maybe you can help us."

"Wouldn't you like to—" the woman began. Lazaire took his hand from the door and shoved it abruptly toward her, the palm open, his eyes on Oliver.

"From the embassy, eh?"

Oliver nodded. "That's right."

The man shook his head from side to side. "Came all the way down here. Must need something bad, then."

He stepped back and turned to go into the house.

The woman smiled at Oliver and beckoned. "Go right on in. It's all right. Just go on in. I'll get coffee. The maid—no, no, I can get it," she said as Oliver began to close the door. "You'd better go on in."

Lazaire had stopped at the door. When Oliver reached it, Lazaire turned without speaking to lead the way through a silent dark living room, where heavy wooden Mexican chairs stood stiff in a semicircle. A coffee table made of a polished cross section of tree trunk shone dully in front of a chintz-covered couch. Oliver caught sight of a pastel portrait of an Indian girl in a headdress. A smell of cold smoke persisted in the fireplace, green pine logs left half-burned in a wrought-iron grate. On the mantel the works of a clock in a glass case jerked quietly from side to side.

The man turned in the gloom of the hall beyond and said, "In here." The den was paneled in vertical strips of mahogany, dark red curtains drawn against the closed windows. A green glass-shaded light with a brass base shone on a desktop. He leaned to turn on a high brass lamp standing next to a red leather chair, a ruffed grouse leaping in the picture on its shade. The bulging reflections of the lamps shown on the dusty screen of a ponder-ous television set in one corner. Lazaire picked up papers from the seat of the other red leather chair and motioned with his head for Oliver to sit down, tossing the papers on the floor. Lazaire sat in the chair by the lamp, the magazine open on his lap, ready to resume reading. He sat in such a way that he did not look directly at Oliver. "So you're from the embassy."

"From the station, actually."

"Why didn't you say so in the first place? How long you been here?"

"Here—in Mexico, you mean?" Oliver sat down in the other chair. Unless Lazaire glanced toward him when he spoke, as he had just then, Oliver saw him in profile.

"Yeah. Here in Mexico. Where else?"

"Oh, less than a year."

"Less than a year. Guess you're an expert by now."

"Hardly. I don't expect to be expert anytime soon."

"Your modesty is—what do you want?" That last was di-rected to the woman, Mrs. Lazaire, Oliver assumed. Lazaire was not looking at her, either.

"The maid's away today." She put on a small smile for Ol-iver. "What do you take in your coffee?"

"Maybe—what'd you say your name was?"

"Oliver. Ted Oliver."

"Maybe Mr. Oliver doesn't like coffee. D'you ask him?"

"Oh, Lester—"

Oliver was on his feet. "That's fine. Black is fine, thank you." He took a terra-cotta pottery cup and saucer from the tray.

The woman set the tray with a squat matching pot on the corner of the desk nearest to Oliver and turned to Lazaire. "It's Wednesday, the day for the cleaners. The two suits of yours—you want me—?"

Lazaire frowned. "No, I'm going. Mr. Oliver won't be long."

"I'll just freshen up, then. I thought I might go in with you—"

Lazaire slapped the leather arm. "I told you. We're not leaving this *house*. Not both of us." He was not looking at the woman as he spoke but at the magazine in his lap.

She wrapped her arms in front of her, hands on her elbows, and tried again to smile at Oliver. "We've been robbed, you see. Three times now. That's why Lester—"

"All right, all right!" Lazaire looked at Oliver. "So?" The woman picked up the tray and went out.

Oliver remembered now that they had called Lazaire—the people who worked for him—Lester the Lizard Lazaire.

"You knew General Robles."

Lazaire turned his head to stare at Oliver without expression. "I knew Carlitos, all right. Who killed him?"

Oliver shook his head. "That's what we're trying to find out."

"Oh? What's the interest? We using Carlos?"

"No. But Robles wanted to get in touch. Apparently he had something for us."

"Carlitos was onto something."

"Oh." Oliver reached for the cup and saucer. "Did he talk to you about it?"

"What I want to know is, did he talk to you about it?"

Oliver just shook his head.

"All right, Oliver. I'm asking you. He tell you people what he wanted?"

"If he had, would I be here asking you?"

"Someone was with him when he was killed. A foreigner, I hear. An Anglo. Was it one of ours?"

"They don't know who it was."

" 'They.' Who are 'they'?"

Oliver shrugged. "The authorities."

"Whatta you bet they know and aren't saying? Who sent you to see me? You one of that bunch from Germany moved in and took over the division?" asked Lazaire.

Oliver finished his coffee and put the cup back on the desk. "I never served in Germany, Lazaire."

"Got rid of all the old gang. And then they couldn't find their ass with both hands, what I heard."

"Robles. How recently had you seen him?"

"Hey, I'm a suspect now." Lazaire laughed. "Think I was the joker with the glasses and the tweed jacket?"

"You got the description, then."

"Goddamn right. We're gonna find that son of a bitch. He set Carlitos up."

"Who are 'we'?"

Lazaire laughed and shook his head.

"Why would someone set him up?" asked Oliver.

"That's for me to find out."

"Robles involved in anything you know of that would make someone kill him?"

Lazaire shrugged. "Could be a lot of things. Or nothing."

"I'll find out sooner if you've got any ideas. Any leads."

"Shit! You won't find anything out, sonny boy." Lazaire grinned at Oliver. "Who'd they send down to replace the old Indian fighter, Art Wilkins?"

"I replaced Art."

"Jesus," said Lazaire, shaking his head. "You mean you're chief of station?"

Oliver stood up. "Okay, Lazaire. Forget I asked. I'm keeping you from getting your suits to the cleaners."

Lazaire remained seated. "Listen, smart-ass. Wait till you're sitting on your butt down here, they send some *chamaco* down to replace you. Sit on your ass all day, read the *Economist* a week old. See how you like it." He brandished the magazine, not looking at Oliver, and threw it on the floor. "You don't fool me, another goddamn import, coming down here—oh, hell, no, nothing ever happened before *you* got here. No, sir. You don't fool me a goddamn minute. You don't give a shit about Carlitos. A piece of paper you gotta take care of, headquarters told you to."

Oliver paused in the doorway. "I guess you know how to get hold of me if anything comes up." Lazaire was staring at the wall, his head trembling, the gasping coming shallow from his mouth.

In the narrow paved space between the house and the door to the street, she was crouched at a border of zinnias that grew in the rectangle of sun next to the wall of the house, scratching with the weeder when Oliver came out the door into the courtyard.

"Thank you for the coffee, Mrs. Lazaire."

"You leaving so soon?" She still knelt, her back to him, but she turned her head partway toward him to smile. "Just a moment. I'll let you out."

"That's all right."

"He's not well. You understand, don't you? Sometimes he resents those of us who are. It was nice of you to come. It does him good to see people." She let out a breath as she forced herself to her feet. "Dear me, I get so stiff." Oliver offered her an arm, and she smiled and shook her head. "Does me good to try."

"Did you know General Robles?" he asked.

"Oh, dear. Not that." She turned to face him. She was not smiling now. "Are you working with—" She looked toward the house. "I don't like it one little bit. He gets so worked up."

"Working with whom, do you mean?"

"Doris!" Lazaire was standing in the shadows by the door to the house. "Can't you see I'm in a hurry?"

She went slowly past Oliver without looking at him, stepping carefully, head down, around Lazaire to get to the door. Lazaire stayed to stare unblinkingly at Oliver. Turning to go out the gate, Oliver deliberately left the door open. As he walked on the uneven cobblestones back up the street he heard a harsh laugh and the sound of the gate being slammed shut.

Chapter 8

The ambassador sat blinking, otherwise stone-faced, at Oliver as he closed the heavy door and came across the carpet toward the desk. Arms resting on the green desk blotter, the ambassador was twirling a pen slowly. A large, round-faced, pink-skinned man in a light blue suit sat in a chair in front of the desk, one long leg cocked across his knee, white flesh showing above a black sock, shiny brown loafers on his feet. "There he is," the man said in a hearty voice as Oliver come toward them.

The ambassador was clearing his throat. "Ted—" he began.

The man in the chair jumped to his feet. "Ted. Remember me? Claude Clinkscale." He put his right elbow to shoulder height and brought his hand down fast to grab Oliver's hand. "Good to see you, Ted." He towered over Oliver, a smile on his wide mouth, large left hand on Oliver's right shoulder. Retaining his grip, Clinkscale turned toward the ambassador, holding the pose as though they were standing for a photograph: "Thanks a lot, Mr. Ambassador."

The ambassador remained seated, twirling the pen. "Mr. Clinkscale is legislative assistant to Congressman Birdsong, Ted."

"Yes." Oliver knew he had seen Clinkscale somewhere before. "Of course."

"I'll get this character outta your hair now, Mr. Ambassador." Clinkscale, laughing, relinquished Oliver's hand but kept his hand on Oliver's shoulder, kneading it. "I couldn't agree with you more, and you can be sure I'll pass that on to the

73

congressman, Mr. Ambassador. Congressman'll be right glad to hear you're taking that stand, I assure you.''

The ambassador nodded and stood up slowly, coming around the desk, and the three of them walked to the door, which Oliver opened. The ambassador and Clinkscale shook hands. Clink-scale went ahead through the door and Oliver followed him. As Oliver turned to draw the door shut the ambassador popped his eyes wide, looking back at Oliver with eyebrows raised high. Then he winked. Oliver closed the door and turned to look at Clinkscale. Now it was Clinkscale who winked at him.

As Oliver led the way to his office Clinkscale seized him by the upper arm. ''Between you, me, and the gatepost, that's one cold fish there. But very high on you, Ted. You're in solid there. Guess you know that.'' He laughed, haw-haw, and squeezed Oliver's arm. ''Slasher tell you I was coming?''

Oliver stopped. ''You're the mysterious visitor.'' He smiled. ''Slasher might have been a bit more explicit.''

Clinkscale grinned and seized Oliver's arm again. ''You know Slasher. The ole cloak-and-dagger stuff, right, Ted?''

In Oliver's office Clinkscale refused coffee. He sat down by the coffee table and, when Oliver sat, said, ''Ted, I came to Mexico to fill you in, understand? Ambassador's not in this at all. At all. Be sure and keep it that way. Gave him some cock-and-bull story, air pollution along the border, the *maquiladoras*, usual bullshit. Okay? Told him I'd like to see you, seeing as how I'm passing through and seeing how you're a good personal friend of the congressman. Can't do you any harm, Ted.'' Clinkscale winked again. ''Ted, it's Bondie Birdsong's turn in the barrel. Bondie's on your intelligence committee now, and I'm his guy there. You came over that one time and briefed us, Bondie and me, on Oriental Oil when he was doing that investigation of Commerce. Knew your stuff too. Bondie saw that and he likes it. *Some* of those idiots. . .''

''You got a good memory, Mr. Clinkscale.''

''Claudie, Ted. Ted, memory is half my business. Memory and people. Faces and names. Where the bodies are buried, Ted, as Bondie always says.'' Thinning shiny brown hair lay flat across the large pink scalp. He tugged at a white tie with small black spots that he wore with a white shirt and jumped up to take off his jacket. "That's okay," he said, throwing it on the corner of the couch and sitting back down. He looked at his 9watch. "Didn't mean to spend so much time in there. They all wanta be in good with Bondie. Got an appointment this afternoon. You doing anything for lunch?"

"We can go across to the Zona Rosa." Oliver went to speak to Mrs. Pott. When he came back Clinkscale was walking around the office. "Been here before, you know. Who was it? Don't tell me. Big golfer. Art somebody. Right?"

"Right. Art Wilkins. One of the old Latin hands."

"Right. Old Art Wilkins. Sorta laid-back, I remember. Sit down, Ted. We gotta lot to talk about. Not much time. Reminds me. Maybe your girl can check my reservation." He jumped up, took a ticket folder from his jacket pocket, threw the jacket back down. "Here." When Oliver came back from talking to Mrs. Pott, Clinkscale slapped both hands together. "Okay, Ted, boy. Here it is. Slasher and I, we're like this, see each other practically every day or so, once or twice a week, anyway. We finally got this deal worked out and so we sent me down here to outline it to you." Clinkscale hunched his chair closer to Oliver and clapped his hands together again. "Here's the deal. This is straight from Slasher. Just between you and me both your director and Bondie put their chops on this. Nothing in writing about any of it. Not a goddamn word, Ted. Slasher covers your ass in headquarters and I cover it in the committee. Director takes care of the National Security Council, keeps the noise level down over there. You with me so far?"

Oliver shifted about in his chair and cleared his throat to speak. "What time's lunch?" asked Clinkscale, shooting his cuff to look at his watch. Oliver started to get up. "Never mind," said Clinkscale, pushing him back. "Siddown."

"One o'clock, I told her. She'll let—"

"Fine. Okay. You got that. Nothing in writing." Clinkscale put a fist to his mouth and coughed. "And no action down here on the Movement. Here's why. Slasher and I—"

"The Movement?"

"Ah, you know. Mexico Irredenta, whatever the hell they call it."

"Well, I'd sure like to know more, Claudie."

"Fine, Ted. I'm here to tell you." Clinkscale laid his right hand on the palm of his left hand. "Listen, Ted. Ethnic politics." He slapped the hands softly together. "That's what it's all about. The coming thing. The hell, you say. It's already here. And you're right, Ted, in a way. But in Texas, Ted, Hispanics are the coming thing. Why? Because someone sneaked around and tipped 'em off they could vote. My God! Everybody just kidding, going around saying what a shame—not exercising your franchise—even Bondie, Ted, believe it or not. It's right there in the record, Bondie, for God's sake! And then all of a sudden they start voting. On their own, I mean. Not because someone tells 'em. Greatest thing since sliced bread. I don't have to tell you what this means, Ted. Blacks, Asians, Hispanics, women. Ethnic politics, Ted. Forget your melting pot, if you ever thought there was one, Ted. It's the Balkans. Remember the general welfare? The for-the-good-of-the-country talk? Forget that too. It's single-issue politics these days."

"Where does México Irredenta—"

"Hold up." Clinkscale raised a large hand. "I'm coming to that. The Hispanics? Don't like the word, Ted? Okay, Ted, I'm with you there—Cubans, Porta Ricans, Salvadoreans, Dominicans, Spaniards, old families, new immigrants, but right now we're talking Mexico, Ted. Chicanos. New or old, legal or illegal, close ties to home. Lot of 'em don't like the PRI worth a shit. The PRI—that's the dominant party, Institutional Revolutionary party—shoot, you know that. Maybe they're not that concerned but not too happy with the PRI, either. I don't have to tell you. PRI's a big fat target. So we got our own little minicrusade. That's where the Movement comes in."

Clinkscale cleared his throat. "Next point." He put his right hand on the left and slapped it, softly again. "Mexico Irredenta. Spiritual leader Don Saturnino Mora. Very well-known, very noted, very fine, deeply respected, or was once, anyway. Maybe a tad obscure last few years, head of some distinguished association no one ever heard of, kind with offices upstairs above your Chinese laundry, society for the Protection or Preservation or Prevention of Cruelty to José Vasconcelos, the great Mexican intellectual no one ever heard of before, either. All very significant and full of import and highly prestigious. Old, now, Mora, a holdout, doing his best to avoid being a paragraph on the obituary page. He'll be there any day now. Main thing is he's on the outs with the PRI. Hates their guts. It's mutual.''

"Where is Mora making his headquarters now? Guanajuato?''

"Guanawhatchit? No. Chiapas.'' Clinkscale jumped up and went to the map on the wall. "Somewhere—along—about—'' His hand swept across Mexico past Campeche, across the Isthmus of Tehuantepec, up to Mérida. He took off his glasses and dragged his nose down the map. "Here. The ass end of the world. Right next to Guatemala.'' His finger was on San Cristóbal de las Casas. "Right there. That's the place.''

"You in touch with Mora?''

"Hell, no. Eats gringo tacos for breakfast. Intermediaries.'' He grinned. "Guess I should say cutouts, right, Ted?''

"You say Mora's old. Is he—''

"Tell the truth, he's sort of out of it, wandering around out there in left field rattling his beads, mumbling evilly. What Slasher calls 'unwitting,' I mean, of our role in this. The guy to watch is young Mora, the bright understudy, a real comer in Mexican politics, a young guy, when I say young I mean maybe somewhere around forty something. Some kind of political genius, the old man's son, and he pops up providentially just when daddy's beginning to go bonkers. When I say providential I mean he's reasonable. Boy-san stands ready to run the Movement. Take what's actually a marginal, nutty little coffee klatch, a nasty old man's grudge fight, frankly, and turn it into something meaningful. With a little help from us.'' Clinkscale grinned. "Okay, Ted, maybe more than a little. Techniques. That's our department.''

"Does the old man know about you?''

"Hell, no.'' Clinkscale's eyes went flat. "Look, Ted, how it all works—none of that matters to you.''

"But the son knows. That's what makes it providential, right?"

Clinkscale winked.

"I don't get your role. I mean, this is Mexican politics."

"Yes and no, Ted. It's also ethnic politics in Texas. Frankly, Bondie needs to get in with the Hispanics. Capture their imaginations, fire 'em up for Bondie. Look at the Movement as Texas business. Nothing that need concern you. Right, Ted?" His hearty manner returned. "Never mind old Mora. The crown prince is intensely loyal to Papa, who, frankly, is propped up on a pedestal, more your ancient guru sort of thing. Ted, Slasher said to keep it on a need-to-know basis. And that's all you need to know and now you know it. So don't worry about it. Shouldn't we be getting started?"

Waiting for the traffic to thin out, Oliver led the way in a dash across the Reforma. At the curb on the far side Clinkscale had his arm in his grasp again. "Wife'll shoot me right between the eyes if I don't bring her back a leather bag. What's the name wait, I've got it written—" Clinkscale slapped his chest. "After lunch."

Oliver led the way through the lunchtime crowds, and at the corner he looked back to find Clinkscale had stopped, was gazing at leather goods in a shop window. Clinkscale saw him waiting, waved a large hand, and came quickly to the corner.

When they got to Bellinghausen's Clinkscale said, "I've been here before. Yeah, right. Art Wilkins brought me here. Hey, this some kinda spook hangout?" He laughed and grabbed Oliver's arm. "Just kidding, Ted. Okay, waiter. Listen carefully. I was dispatched down here by General Pershing personally, who's so busy up north chasing Pancho Villa around he couldn't come himself. As I am his trusted aide-de-camp, he sent me in his stead to tell you how to make a genuine martini." The waiter looked questioningly from Clinkscale to Oliver. "Okay, my good man. It appears we have a communications problem. I may just have to ask my good friend here to help out with the language. Ted?"

When the waiter left, Oliver asked: "So México Irredenta is your answer to ethnic politics. That's interesting."

"Ted. I told you. Forget the melting pot. Smart money's on the ethnic game. Your flag-waving's all right, but beneath it you've got the demands of your minorities, bilingual education, affirmative action, and woe be unto the politician who gets on the wrong side of the women. Guess you heard, Ted. The last of the male WASPs are being boosted into the tumbrils for a little trip over to the Place de la Concorde. They're using the old name: Place de la Guillotine. Band in background playing melancholy renditions of traditional New England airs. *Chunk!*" Clinkscale laughed, showing his fillings. "Sorry about that, Ted. Wish I had a camera. Oughta see your face." He laid a hand on Oliver's arm. "Just kidding, Ted."

"You're preaching the politics of division."

Clinkscale shrugged. "We don't say that, Ted. Waiter, you've just been given a jump promotion of two grades. To show your gratitude you might well return with two more of these."

"Holy—" Oliver exclaimed.

"Relax, Ted. Just tell him what I said. You worry too much. Slasher does too. Hey, I'm crazy about that director of yours. What a guy! He and Bondie are just like that! Bondie may be a dyed-in-the-wool yellow-dog Democrat but he's not one of your bomb throwers. Hell, you know Bondie. The Movement? Okay. Bondie discovers the Movement. He doesn't mention PRI, come out directly against it necessarily, just starts building up the importance of a new dispensation in Mexico. Like that? 'A new dispensation.' Bondie can make it sound vurra religious in Spanish. I am informed by my experts that Bondie displays a rare talent for mangling that language. He's no Winston Churchill when it comes to English, for that matter. I am able to state that as a result of my own independent observation. But the voters listen. In return Mora—not Mora himself, you better believe, others acting on his behalf—start passing the word what a great guy Meester Birdsong is. Psst. Pass it on. And it doesn't cost Bondie a damned thing. There's no downside, Ted."

"What's the strength of the Movement? Numbers, I mean."

"Ted, you're dating yourself. Numbers don't matter anymore. Forget your quantitative measurements. It's done with mirrors."

"No, really, Claude."

"I tell you, techniques. The creation of illusion. If there were nobody at all in the Movement, we could create the illusion of a party. It's a play! It's a movie! It's on TV!" Clinkscale guffawed.

Oliver shook his head. "What does the agency have to do with all this?"

"I'm trying to tell you, Ted. Nothing, nothing at all."

"Nothing in writing. No reporting on México Irredenta."

"Okay. I told Slasher he really ought to get you up there so he could go over it with you. The Movement is going to need a little developmental help, and Bondie can see they get it—"

"Through the agency?"

"No, no, Jesus, Ted! Relax. You do nothing. Develops strictly on its own. The PRI's on the skids anyway. The best minds in Washington know that. Something is going to replace it when it goes, and Bondie's on the ground floor with the Hispanic vote. Statesmanlike. And if the Movement doesn't replace the PRI? So what? It's not power you want, necessarily, but influence. Get your piece of the pie. Either way Bondie's got the statewide thing in mind, Ted, but don't quote me."

"Texas congressman heads up new political party in Mexico."

Clinkscale grinned. "Ted, that's exactly how your unfriendly media would play it. It's not that way at all. It's just good ole Texas politics. Take my advice, Ted, and leave it alone. You're good at what you do, but get into Texas politics and you're way over your head."

"Ethnic politics. Couldn't you say that was what Hitler practiced?"

"Hey, watch it, Ted. Gotta be careful who you say that to." Clinkscale pretended to look about them furtively, then guffawed. "You're safe saying that to Claudie. But, no kidding, be careful with that. Know where Hitler went wrong, Ted? The herrenvolk business. His message was too limited, know what I mean? If you weren't German, Aryan, forget it. Ah! That was fast. I like this place. Just what I need. Jesus, Ted. You don't know how I'm enjoying this. You have no idea. When were you last in Washington? Oh, yeah, of course. But even since then, the rat race. Don't care if the—what'd you call that fish, Ted?''

"*Huachinango*. Red snapper.''

"Yeah. I don't care if the watchyertango never comes. Go on. Drink up. You can't work all the time. All work and no—you and Slasher old buddies?''

"Well, not exactly. We've never worked together, before this, I mean.''

"Slasher and I are just like this.'' Clinkscale put his forefinger and middle finger together and stared at them for a moment. "I've got no secrets from Slasher and he doesn't keep a goddamn thing from me. Know what I mean?''

"I'm having a problem, frankly, with the idea of being told that we shouldn't report something if—for instance, did you know that someone got killed recently, over, uh, apparently, over the México—the Movement?''

Clinkscale's eyelids fell a millimeter or two. "Slasher said something about that. Sounds like someone stuck his nose in where it didn't belong. That can be real dangerous. Hell, Ted''—Clinkscale laughed now, nudging Oliver—"Mexicans always killing each other, Ted, aren't they? Wouldn't be Mexico—once more, Ted. The deal is this. We keep headquarters advised on the Movement and you down here keep to hell away from it.''

"What do you mean, 'we,' Claude?''

"By 'we' I mean 'me,' Ted.'' Clinkscale winked at him and raised his glass. "To the ladies. You got any on the string, Ted?''

"Look, Claude—''

Clinkscale laughed. "Forget it, Ted. This is one visitor can take care of himself. You'll never have to pimp for Claudie, Ted. Bondie, now, that might be something else.'' He winked.

"Wait, Claudie. We're going to have the Congress furnishing intelligence to the agency? And the deal is the agency, the station, just ignores the development—assuming there is such a thing—just sits here and ignores México Irredenta? Pretends it doesn't exist?''

"Right. You got it, Ted. Call it the Movement. I do. One hell of a lot easier to say.'' Clinkscale laughed and sipped. "A good martini, if I do say so. How do people stand 'em with vodka?''

"What is the agency getting out of this?"

"Nothing. Not a damn thing. Ted. Of course, Bondie being on the committee will appreciate—what I mean—he's not going to make life difficult for your boss."

"Oh."

"Ted, let me make it very clear. This hold is for a limited time only. Stay out of it, and once it's under way you can stand back out of the way and you'll see the media reporting on it to a faretheewell. No role for the agency at that point, right?"

"No, but—"

"You begin with the op-ed pages. In the States, I mean. In some crazy way you can do all this in the States now, what with television. You don't need the grass roots anymore at all. You do the grass-roots bit with mirrors. TV. Press releases. Opinion leaders, and it's not Mexican opinion you're after, either."

"You mean—"

"Hell, Ted. I'm talking too much. But television! Nobody reads anymore, you know. You just lay off the Movement long enough for it to take on a life of its own, live on its own outside the incubator. That's your director talking, Ted. Once it's rolling, you'll see. Hell, they all talk about the same thing. Talk shows. Magazines. Interviews. They gotta have material to keep the damn thing going. God, Ted, sometimes I wonder where the hell the country's going."

Clinkscale waved a large hand. "Funny you mentioned Hitler. Not many people left to make that connection these days. Remember Bondie? I mean what he looks like? Your west Texas Anglo-Saxon genetic compromise, medium build, about your size, blondish, pale, damp, overall effect sorta blah. Nothing wrong with that. But what you need is a big guy, really big, or else a little feisty fellow. Napoleon. I'm talking charisma now, Ted."

"Hitler was no great shakes physically."

"I grant you that. But he had a lot of other things going for him, among them being one hell of a lot of charisma. An expert rouser of the rabble. At the same time able to scare people shitless. Look at the Prussians, the general staff, the businessmen, all sucking up to the common upstart, the Austrian corporal. Anyone, I repeat, anyone could have stood up to him at one time, one puff, blown him over. They never did. Why, Ted?''

"You're pretty good-sized yourself, Claude. Try the fish."

"No, sir, Ted. Not Claudie. I don't have it and I wouldn't want it. You gotta pop your eyes, like Hitler, roll 'em, show the whites of your eyes like a mean horse. People like Bondie all right, but Bondie couldn't scare a jackrabbit."

"You don't really believe we're going that way."

" 'Course not, Ted. I mean, no one does things exactly the same way. You're the one brought up Hitler. Hell, you know your history. Look at the Irish thing, the anti-British thing, the situation here in the nineteenth century. Hell, still going. Northern Ireland. Okay, you say it's an histology—fsst—an—historical—analogy—of limited application, okay, but Bondie can play the Hispanic thing, pull it off in his district, anyway. What's that on the fish?''

"Cayenne, maybe."

"Not old Claudie. No, sir, Ted. Another thing, I'm not from Texas. Kiss of death. Thing is, tell you the truth, Bondie may be from Texas but he ain't got it. What's more, he knows it. Jesus! What time is it? Hey, I gotta run." Clinkscale began to stuff fish into his mouth. " 'Sokay. Goob," he said. He pulled his wallet from his jacket and flipped through a pad of notes. "How far's it?"

Oliver leaned over to read. "The metro at Insurgentes? Close by. I'll get you over there."

"No, no. Gab a taxi," said Clinkscale, wiping his plate with a piece of bread, stuffing the bread into his mouth. "I gotta run."

"It's no trouble, Claude."

"No, no. Gotta run."

Oliver put an insistent Clinkscale into a taxi, and once it had moved off, he walked rapidly up Londres, skipped at a half run across the corner to hurry down Genoa, slowing as he neared the corner where Avenidas Oaxaca, Chapultepec, and Insurgentes come together. He stood back to scan people on the street, wagering that he had covered on foot the distance Clinkscale in his taxi would find slower going.

Then Oliver stepped quietly back into the shadow of a shop doorway. Debbie Kraus was only a few yards away from him, in front of another shop, near the corner by the metro entrance, looking at her watch as a taxi drew up to the curb. When the rear door opened enough to reveal Clinkscale in the backseat, Debbie waved and ran to join him in the taxi.

Chapter 9

The walk back to the office gave Oliver time to consider the meaning of Claude Clinkscale's meeting Debbie Kraus. Their connection could be merely sexual, as Clinkscale's remarks toward the end of lunch might be taken to imply—making it a remarkably small world and the odds favoring a world that small lying on the farther side of the scale between improbable and impossible.

The obvious link between Clinkscale and Debbie was México Irredenta aka the Movement: a conspiratorial connection, thus, from Oliver's viewpoint. Yes, Clinkscale's being away from home could inspire in him a suprapolitical lust with Debbie a convenient object. Nevertheless the afternoon rutting of a visitor from Washington could have only minor meaning compared with the principal connection. The relative elegance of the leather bag Clinkscale would take home to his wife might be the only tangible sign that the meeting was romantic as well as organizational.

What if—Oliver then asked himself as he stood at the Reforma waiting for a pause in the flow of cars—what if he had not given in to the unworthy impulse to see who it was Clinkscale would meet at the metro station? He had been abashed by what he was doing, finding himself furtively hurrying to beat Clinkscale's taxi to the rendezvous. Would Oliver have stooped to this unethical and professionally unacceptable surveillance of a legislative aide had he not drunk two martinis? One and a third, actually. Oliver had not finished the second, pouring a large dollop of it into his water glass when Clinkscale was absorbed in the deliv-

ery of one of his eloquent paragraphs on ethnic politics. If one
looked at it that way, one could maintain that it was Claudie
himself, with his martinis, who had provoked the act that led to
Oliver's discovering the connection between Debbie and Clinkscale. Oliver hurried across the street with an anxious eye on
the phalanx of automobile hoods rushing toward him. That last
is sophistry—Oliver pointed out to himself, running the final few
feet—that pretense of blaming the victim (Clinkscale) for the
crime (of Oliver's surveilling him). Don't muddle the picture,
Oliver warned. The evidence was full of portents that would
lead him to an outline of meaning once he could sit down—
Oliver promised himself—and think the thing through.

As General Pershing's gin martinis—that origin seemed unlikely—ended their exhilarating course through his brain and
began their midafternoon thumping in his head, Oliver wanted
particularly to close the door to his room, put up his feet, have
a chance to think without a whole lot of interruptions.

Mrs. Pott would not permit that. The minute Oliver came
through the door she was right at him: "You must call Mrs.
Oliver. It's urgent." Adding with an abnormally severe look:
"You've been so long." (Rare experience of disapproval by
Mrs. Pott.) "That person kept you, didn't he?" (Compassionate
shifting of blame to Clinkscale.) *That person.* (Mrs. Pott found
an unacceptable level of vulgarity in Clinkscale.)

"What she want?" asked Oliver, his eyes small in the glare
from the window behind Mrs. Pott.

"She didn't say. And the Mexican gentlemen called."

Diego, she means. "Sheesh!"

"I'll call Mrs. Oliver first."

After he had spoken to Marge, Oliver said to Mrs. Pott, "I
have to run on home."

"The minister."

"Oh, all right. I'll get him myself." Oliver's dialing rang a
phone on Diego's desk.

Diego was discreet. "The authorities have confirmed that the
general had been making inquiries about the leadership of that
political faction. He had been asking questions of the so-called
representative of that faction in that city, among others."

Robles had been asking questions of others than Oliver—others than Lazaire, who had implied that Robles had said something to him. So he had talked to the México Irredenta representative. Oliver was rubbing his head where the ache seemed to have concentrated itself under the scalp near the top. "Well, I suppose we should not be surprised at that."

"I did not call you in order to surprise you. I want you to be thinking of this question. What could he have been asking about that might cause someone to kill him?"

Oliver quelled an impatient rejoinder: That's the only thing I have been thinking about, Diego, old buddy. "Well, sure," was what he said.

"The implication is that he uncovered something so sensitive, so shameful, that the exposure of it would bring ruin to this corrupt concentration of degenerates as they seek a respect they have not earned, as they clamor for a recognition they do not deserve. What did he find out? That is what interests me greatly. I want it to interest you. Think about it."

Oliver put the phone back on the hook. Corrupt concentration of degenerates—Diego was letting México Irredenta get under his skin. Corruption was endemic to Mexico, to politics—as American as apple pie. What could possibly be so sensitive, so shameful, as to ruin a political movement in Mexico?

Oliver let out his breath and got slowly to his feet as a sense of horror turned his headache into a minor nuisance. The one accusation that could threaten a Mexican political group was the hint of foreign support, intervention in Mexican politics from outside. Did Diego suspect? Could he be thinking? Oliver's own thoughts took him straight from Bondie Birdsong and the director of Central Intelligence to Slasher O'Rourke to Claudie Clinkscale to Debbie Kraus to Ted Oliver and what would appear to Diego as evident CIA support of México Irredenta.

Oliver sank back into the chair behind his desk. How could General Robles have suspected it? Was Robles going to warn Oliver that the secret was discovered? What did Canada have to do with it?

"You said you were going home." That was Mrs. Pott.

"Oh, yeah."

"You needn't come back. I'll put your things away." As Oliver left, Mrs. Pott added, "Let me know if there is anything I can do. It's not like Mrs. Oliver to call."

"Here, Tom. This one's yours. That one's Nancy's." Tom began to rip at the wrapping paper. "You say you saw him more than once?" Oliver was trying to get his mind on Marge's report.

"I certainly did. I went out not long after you left, and when I came back he was there. So I drove out again, oh, maybe half an hour later just to see if he was still there, and he was. When I went out again about ten he wasn't there."

"You know, I left pretty early this morning. He could have missed me."

"Something about him that didn't fit our street. Please don't get those awful plastic things all over," said Marge. "Here, Tom. Let me. Remember that car we saw, Nancy?"

"Dad! Look! What is it?" asked Tom.

"All right, Tommy. Where are the directions? Give it here."

"Let's see," said Nancy.

"Get away!" said Tom. "You don't even know what it is, dummy!"

"Tom! Don't talk to your sister like that. I didn't like it," said Marge, "coming after whatever it was that happened or didn't happen"—she looked sidewise at Oliver—"in Guanajuato. That's why I called. You think I'm being silly."

"No, I don't. Of course you should call. You know that. Doesn't hurt me to come by and take a look—not good for much else after that martini lunch. Come here, Nancy. Sit up here."

"Why a martini lunch?"

"Oh, some guy from Washington. On our committee."

"Was it bad?"

"No, it was all right." Actually it was pretty bad. And it still is pretty bad, Oliver added to himself. "A white Ford Country Squire station wagon?" said Oliver.

"With that imitation wood business on the side. Now, you two—we're going to sit down and write thank-you notes to Grandma and Grandpa before we do anything else."

"Well, he wasn't around when I came in. Maybe I'll just stick around in the morning. But he didn't follow you?"

Marge shook her head. "I don't think so. I would have seen him. That's a very distinctive car, and I was watching."

"Hardly the kind of car for surveillance."

"It may turn out to be quite innocent."

"Or just another one of those unexplained—Wait! What did you say?"

"I said it may be something completely innocent. I know, but nevertheless—"

Oliver put Nancy down. "By God, that may be it," he said slowly.

"What do you mean?"

He gave a short laugh. "The explanation is innocence. What time is it? Hell. I'm going back down to the office."

"It's all right, Mrs. Pott."

"Really? I'm so glad."

"There was some guy hanging around near the house, up the street actually, and Marge didn't like his looks."

"Oh, dear. You don't think of that sort of thing in Mexico."

"Well, I don't think it's that sort of thing exactly. Do you have the combination of the archive storage files?"

"You look very tired. Can't I find what you're looking for?"

"I don't know what I'm looking for exactly, Mrs. Pott. Maybe open the safe. I have to see it to see if it's what I'm looking for."

Oliver was leaning on an open safe drawer, thumbing through file folders, when Sanders walked into the file room to put a folder away. "Whoo!" he said, waving the folder about his head. "Smells like a brewery in here."

"Not at all, Sanders. If you intend to be an intelligence officer, you must strive for precision. It smells like a distillery in here. We got a lot to talk about."

"Okay."

"But urgent investigation intervenes. Fate dealt another hand just when I was on the verge of concluding that I was doomed

to ride forever on the same painted pony on the same old merry-
go-round, reaching out for the same old brass rings.''

''Some distillery!''

''Looking out the windows of a train, discovering that the
scenery isn't random, that it classifies itself into certain broad
categories, begins to repeat itself until, finally, one day—golly,
look at this folder. 'The Tlatleloco Affair—1968.' I'd like to see
Diego's file on that.''

''I read it. All you learn from what's in there is that nobody
knows how many were killed.''

''Still worth reading, though. Listen, Pete, while I relate to
you an anecdote that if you have the wit to contemplate its inner
meaning may help you in your budding career. There was a guy
back in Washington assigned as chief of station, Buenos Aires.
Never been near the place. Argentine desk officer comes in
pushing the usual wheelbarrow full of files for the new fellow
to read before he goes down to BA. 'Oh, no,' sez our senior
whiz, 'I never read files. Might destroy my objectivity.' ''

''No kidding.''

''So help me God. Chief in Argentina for a full tour. Never
did get the drift of it. To be fair to him we should remember
that no one else ever figured out Argentina. But, listen. Any
time you give to the old files pays off. About to furnish you a
striking example if you'll just try to show a little patience.''

''When do you want to talk?''

''*Mañana.*''

''*Siempre mañana.*''

''Soon we'll have half a century of history behind us. Lankester reads his histories of Mexico. In these files is concealed a
history you won't find in his books. Retired files. Terminated
projects. Old cases. The good guys, the bums, the liars, the
cheats, the fabricators, the ones we recruited, the one's we
couldn't recruit, those we never figured out and who live eter-
nally in mystery. A lot of those. Our failures, the kind that make
your toes curl up in shame. Who we all were. The station's
character, the generations of ops officers, the way the country,
the national character—ours and theirs—shaped the work. Forget the official histories in the binders up in headquarters. Con-

ceal as much as they reveal. The truth will die forgotten in our heads. But dig in the files. Get the names, at least, in your head." Oliver drew in a breath, pulled out a file, and smiled at Sanders, who was leaning on another safe, grinning back and shaking his head from side to side.

"The warm elixir of self-satisfaction," said Oliver, "is bathing my whole frame because I'm so damned smart. Or think I am. That will pass soon enough. Some shower'll come to spoil it. Or the sense of dread that is waiting to spring on me, like a panther, the moment I—but I knew there was something. Blessed are the file clerks, for others shall reap their reward."

Around four the next morning Oliver dreamed that he was walking through thick woods, in dark grounds unknown to him but familiar to the predator in ambush. He stopped, slowly raising his eyes for a glance at a heavy shadow on the thick limb over the path, dreading to see what was there. Before his eyes reached the shadow it sprang hissing through the dark toward his head. Eyes open, Oliver went rigid, unable immediately to see the shape of his dread. It came on him with a rush: Diego, on the scent of México Irredenta. Oliver did not sleep again.

For the third time since 6:30 he walked to the wall at the front of the house, unlocked the gate, and looked up the street before going out. At the top of the street was a bend a hundred yards beyond which the street met the extension of the Reforma on its long upward run through Lomas to where it joins Avenida Constituyentes. Oliver walked as far as the turn, keeping close to the wall, to peer through a cluster of fuchsia blossoms of a bougainvillea cascading from the top of the wall. There were three cars parked on the right side of the narrow street. Among them he could make out what looked to be the tailgate of a white Ford Country Squire station wagon. There was a hat on the person slouched in the driver's seat and the hat moved.

Oliver slowly pulled his own head back and walked briskly back to his own gate.

"Marge. He's there. Drive me up there and stop just beside him and I'll jump out."

"I can't leave Nancy by herself."

"Well, hurry up."

Oliver opened the gate to the street. Getting in the backseat on the right he said, "Just let me out when I say and double around back and stop the car in the street just up from him."

"I really don't think that's a very good—"

"C'mon. Let's go. Hurry up. Let me off and turn right around and come back."

"There's the bad man," said Nancy, standing on the seat next to Oliver, who had his arm around her. Marge slowed the car as they reached the white station wagon. Oliver had a glimpse of the whites of brown eyes in the shadow of the brim of a fedora.

"Right here! Siddown, Nancy." Oliver jumped out and ran up to the other car before the driver could press the button that would roll the window up. "Inocencio!" he said.

The man was watching Marge making a U-turn at the corner. At the same time his hands were fumbling at the controls that would get the station wagon moving.

"Inocencio," shouted Oliver, rapping on the rising window. The man was still watching Marge in the Toyota. It was he, all right, under the fedora—one of his trademarks, said the file. High sloping forehead, the lean face a creamy brown, more gaunt than the full face and profiles in the file folder, but with the same hawklike nose, the wide thin-lipped mouth, a spare, bony-looking face. Inocencio bared his teeth like a mandrill on seeing Marge slow to a stop, leaving no room for him to pass by her to escape the narrow street. He shook his head slowly from side to side and started the window back down.

"Inocencio. You and I gotta talk."

"No hablo inglés," said Inocencio.

"You speak English better than I do."

The man took a small blue wallet from his suit pocket and flipped it open. "Gobernación," he said, still staring ahead, and speaking again in Spanish. "Tell that woman to move that car."

"Let's see that," said Oliver, continuing to use English. "Come on, Inocencio. Who you kidding? Lester know you're using expired credentials?"

The man took the wallet back, put it on the car seat, looked straight ahead through the windshield, hit the steering wheel hard with his right fist, and said, in English, "Shit!"

Oliver waved Marge toward their house. "Come on in and have a cup of coffee. Give me a lift back down, okay?"

Inocencio Brown turned the wheels into the curb in front of the Oliver house and set the emergency brake with a ratcheting click. He got out of the car, lifted his hat off, revealing a glossy scalp the rich color of *café con leche*, took a white handkerchief from the breast pocket of his suit jacket, and ran it over his head. When Oliver came around to that side of the car, Brown was putting his hat back on, using two hands to do so, and pressing a button to lock the doors. He sighed, slammed the door, and looked at Oliver for the first time.

"Ted Oliver," said Oliver, putting out his hand.

"Yeah," said Inocencio dispiritedly, in English. "I know." He touched the hat brim with his right hand and then put it, limp, in Oliver's. "Inocencio Brown. I guess you know that."

"My, little lady." Brown had put his hat, the good black-banded homburg of the same rich brown as his skin, on the dining-room table and pulled out a chair, sitting in it to get to the level of Nancy. "You and Mama a pretty good team."

Oliver was at the kitchen door watching Marge pour the coffee. Marge mouthed at him with eyebrows raised high: "Who in the world is that?"

"Nice going, up there. But next time you ought to—"

"Must there be a next time? Who *is* he?"

Oliver smiled at her and picked up the coffee. "Yesterday, when you said the explanation might be innocent, you lit a fuse in my head. Come on," he said to her as he turned. "You take cream and sugar?" he asked Brown.

"Some cream. Lotta sugar."

"This is Mr. Brown—Mr. Inocencio Brown."

"Pleased meetcha, Mrs. Oliver. You pull a good block on me, back there. Nice lady like you. I'm surprised. You don't want to do that with the wrong guy." Before Marge could answer, Inocencio was saying to Nancy, "Inocencio gotta granddaughter your age up there in California—how old you, Nancy?"

Nancy held up a hand with the thumb tucked in. "I'm going to be five." She looked at the hand and extended the thumb.

"Five years old! Well, our Delia, she almost six."

"Would you like some toast with your coffee?" asked Marge.

"You know, I sure could use it, get up so early. But I don't want you should bother," said Brown.

"It's no trouble at all. Come on, Nancy," said Marge to the girl. Nancy was standing two feet in front of Brown, examining him, mouth open. "Nancy! You can make the toast."

"You still have family back in Blythe?" asked Oliver.

Brown gave a short laugh, putting his head to one side. "You know about Blythe. You made me, all right. I know I'm a goner when I hear 'Inocencio.' Yeah. The oldest daughter, she lives up there, California, with her husband. She got married up there. Blythe. Doing all right. Got a good job in the bank. Tell you the truth, Mr. Oliver. I never saw you. I never forget a face, know what I mean?"

"I'm new here. Didn't Lester tell you? Why did he put you on me, anyway?"

Brown slurped some hot coffee and put the cup down. "Lester, he's got this case he's working on. He gives me a name. I don't have to know why. I work it from there."

"Kept up your contacts in the embassy. Ran me down that way." Oliver waited. Brown winked at him, but said nothing. "You're working on the Robles case. So am I."

"You talk to Lester, something like that, Mr. Oliver."

"Lester thinks I was with Robles when he got killed. That's it, isn't it?"

"Well, Lester, he's got contacts, preliminary results of investigation. Subject sitting there with General Robles." Brown's eyes went quickly up and down Oliver's body. "Maybe a subject fits your physical description."

"And I set up Robles. He's wrong about that."

"Better talk to Lester."

"Lester tell you what Robles said to him?"

"General Robles, he's asking Lester help him get in touch with the outfit."

Lazaire could have told me that much, thought Oliver. "Well, I wonder why Lester didn't let us know."

"Lester said all the old gang was gone."

Angry Lester, grousing in his bunker. "Wonder what Robles wanted from us?"

Brown shrugged his shoulders. "Lester didn't tell me that." He looked at his coffee cup, turned it on the saucer. "Tell you the truth, Lester doesn't know."

"Yeah. I want to give you a note to Lester."

"Just telephone Lester. I listen in. Get it all settled fast."

"What I want to say I don't want to say on the phone."

"I can see that too."

"Look, Inocencio. Have some more coffee. Guess I'll have some too. Listen, I've got a lead. A lead maybe we can work. No point sitting around up here in that station wagon."

Brown held in the air the spoon he was using to ladle sugar into the second cup of coffee. "Just going to establish your pattern."

"Sure, that's how you have to start. But you can skip that with me now. We'll be—"

Brown put the spoon down and shook his head. "He'll chew my ass, Lester. You're COS, aren't you?"

"Didn't Lester tell you?"

"No. Lester, he don't tell me much. I seen a few chiefs my time. But Lester, he really going to chew me. I don't care, maybe make him feel better."

"It's that station wagon. Might as well use a fire engine."

"Oh, hell, Mr. Oliver. I know that. I do this for Lester, you know. On my own. Old times' sake. No ops expenses. Personally owned vehicle I bought, use parta my termination bonus. Take good care of a vehicle, it'll last you. Tourist guide, you put on the mileage. My own boss. Work the Hotel Cortés, mostly, the Majestic, that part of town. Tourists, couples, families, mostly. All nice people. Want to go out to the pyramids, the *sonido y luz*, maybe the bullfight, go to the market, get something to eat, you name it. Need a big car. Ops funds, then

I rent something, know what I mean? Don't use the personal vehicle.

"Now, Nancy, that's a real nice girl. Thank you very much. You make this toast all by yourself for Inocencio. Well, I—you know Lester Lazaire, Mrs. Oliver?" Marge shook her head and looked at Oliver. "Mr. Lazaire and me, we go way back. Play golf at the little nine-holer outside San Miguel until maybe two years ago. Lester, he can't play no more. Just sit around. I hate to see it. Heart." Brown placed his right hand on his own heart. "Mrs. Lazaire really worry about him. The altitude too. Lester, he change a lot." Brown looked somber and picked up a piece of toast.

"Any of the old people left, Inocencio?"

"Like who?"

"Well, the team leader before you, Antonio Macedo."

"Toñico. I took over from Toñico. We're cousins, you know that? Toñico's dead now. Died about three years ago. Cancer. Eastertime. Went real fast. First I hear, then maybe a month later in Mexicali for the funeral. Good Friday. His wife's folks from up there. Mexicali."

"Anyone left here?"

"You mean we could use? Same Lester asked me. I dunno. You see, there's Benito. Benito Díaz. I put him on the base station. He doesn't work out too good on the street. He's sour. We pick him up late, brother-in-law Nelson Rodriguez, one we call El Rubio. You want relations you can trust. Sovs or the Cubes always trying find the team, you know. Big money for the wrong kinda guy. Coming on the team late, Benito's termination bonus not too big. He didn't get as much. That's fair. But Benito, he hasta go 'round finding out what everyone else gets and ends up real pissed off. No, not that Benito. Sour. And Nelson, he getting good money with DEA now. There was a good man on the street. He and El Vasco always like to work together." Brown took a sip of coffee. "I'm talking too much. You miss the old days."

"No, I just thought maybe some were left around."

"El Vasco, I make him deputy team leader when I take over, even though he's a youngest. El Vasco, he's named Elizalde.

He's living somewhere outsida Caracas now. Wife's people have some kinda dairy farm down there. She's Basque, too, and she comes from down there. Real pretty red blonde what they call strawberry but, Christ, what a temper you never see! I guess he's doing okay. I get a postcard from Venezuela, no name, I know it's from El Vasco. He was one hell-raiser. She didn't trust him worth a damn and sometimes she'd come along on a job, keep an eye on him. Okay by me, you want a woman, lotta jobs, make it look normal, what I mean? Too bad we had to break up. We had a good team. Best there was. Ask Lester one a these times. We do everything. You work it too long you get burned.''

"I know. Your team was famous in the old days. No one left to give us a hand if we need it.''

"Problem is—you ask Lester—time came to terminate, outfit came up pretty stingy, you want the truth. Not Lester's fault. Lester always stand up for his people. Buncha slimy bastard bookkeepers up there in headquarters—that was Lester. Up there in Washington they don't always understand what it's like all day on a case, maybe all night. Know what I mean? How it is with the troops in the field, you know? Most the boys, they pretty unhappy. Some blame Toñico and me, think we work some kinda deal. I didn't work no deal. I get a better bonus, team leader, that's all. Amicable termination, what they want on the Mexico desk. I stand up for the outfit and I stand up for the boys, end up in the middle. Know what I mean?''

"It's too bad,'' said Oliver.

"Yeah, too bad.'' Brown looked around the room. "Nice place you got here. Guess you pay plenty rent.''

"I'm going to type a quick note for Lester, Inocencio. Here's today's paper.''

"I just walk around out there, your garden.''

Chapter 10

When Oliver went out on the veranda, Brown was coming back up the walk from the garden. "I got this same flower, dahlia, they call it," said Brown, pointing. "They come from down here, Mexico. Lotta people don't know that. Like that margarita—what you call it?"

"Daisy."

"Yeah—daisy." Brown looked doubtfully at the envelope Oliver held out to him. "You want I take it to Lester."

Oliver opened the envelope, unfolded the note. "Take a look."

Brown read it carefully then looked at Oliver. "Okay. I'll take it down there, San Miguel. Today." He frowned. "You don't have to tell me but what kinda assignment? Locate subject, establish a pattern, easy. More than that, break off subject, identify contacts, then you needa team. Another car, anyway, not the wagon."

"No, I know. What I've had in mind—you see what I say there—is an investigation. Look for vulnerabilities. Plan the approach. Aim at laying on a recruitment pitch, but anyway plan an approach. There's a pretext for an approach now, but I doubt I could pull it off. Might be better for someone younger to try with another pretext."

" 'Pretext.' " Brown grinned. " 'Vulnerability. Approach.' Words I haven't heard a long time."

"Problem is that the target, it's a woman—"

"Oh, oh. Watch out. They the tricky ones."

"She has no motive I can see for cooperating, no obvious

vulnerability. Then something came up yesterday that knocked it all into a cocked hat. One of those times you want to hold off, do nothing, see what develops. Anyway, yes, rent a car. Once you're on this, you'll have some ideas."

"Yeah, maybe you right. Waiting around this morning, I'm too old, this kinda shit. Maybe not now. One other thing, way I see it, maybe good for Lester."

Oliver was holding the phone in the study at home that night listening to the gruff voice of Lester Lazaire say, "Read your letter. So go ahead. I told Inocencio to work with you. Keep me posted."

The old hands like Lazaire might spend half their careers working with phone taps and never get it through their heads that others could listen to them. And it wasn't a telephone line anymore but microwave and the whole world listening. "Want me to run down there? We could kick it around, if you like."

"T'hell for? Inocencio's gone. I told him to report to you in the morning. So go ahead. What's to talk about?"

"Well, fine, then."

"Take good care of Inocencio. You got a good man there. I hope you know that. Look after him. See to it nothing bad happens to him."

"Well, fine, but don't forget how this thing got started."

"Carlitos? Hell, no. What I'm talking about, big noise from Winnetka blows into town, doesn't know shit about the past, and doesn't give a shit, either, out to make a name for himself. Devil take the hindmost. Chews—"

"Look, Lazaire."

"—up the troops, leaves 'em lying there, he's up and away." Lazaire paused for a breath, his breath coming in rapid short gasps over the line.

"Don't worry."

"Well, Inocencio says you're all right." Lazaire's voice was even more gruff with the effort it cost to make that admission. "Says you think more like a CO than a COS."

God! You had to wonder who might be listening. "I take that as a compliment."

"You better, coming from Inocencio." He gave a harsh laugh. "Someone up at headquarters says that, look out for your back. They're sharpening the knives."

"Yeah, true enough."

"By the way, I told Inocencio I was pretty sure that was you with Carlitos over in Guanajuato, Oliver."

"Look, Lazaire, we'd better—" Oliver started to speak against the sound of Lazaire's harsh laugh. Lazaire had hung up.

Oliver blew his breath out, shaking his head as he put the phone on the cradle.

"What do you take as a compliment?" asked Marge from the wing chair where she sat reading.

"Oh, Inocencio Brown told somebody I'm more like a case officer than a chief of station."

"What's so wonderful about that?"

"I dunno. I guess that I'm not a stuffed shirt."

"Oh? I could give Inocencio Brown a few examples to the contrary."

Oliver snatched up her book.

"Stop it! Oh, darn it. You'vc lost my placc."

They were sitting in the rented Datsun on the street near the Central Library and Oliver leaned forward to look past Inocencio at the mosaics the architect Juan O'Gorman had designed for the library walls. Next to him, sitting in the driver's seat, Inocencio followed his gaze.

"Toñico and I argued about that what-do-call-it mosaic stuff. I say it's ugly, all those little stones. They do it to get attention, make an impression, just something new." Brown shook his head and smiled. "You shoulda heard that Toñico the way he talked—he'd go on about those mosaics, how they 'embrace the soul, essential spirit of the Mexican,' crap like that. Not my soul, '*mano*, I tell him. Just some thing he read somewhere. You'da liked Toñico. Give me a nice adobe, stucco, do you know what I mean? Maybe outline your door in stone, wood, doesn't matter, old-fashion way, same with the window, leave the rest alone, a blank wall. Maybe a statue, your coat of arms.

Simple. The old way. Your palaces, your churches, houses. Keep the outside simple, inside do what you want. They knew what they were doing, not all this modern—more people coming now." Inocencio motioned with his chin.

They were parked five cars behind the red Nissan. The sun was bouncing its blinding rays from the windshields of the cars, so that Oliver did not need to crouch down when finally he spotted Debbie and Susie. The same angle protecting Oliver from their vision backlit their figures, so that they were almost in silhouette. "The two women with the books. Coming toward the Nissan." Chato Escobar got out of the car, slammed the door, and walked around the car to go toward the women. "Catch the guy going up to them."

"Hey!" said Inocencio.

"What's the matter?" Oliver kept his eye on the three people who now stood together.

"I don't know. Tell you later."

Escobar was talking to Debbie, shrugging his shoulders up around his ears, putting his hands up against his chest. Debbie had her head out toward him, her lips stuck out, then her mouth wide and ugly. Escobar thrust his head right up in front of Debbie, and for a moment they stood like a pair of finches quarreling over sunflower seeds. Then Escobar stood back and extended one arm in a quick gesture. "Get in!" he would be saying.

During this, Susie Sanders had stood back, biting her lip, looking away from the quarreling pair. The way she held the books in her arms made her even younger, more like a college student than a CIA wife. When Debbie got in the car Escobar slammed the door and quickly caught up with Susie, who was strolling slowly now toward where the two men sat in the Datsun. Escobar took her by the elbow to turn her toward him. He talked rapidly, managing to keep his smile flashing at Susie as he talked. Susie was nodding as he spoke, frowning, looking over her shoulder toward the Nissan occasionally.

"What's that bastard up to?" growled Oliver.

"That's lover boy, there," Inocencio commented.

Susie was shaking her head. Escobar had reached up to take her by both elbows, books tucked in her arms. Susie broke away, shaking her head, walking quickly toward where Oliver and Brown sat. Escobar was calling something after her, laughing.

"Hell!" said Oliver, scrunching down in the seat, hearing her heels on the walk. Inocencio slumped and pulled his hat over his eyes as Oliver bent to put his head under the dashboard, forcing the breath out of his lungs.

"Okay, she's unlocking her car." Inocencio had his nose against the window, looking in the side driver's mirror. "About six back. There goes lover boy."

Oliver could hear the crepitation of the Nissan exhaust as Escobar pressed his macho foot on the accelerator.

"Okay. She's pulling out, she's going by."

Susie's car swished by and Oliver brought his head up and took a deep breath. "All right, Debbie Kraus is the one that was quarreling with her boyfriend, the ballroom dancer. She's the one I'm interested in. He's named Escobar. Full name unknown; nickname, Chato. He's with Relaciones Exteriores. The one getting the treatment from Chato is Susie somebody and she's an embassy wife. Let's go."

"Husband better look after that one. Listen, Mr. Oliver, that Escobar FNU, the gigolo there. I seen him before. Some case, I'm pretty sure." He started the car and turned to drive up Insurgentes away from University City.

"No record, Inocencio. I ran him through the files. Only that he's an employee of Relaciones. Haven't asked to see if anyone in the embassy knows him. Can't just go around asking. What kind of case was it?"

"Never forget a face, but damned if I can remember—getting old, I guess. Debbie Kraus's the one you interested in."

"Yeah. I wouldn't be interested in her if I had a better peg to hang an investigation on."

"Got to start somewhere. Why her?"

Oliver did not answer right away. As much as he would have liked to be able to unburden himself of his dread—talk about it and get another opinion—he didn't know Inocencio well enough to trust him with more than the half of Debbie unconnected with Clinkscale. "Someone sent Debbie at me to find out if I had been with Robles in Guanajuato."

"Were you?"

"Yeah. Robles wanted to talk to us about a political group called México Irredenta—ever heard of it?"

"That's that old Mora. Something I read the other day. Funny. I forgot about him, thought maybe he just gone off somewhere and died."

"What d'you think of him?"

"He was always what you call a nut, that's all I remember. You tell Debbie you saw Robles?"

"No, sir, I certainly did not. She's tied up with this México Irredenta."

"How'd she know you're with Robles?"

"She didn't. The police got my name from Robles's memo pad."

"What pretext for an approach you got?"

"Just get hold of her, since she came to see me. But no real reason to think she'd cooperate." Awkward not to be able to give Inocencio the whole story; after learning of Debbie's connection with Clinkscale, Oliver had strong reason to think she would not cooperate. "Pretty weak case, at the moment."

"So stay on her, establish pattern."

"And the gigolo, too, I guess."

"He the one who sent her?"

Oliver shrugged.

Inocencio shook his head. "Thought maybe we had more to go on. Like you said, a pretty weak case."

Chapter 11

"I'm not sure it helps to refer to him as 'that gigolo,' " said Marge as they sat over coffee after dinner that night.

"Well, anyway," said Oliver, having told her about Escobar and Susie, "what do you think?"

"What can I think? It's not at all clear what it is you're worried about. Are you suggesting the chief-of-station's-wife act? The station hen mother? Because if that's what you have in mind—"

"I don't want you to do anything." Not entirely true—Oliver had thought that Marge might come up with an idea for female handling of what he saw as a problem that needed to be nipped off right away.

"—those days are long over. I can see myself telling Susie she should be more careful whom she associates with. Can you imagine her reaction?"

"I didn't want—you're getting it all wrong."

"I think you have to decide what it is you're worried about, and once you can define that clearly, then decide if you should bring it up with Pete somehow."

"Yeah. If you saw the guy, the kind of car he drives!"

"His car? Is it a car that's bothering you so? What I don't understand is how you happened to see his car or what you were doing that you saw him with Susie. If you've taken to following Susie around Mexico City, maybe I'm the one who should be worried."

"Very funny. Just between us, I've got good business reasons for being interested in the other girl, Susie's friend, and the gigolo—and the distinguished official of Exterior Relations. Do you find that description more pleasing?''

"Hey, Pete. What's up?" Oliver heard himself call out in an unnaturally hearty greeting to Sanders the next morning.

"Something pretty funny." Sanders came into the office with Lankester right behind.

"Funny ha-ha or funny queer?"

"Wait'll I tell you. Debbie Kraus called last night."

"I'll be darned," said Oliver.

"Could this be in any way connected with Clinkscale, do you think?" Lankester asked Oliver.

"Hah!" said Oliver, who had been preoccupied with Escobar–Susie rather than with Debbie–Clinkscale. "That's a thought, all right, Chas. Clinkscale," repeated Oliver slowly. He had given Lankester and Sanders a straightforward if abbreviated account of the conversation with Clinkscale, unable to avoid letting slip pungent expressions of his dismay at Clinkscale's orders to ignore México Irredenta. And he had told them of seeing Clinkscale keep his appointment with Debbie Kraus.

On hearing Oliver's report, Lankester had accepted the directions transmitted by Clinkscale, verified by Slasher O'Rourke's instructions, as valid orders, not to be questioned. Sanders had asked if the delivery of oral orders to a CIA station by a congressional aide was not unusual procedure. Oliver had dryly replied that in his experience it was more than unusual—it was unique.

Oliver had said nothing to either of them so far about the recall of Inocencio Brown to active duty, reenlisted by Lazaire and confirmed in service by Oliver. Nor had he said anything of the surveillance the day before at the university. He would say nothing now.

"Anyway, Debbie said she had to talk to me. Alone. I said, 'What do you mean, alone?' She said she didn't want Susie involved, as some of it concerned Susie. So I said if it concerned Susie, she had to be there."

"It seems to me," Lankester was saying, "that Pete should not, definitely not, see Debbie Kraus."

"Why not?" asked Sanders, surprised. "Anyway, I've already seen her."

"You should not have done so," said Lankester.

"Wait a minute, Chas. Look, she's a friend of yours, right, Pete?"

"Not exactly," said Sanders. "More an acquaintance of Susie's, actually."

"There you are," said Lankester. "The obligation to see Debbie, were there one, would have been Susie's. But she should not be involved, either."

"Hey, hold it, Chas. I tell you, I've already seen her," said Sanders.

"You shouldn't have," Lankester repeated.

"High marks for punctilio, Chas, but you've taken my more or less faithful account of what Claudie Clinkscale gabbled about over two strong gin martinis at lunch and turned it into a whole set of self-denying regulations—"

"I'm only trying to keep Pete from—"

"—keeping in mind a legislative assistant to some Texas congressman has no feel for how the executive branch works. Even less the agency. A different culture. He's used to whooping it up with lobbyists, that ilk—hints and winks and nudges and innuendo. Congressional sleaze. Alien to our ways."

"I can assure you the director would have known exactly what he was doing when he chose Clinkscale as the instrument to inform you."

"Okay," said Oliver, trying to run ahead and shake off Lankester. "But what are we arguing about? Pete saw her. And—?"

"Susie was there listening and she told me to go ahead and see Debbie. So while we were waiting for her to show up, Susie told me Debbie and Escobar had been quarreling. And Susie says that Escobar has started to make a play for her."

"That SOB!" said Oliver.

Sanders paused to look at him, surprised at the strength of Oliver's reaction. "Susie doesn't like the way he treats Debbie. Susie's not at all impressed by what she calls the childish ego of the Mexican male."

"Hooray for Susie!" Oliver exclaimed, immensely relieved.

Sanders paused to stare for another moment at Oliver before going on. "She's disgusted with Debbie, too, for being so sub-servient to him. Anyway, Debbie came and Susie said hi and said she understood why Debbie wanted to talk to me alone and that was all right with her. I was proud the way Susie handled that. Debbie came on very common—as Susie observed later—tilting her chin up at Susie and not looking at her. A big act.

"I can make this part short and sweet. Debbie gnashing her teeth with jealousy. Came to warn me about Susie and Chato. I cut her off fast. She could talk to me about it or she could talk to both of us about it, but I was not about to have her blaming Susie for Debbie's own problems with Chato. And the best thing might be, as far as I was concerned, that we all stop seeing each other."

"Good," said Lankester. "You handled that part very well."

"Well, I'm not through yet. Debbie gave a couple of hiccups then and got some tears started and said how very, very sorry she was and how grateful she was to me and how Susie was her only real friend and how incredibly insightful I was and oh God she had to apologize to Susie. I started to get Susie back ASAP for Scene Two where Debbie falls on Susie's neck, whatever, when Debbie said, stop, there's something else I need to talk to you about."

"You see? I was afraid there would be—"

"Let him finish, Chas."

Sanders addressed himself to Oliver, his eyes wandering over to Lankester as he spoke. "She wanted to ask about you."

"There!" said Lankester.

"What about me?"

"Said she had met you one time. That's all. Just that she'd met you once. Asked if I knew you. I said I knew who you were, sort of. It's a big embassy. Then she asked if you weren't involved in covert action, that's how she put it."

"A made-for-TV movie," said Oliver. "*México Irredenta*, starring Debbie Kraus, girl guerrilla. Did she give you any idea what her concept of covert action might be?"

"Look, maybe I didn't make it clear. She's in sort of rough shape. Susie thinks Escobar pushes her around from time to time. Anyway, emotionally in poor shape despite the histrionics.''

"Okay, sorry," said Oliver.

"I said I'd be surprised if you were mixed up with anything like that. I used the story Diego gave the judge in Guanajuato, something to do with scholarships. Cultural exchange, good, vague sorts of things.''

"Someone must have told her.''

"Clinkscale?'' Lankester suggested.

"Could be,'' said Oliver.

"When I gave the cultural-exchange bit, she looked at me as though I was some kind of idiot.''

"What does she think you do?'' Lankester asked Sanders.

"It's never come up, Chas.''

"Go on, Pete.''

"She asked if I had an incredibly important question to get the answer to, would I ask you. I asked what kind of question and she said she could not explain. She only said she didn't want to get into trouble.''

"You musn't see her, Ted,'' said Lankester.

"Well, anyway,'' said Sanders, looking at Oliver and not Lankester, "she went on to say she was thinking maybe she should see you again. So I said, well, sure, if it would help her get an answer to her question.''

Oliver laughed. "Gee, thanks, friend.''

"Well, I thought you'd—''

"No, no, that's exactly what I want.''

"Really, Ted, you must not see her,'' said Lankester again.

"She wants to see me, Chas. I put her in the category of a walk-in and the rule is you never turn one down. I can sit and listen to her again without violating the Constitution. She going to call me?''

"Uh, she asked me to talk to you.''

"I hope you refused to do so,'' said Lankester.

"No, I said I would. Look, she's shaky, in bad shape.''

"So? Now you are implicated.''

"Oh, well, Chas,'' said Oliver. "What could the guy do?''

"You can't just toss it off like that. If the chief of the CIA station arranges a rendezvous through Pete, doesn't that confirm her suspicion that Pete is with the agency?"

"She doesn't suspect—"

"What makes you think—" Oliver and Sanders had spoken together.

"I'm going to see her, Chas," Oliver continued, "and the question is where."

Lankester stood up and began pacing about the room.

"I think she's scared. How about the safe house on Amberes?" asked Sanders.

"We can't throw away a nice brand spanking new clean safe house, compromise it to Debbie. Not till we know what we're dealing with. Here's what. Have her be at the coffee shop across the street again tomorrow at eleven. That's the place she herself chose before, and that way it doesn't reveal anything more about you or about me, doesn't commit us to anything."

Lankester stopped and put up one hand. "Has it occurred to you that she may be luring you out? That they intend to make sure of you this time, having missed you before in Guanajuato?"

"It certainly has, and it doesn't do a whole lot for the old morale to have you reminding me of it, Chas. However, way I see it, the odds are greater I'll be run over right out in front here trying to get across the Reforma."

Sanders grinned while Lankester frowned heavily and resumed his pacing but, instead of reversing direction, marched straight out the door. Sanders raised his eyebrows at Oliver but remained seated. Oliver sat back in his chair, stretched his arms, and looked at Sanders. "For your information, you and I constitute a quorum." He repeated the meeting instructions for the morrow. "What's Debbie up to?"

"Hard to know, hard to sort the emotions out. Susie came back and I went back to my book. They worked it all out and went on for a while, you know, saying the same thing over and over again. Susie thinks that there's more to it than the jealousy, over Chato, I mean, and that Debbie's worried about something else."

Lankester came back, red in the face. "I must insist on this point. I repeat. We have been forbidden by headquarters to have anything to do with—even, as you point out, to write about— this Irredenta affair. Your coming on the connection between Clinkscale and Debbie may have been inadvertent—''

"Hardly," interjected Oliver, winking at Sanders as he recalled his abandoning decorum to dash through the Zona Rosa to intercept Clinkscale.

"—but nevertheless it has put Debbie definitely out of bounds."

"Okay, Chas. Your point has been taken and duly recorded in the ship's log."

"Your attitudes are inconsistent. When we first were asked by the NSC to report on the Movement, you said it was none of our affair. That it was State's, the embassy's business."

"So I did."

"Now that we're ordered to have nothing to do with it, you're hell-bent on becoming involved. Can you explain that?"

"Sure. But not right now."

Lankester continued: "You yourself object to receiving oral instructions. I suggest you put your present orders to Pete in writing so that he will later be able to defend himself when he is accused of disobeying a headquarters directive."

Oliver got up from his desk. "Chas, you make it sound like the Nuremberg trials. Go on, Pete. Get hold of Debbie."

Lankester stalked out again before Sanders could get through the door.

Sanders called Oliver at home that night. "Our friend doesn't like your choice. Says she'll be in front of the Sagrario at tenthirty, you know, next to the cathedral."

"I don't like her choosing the place."

"I'm not sure I can get back to her."

"No, that's all right. I'll be there."

Chapter 12

CONFIDENTIAL

SUBJECT: Meeting with Debbie Kraus, 1030, Wednesday, 7 January.

1. Kraus waiting in front of the Sagrario in the *zócalo*. Didn't spot me at first and I had to get out of car and walk her back to it. Had expected me to come on foot. I spotted no one, but that wide walk on the cathedral side of *zócalo* is full of vendors and artisans looking for work, people wandering around, let alone whoever might be watching from the grounds of the cathedral or the Sagrario. Stepped along as lively as etiquette allows because I couldn't help wondering if Guanajuato bunch might think morning ambush would amuse the tourists. If so, they running late which okay by me. Kraus pale, dressed as she was in coffee shop only this time a beige sweater and matching ribbon on the ponytail. Not as neat, something awry, her appearance tending slope away from smart toward frowzy. Even without Sanders account I think I'd have guessed something happened since I last saw her.

2. Wary about car: "Where we going?"

Told her just drive around while we talked. Asked her if she had waited long.

Said no in dull voice.

Did anyone know she was meeting me?

Petey (sic!) Sanders just might suspect something, she said, giving me a look by which I mean a look of contempt.

Yes, he called last night, I said. Seems to be a nice young man. Friend of yours?

Susie, she's Petey's wife, was my best girlfriend, or I thought she was until I found out how she operates. I used to think Susie was so really cute—cute, cute, cute. (Comment. I'm not making any of that up.)

Found what out?

Never mind. I like Petey. He's really neat. A class act. He deserves better.

What's wrong with Susie?

I don't want to talk about it. Susie's real stuck on herself. End of commentary on Sanders family.

Anyone else know we're meeting?

Why do you ask?

It might be important.

What makes it so important?

This sort of conversation disturbing to my thought processes, so I don't answer, take up driving as therapy.

Well, if it's so important, no, no one else knows. I'd have to be literally raving mad to tell anyone I'm seeing you the mess I'm in.

Tell me about mess.

Instead she looked out car window in hopeless way as though she wishing she somewhere else with someone else.

3. Tempted fate by looping around to Reforma Norte, taking Eje 2 Nte to Insurgentes Nte, out toward Tepeyac and Indios Verdes. As dwelling on latest episode Debbie's soap opera rather than maneuvering had more than usual ration of narrow escapes in traffic stimulating artificial attempts at merriment on my part, cheering her up slightly, leading to conversation on Mexican drivers, air pollution, death of trees, squatters, poverty, stimulating comments on ineptitude/callousness of government/Institutional Revolutionary party, crying need overthrow government/PRI preferably with blood running in gutters, if that not feasible maybe through elections, latter clearly last resort and far less fun. My inability reciprocate her delight at prospect of Leninist processing of class enemies may have contributed to silence coming down over us again.

So I said, Debbie, what can I do for you? Why did you want to see me?

I've got to think, she said.

Of course, I said. Go ahead and think but in meantime what was it you want to talk to me about?

Attack of lip chewing. Then she burst out with following. Oh, God, I'm like what do I do now?

What is it, Debbie?

Listen, I've really got to know. This is incredibly important to me. What do you really do?

Told her the question not what I do but what she doing. She can certainly speak to me in confidence. I would not be driving around Mexico City with her now if I wasn't ready to help her.

How do I know I can trust you?

Look, I said, Debbie, your calling me out to coffee shop, giving lecture on México Irredenta (hereafter MI), trying to find out whether I had been in Guanajuato, was pretty strange behavior. When Mr. Sanders came to say you wanted to see me again, I told him our previous conference was odd, except that I did do a memo on MI because I thought that part of your remarks interesting.

Oh, Jesus God! That's just what I was afraid of. Don't tell me. Who all'd you give it to?

Oh, just to a few key people in the embassy. (Did not actually do anything of sort, of course.)

I really wish you hadn't done that.

Why?

Well, God, who all's going to see it? Did you say I was the one who told you?

No, I wouldn't do that. Although you didn't ask me to keep your name out of it. But you were very clear that the embassy should know all about MI.

God, I know, I know. Thank God. I shouldn't be tied in with MI in any way at all, don't you see? I just completely, but completely screwed up. Literally screwed up. I should never have listened— Pause.

Listened?

Ignored question. More lip chewing. Then: I'm in way, way over my head. Way, way over. It's unbelievable.

How so?

It's an incredibly bad idea to get involved in other people's politics. Do you know what I'm saying?

Sure. That is the beginning of wisdom, Debbie.

4. We finally got to a point or two. Viz.

    a) She has been working with or for MI because MI literally only possible way out for Mexico. Otherwise just forget it. The political basis for her thinking all this is not so edifying as to merit more elaboration than given earlier: trendy left, adequate shorthand summary.

I get back to asking: Who in MI sent you to see me the other day?

That's not important.

It is to me.

More important my health not to tell you.

Shelved that for moment although my leading candidate is Chato Escobar.

    b) Sudden outburst: Listen, if you want to know, the MI killed someone. Then hastily: Not that exactly but MI had someone killed. No, I don't really know that. But I know someone got killed. I can't hack that. I've been around and can handle, like, just about anything, but don't give me killing. I've gotta find out.

Who killed?

Someone in Guanajuato.

Who?

Some Mexican general. He doesn't matter, it's the principle.

Why was he killed?

I don't know.

Tell me what you know. Did the general know something that would harm MI? What was it he knew?

I don't know, swear to God, how he could possibly have found out. Maybe just suspected.

Found out what?

I told you. People shouldn't know about me, word gets around an American working with MI, could be misunderstood. Why I wish you hadn't written that memo. She

looked scared then and said, What I mean, if they kill
    him, who else they going to kill?
You're worried about what they might do to you.
Not really. But why did they have to kill him?
All right, Debbie. Do you think someone killed him be-
    cause he found you, an American, are working with the
    MI? C'mon. That's not worth killing, is it?
You don't understand. It's not just me.
What's the whole story, Debbie?
I've really got to think very hard about this, hard, hard,
    hard.
Sometimes it helps to talk to someone else who's not
    so close to it. Her chin trembling now. We were up
    at the shrine of Guadalupe and I pulled over and
    parked.
c) When you came to see me that time in the coffee shop,
    you insisted I had been Guanajuato. Why?
It was an assignment.
Describe the assignment.
Gives me her look. Like I said. Find out if you had been
    in Guanajuato.
Huh, I said, disingenuously. You mean find out if I went
    down there and killed some general.
No, she said, not that. If you were the one talking to gen-
    eral, whether he talked about MI and what he said.
Did person who sent you tell you: Find out what general
    said about this thing or about that thing?
No, just whatever it was he thought he knew, what he told
    you.
Why me? Why would he want to tell me?
Maybe because what you do. You'd be surprised number
    of people out to get Mora. Reactionary sectors terrified,
    privileges threatened. They know Mora's honest and
    can't be bought, co-opted Mexican style, they hate him
    and fear him.
What would give anyone idea I had gone to Guanajuato?
    Why me?
How do I know? Forget it. That was some kind of screw-

up. But at the time they knew general was going to meet someone.

So the MI killed him, right?

I never said the MI killed him.

Excuse me but you did, just a minute ago. That MI had him killed.

Pardon me all to hell, Mr. Oliver, I said nothing of the sort. Who told you they killed him?

See? You're the one saying it, not me.

What could some general in Guanajuato say to me or anyone else about Mora that was so bad as to make it necessary to kill him?

How do I know? People are killing other people all the time for no reason at all, aren't they? Look at the CIA in Central America.

Gave me triumphant squint-eyed look with that. I ignore it. Did you learn about killing from same person who gave you the assignment?

Stop it! Just shut up, can't you! Oh, God, I'm sorry. Tears. Had own Kleenex in her purse. Why do things happen the way they do? Why is everything so complicated? Why is it just when you think you've really got it made, all of a sudden it all turns into shit?

d) All right, Debbie, I'm sorry. But tell me about MI.

Okay. (!)

Turns out she has been to San Cristóbal de las Casas for audience with Mora. (We already had pin in map there from Clinkscale.) Mora: Unbelievably unique, this really marvelous incredible fabulous man, etc. Mora incredibly old, very, very wise, can interpret Mexican history so you understand what happened. These unbelievably deep political ideas. Very very but very anti-PRI, anti, anti, anti! Fantastically dedicated to reviving Mexican traditions.

Vasconcelos?

You bet, Vasconcelos! Literary mentor. Someone like you would think Mora real radical. But let's face it, fundamental changes needed. Mora resents U.S. relations with

PRI. But not anti-American at all. Blames U.S. government but no quarrel American people who Mora thinks really marvelous. (Where have we heard that before?) Get U.S. and foreign banks off Mexico's back. U.S. must understand Mexico. Help but no strings. Let Mexicans work out destiny without foreign interference. U.S. should not fear MI.

Who said it should?

Well, like I said, program sort of radical but that is appeal needed to stir Mexican masses, and U.S. shouldn't take each and every little word of it too seriously. (Where have we heard that before?)

Mora very articulate, I take it.

Well, he gets tired, being real old and all that.

What happens to MI when he gets too old?

Well, he's not in this all by himself, you know. I mean there's an organization behind him.

Elaborate on that. Lots of people all over Mexico, for instance?

Shakes head. You don't understand. You don't need the grass roots anymore. (NB: Exactly Clinkscale's words.)

What have instead, then?

She smiled at that. That's where I come in. (At this point I recall Petey saying she television expert.) Getting word out in other countries, get people talking, asking questions, Mexico is the apparent target but you're really aiming elsewhere, see? Mexico itself comes later. Really exciting, incredibly unique way of going about—a first— we've learned a lot about election spots, you know. This goes global.

e) What's future of MI, Mora being this old crock?

I told you MI, well, aware of that and there's this incredibly clever, clever plan for future.

Such as?

She shook her head. It's very very clever and also something you and I don't talk about. Very cute, very innovative, very tricky. The timing. I love it.

How can that be so sensitive?

If I explained why, then you'd know why it's no one else's
business at this stage. Pardon me for not wanting to get
into deep, deep, incredibly deep trouble any more than I
already am in up to my little neck.

What do you mean by timing?

I already told you, coordination, stuff like that. Things have
to be in place. I got that literally drummed into my little
head again. That's why I know I shouldn't have opened
my big mouth. (Clinkscale?)

Hey, Mr. Oliver, I've got to get back. Come on, Ted. If
you don't mind. Let's go.

Start car and drive back toward center.

You're scared, aren't you, Debbie?

Listen, I told you. Killing people, that's what scares me.
Can't hack it. I feel better now.

Debbie, the person who told you to come see me that day.
You afraid of that person?

Shakes head, chews lip.

He tell you to see me again?

Shakes head.

He know you seeing me today?

Christ! No.

Why didn't you want to meet in coffee shop today?

I'm afraid, if you want to know.

Of what?

Being seen with you.

What's wrong with me?

It's nothing personal, I assure you. Okay, I was supposed
to see you once, but if I see you on my own, then I'm in
trouble. I don't like being in this car even.

Look, I really do want to help you.

Shakes head. I know it but.

5. Back downtown. See you tomorrow.

No.

Well, we have to meet again.

Not so sure about that. Have to think about that.

Don't do it alone. Helps to talk it out. What if I provide

discreet place to meet? Against better judgment tell her I have use of apartment downtown not far from embassy.

You've got to be kidding. Unpleasant laugh. We haven't reached that stage in our relationship yet, Mr. Oliver. Loud, coarse laughter. You gotta be—more of same laughter.

Phooey. It's not a *casa chica*, Debbie.

You gotta be kidding.

6. Made morose by all this, I let her off at the Insurgentes metro station. My little surprise for Debbie; as you'll remember, she had her rendezvous with Clinkscale there. When I pulled up there she gave me a new kind of look, wondering about whether this is a really incredible, unbelievable coincidence.

Look, Debbie, how about it, let's say tomorrow, okay? Meet you right here at ten-thirty.

I'll call you.

Don't. I'll be out. I'll be here at ten-thirty, tomorrow.

She didn't say yes but she didn't say no.

COMMENTS.

a) Why did Debbie want to see me? To see what I know or what I've done or said about her. For instance, upset when I claimed I'd done a memo on MI. Maybe she wanted to learn if I had told Clinkscale about the first meeting with her. That's doubtful, though. If I had, he would have said so to her, I think.

b) Add this hypothesis: Clinkscale talked about his reason for coming down, filling her in on what's going on in Washington, and then blabbed away about seeing me, by name and position. Debbie horrified at finding she had been told—by someone in MI, not Clinkscale—to see me. Am worst possible person from her point of view to whom she should have talked. Wants to find out what I know and what I'm going to do about it. (She assumes I did not mention her to Clinkscale and I assume she did not tell Clinkscale about seeing me.)

c) She honestly scared by learning general killed.

d) I do not find Debbie easy to deal with nor do I understand how she thinks. I plan to keep on listening, bore in there, get some names beyond old Mora, something we can get a grip on.

Chapter 13

Lankester finished reading Oliver's contact report on the meeting with Debbie Kraus and looked up at Oliver to say, "If you don't mind my saying so, I don't see that your meeting with her resulted in anything useful. Nothing that we didn't know before. Not worth the risk or worth defying headquarters's instructions."

"Well, I don't know, Chas. It's not so much what we learned as confirming that Debbie knows quite a bit that she isn't telling. That she has a role. That's the lode I'm working. And I'll see her tomorrow, and who knows what she'll have?"

"And what about headquarters? Are you going to admit that you saw Debbie?"

"Chas, I sent a cable saying that she asked to see me again, repeat, asked again, and that I saw her, and I gave the gist of the meeting."

Lankester nodded, frowning, and said, "Frankly, I'm relieved to hear that. However, you should know that I have started keeping an account of this matter—a written log—and have noted there my repeated objections to your flouting of orders from headquarters."

Oliver spoke without thinking. "Oh, Lord, Chas, that's so dumb!"

Lankester came to his feet. "I am sick and tired of being treated by you and by Sanders, too, as though I were—" he sputtered.

Oliver got up too. "Come on, Chas. I shouldn't have said— I didn't meant that. You have every right—sit down a minute and—good, look, I'm really glad you told me about that."

121

Lankester sat down, red-faced, on the edge of his chair, not looking at Oliver. I'm Captain Queeg, thought Oliver, and here's Chas taking a courageous stand on the side of good order and discipline. "I know how you feel. Keep a record, by all means. Go ahead. I should have tried to tell you earlier how this looks to me."

Lankester was not looking at Oliver but he was listening. "Debbie looked me up. I didn't seek her out. Look, Chas, I don't know that this nutty movement we're been told to stay away from is the important element. As you know, I find this cozy arrangement headquarters supposedly has worked out with Bondie Birdsong objectionable. But that's not the reason I'm following through with Debbie." Oliver paused to question whether that statement was accurate and added, "Not the only reason. I promised I'd find out who killed Carlos Robles."

Mrs. Pott came in at that moment to say, "A Mr. Ford on the phone."

"Oh, good. Yeah." Oliver picked up the phone on his desk. "Good day, Mr. Ford."

"Didn't see anyone at the pickup. But you know that place. For sure nobody was on you when you left. I parked behind you at Guadalupe. Didn't see anything."

"Fine. You see where she got off?"

"Yeah, where you said."

"Have a tentative date for ten-thirty tomorrow there. Can you get there a bit early?"

Rather than being curious about the call, Lankester was immediately ready to pick up where Oliver had left off. "But who killed Robles is not our affair. Whom did you promise? Not headquarters, surely."

Oliver thought about that. He could have said that he had promised Jack Winters. Promised Lester Lazaire. Had Lankester known about Inocencio Brown, Oliver would have said that Inocencio was working with Oliver to investigate the murder of Robles. Oliver thought that Inocencio was happy to be back working on a case, back on the street, never mind the occasion. "Chas, this looks to you as, ah, personal, is that it?"

"How else can it be viewed?"

"Yeah." Oliver slumped in his chair. "Well, you see, it wasn't just a casual killing—"

"In that you were there. That makes it important to you."

Oliver shook his head while filing that idea away to be examined later. "No, it's not only that. There are reasons behind the killing that we should know."

"Why?"

"I don't know how to explain it, Chas!" Oliver spread his arms. "Other than saying I'm an intelligence officer. It's in the blood to ask questions and to get answers. You know!"

"But headquarters must decide what questions are important."

"Not when we in the field have a hunch the answer matters."

"We have to trust the director. People in the field can't be second-guessing him. What happens to an organization then?"

Oliver sighed. "I know. Listen, Chas, I wasn't going to get into this. But Clinkscale presented this as a mutual backscratching operation, right?"

"I suppose you could put it that way."

"Bondie gets votes by talking up the Movement, runs in Texas on a Mexican ticket."

"Nothing unusual about that. Look at all the ethnic groups. Politicians appeal to their emotions, get contributions from those groups, and in return support foreign-policy objectives that appeal to blocs of those voters. This example just happens to be a few miles away across the border, rather than Ireland or Israel. That's what bothers you, I think. It impinges on the country you're in and a country you feel very protective about."

"It's not that way at all, Chas. What upsets me is the agency's collusion in this."

"Collusion. That makes it sound somehow underhanded. Ted, frankly, it doesn't matter what you or I think, does it? It's done all the time and obviously people accept it. It's part of the American scene."

"The American scene. In return for our not noticing Bondie's electioneering in Mexico, Bondie scratches the director's back by supporting the director in crucial matters on the intelligence committee."

"Well, that sort of horse trading goes on all the time too. That's Washington."

"Makes me wonder how many other deals the director's got like this."

Lankester resettled himself in his chair. "Oh, I doubt that he does, but if he does, so much the better. I'm sure you object as much as anyone to congressional interference, their attempts to micromanage the agency, don't you?"

"Yeah, I sure do."

"Well, then," said Lankester. "What is your objection to this?"

"My objection? For one thing, Clinkscale didn't give us the whole story. I bet he doesn't know it. You and I know it, though."

"I don't know what you mean by the whole story," said Lankester.

"Yes, you do, Chas. You know that the director has a long-standing grudge, a permanent chip on the shoulder about Mexico."

Lankester stood and walked up and down the rug. "I think that to be a distortion of his views because of your own proprietary attitude about Mexico."

"It's not proprietary or protective. It's a matter of judgment. This is really out of bounds, Chas. All this started before you came over from the NSC, Chas. He went after the government, the PRI, once before. That's where the director and I had our run-in. He's pulling the wool over Clinkscale's and Bondie's eyes. They have no idea he's using this American-as-apple-pie backscratching operation as cover for covert political action against the PRI."

Lankester came back and sat down. "Frankly, I think that's an absurd reading of what's going on. If that were true, however, you could be sure the National Security Council would have directed it," said Lankester.

"I told you what Clinkscale said, the NSC, everyone else cut out of the picture. They want no discussion of it."

"Clinkscale doesn't have to know all the facts. The NSC might want to pull the wool over his eyes if they could. A clever cover story, as you say. Or maybe he and Congressman Bird-song know the whole plan. We just are being told a part of it down here. They decided we have no need to know.''

"Chas, you've got a touching faith in the system, a well-oiled machine. My experience is that you have to be repairing it every day, you can't relax a single minute, someone'll be trying to jimmy it around.''

Lankester smiled tolerantly at that—after all, Oliver had never served on the NSC, never seen government work at that high level. Then he said, still smiling, "You know, if you really believe what you say, why don't you blow the whistle. Why don't you do that?''

"You know what would happen if I did? It would leak. The agency would be right back in the dock, pilloried, with the media, the congressmen, all jumping around and baying like hounds again. Never mind the director. A mob scene. They'd be swarming out of the woodwork to go after the agency. That's why, Chas.''

"I don't think for one minute the theory you proposed is correct. But even if you believe it, you also are saying there's nothing you can do about it. Isn't that right?''

Oliver thought a moment before answering. "By whistle-blowing you mean something public, going to *The Washington Post*. I wonder whether the inspector general knows about this.''

"How would he?''

"Good question. He wouldn't if the director or Slasher didn't tell him.''

"Despite everything you have said—perhaps all the more—I feel I must continue to keep a record of actions taken in the station.''

"Yeah, sure. Go ahead.''

"One other thing. There ought to be a standard format for the preparation of contact reports here in the station,'' said Lankester, who all this time had been holding Oliver's contact report of his meeting with Debbie Kraus. "You and Sanders have highly individual ways of putting accounts of your meetings on paper. These should be standardized. A standard form would mean that nothing is overlooked. If you don't mind, I'll see if I can come up with something.''

''Good idea, Chas,'' said Oliver, insincerely but at the same time glad if it would give Lankester something to do. ''Why don't you pull something together?''

Oliver was on his way to meet Debbie the next morning when Mrs. Pott called out, ''Mr. Oliver! Phone.'' She had a hand over the mouthpiece. ''Washington. Mr. O'Rourke.''

''Damn!'' said Oliver, his body vibrating with the temptation to keep going right on out the door. He took the phone on his desk and told Mrs. Pott to stay on the line. They could hear the muffled voice of O'Rourke's secretary's saying ''—just coming on, Mr. Oliver.''

O'Rourke came on clearly enough. ''Just wouldn't listen, would you?''

''And a good morning to you, Slasher.''

''Get your ass on an airplane.''

''What's up?''

''You saw the girl, what's up. Outta my hands now. Someone else wants to see you. Bad. Get on an airplane.''

Oliver closed his eyes, took a deep breath. ''Anything else?''

''Yeah. Be here first thing in the morning.'' There was a click and the sound of remote cracking and humming, someone speaking Portuguese. Oliver listened to space.

''I shouldn't say so but I don't think he's at all nice, Mr. Oliver.''

''You can say it to me as much as you like. See what you can get, would you?''

''There's that United flight. Let's see what days—I'll look. Why couldn't he just say who it is that wants to see you?''

''Regrettably, he did not have to,'' said Oliver as he went out the door.

Oliver turned the Toyota at the corner to slow down as he neared the metro stop at Insurgentes, looking for the place where Debbie had been standing the other day when she had hurried to get into the taxicab with Clinkscale. Oliver was anxious to see her. It was important that she be there, important beyond the obligation he felt toward the Robles case. Lankester's keeping a record forced Oliver to consider the seriousness of his flouting headquarters's orders, as Lankester put it. With Slasher's command to come home, Oliver was almost desperate to get something from Debbie that would justify his insubordination, something that might serve to lessen the gravity of his defying the oral instructions from Washington.

You don't go into an interview putting personal motives first, it can throw off your aim, muddy your objectivity—all that and more—but right now Oliver needed Debbie badly and he rejected the rule. He planned to zero in on the place of Chato Escobar—then he could justify having seen Debbie.

But instead of Debbie Kraus it was Pedro Sanders who hurried across the walk, threading his way through the people on the street, to run up to Oliver's gray Toyota. Oliver shook his head as he opened the side door to let Sanders in.

"Greetings, bearer of bad news. Out with it," he said.

"She's on her way to the States. I thought I'd better catch you here."

"Christ almighty!" Oliver hit the steering wheel.

"Called me this morning to say she was leaving."

"Time to catch her?"

Sanders shook his head. "She's on that Mexicana flight that stops at Cozumel."

"Leaves at eleven, doesn't it? Wait here a minute." Oliver got out, walked to the middle of the sidewalk, stood there a moment, rubbing his hands together as though washing them, before coming back to the car.

"Who was that for?"

"Well, I'll have to fill you in on that one of these days. In the meantime I've got to go to headquarters. Or did you know?"

Sanders nodded. "Mrs. Pott told me."

"I was really counting on Debbie."

"Yeah."

"Oh, well. You might say I've been asking for it."

"I bet Chas would."

* * *

At noontime Inocencio called again.

"Hadda no show."

"Right. She's gone to the States."

"Lost the gigolo. He go too?"

"Don't think so. Have you looked in Chiapas?"

"Gigolo's not the kinda guy goes to Chiapas."

"I've gotta be in Washington a couple of days. Tell San Miguel, will you?"

"Anybody over there to talk to, you gone?"

"No. Take a break unless the gigolo turns up. You still can't remember where you saw him before?"

"Naw. It'll come to me one day. Okay. *Buen viaje.*"

Tom and Nancy were interested in what he would bring them. Marge wanted to know why he was so glum about going.

"Who wants go to Washington?" Oliver answered. "I guess this blue suit is clean enough, isn't it?" he added. Glum was right. He had been counting far too heavily on Debbie. Now that she was gone, he had nothing. He was going to Washington without a single high card he could play, not one trick he could take.

"Let me see it. I wouldn't mind a visit to Washington. If I were asked."

"I'm only going to be there a day or so. You wouldn't be so eager to go if you had to sit there with Slasher O'Rourke blabbing away at you."

"I don't know. I'd like to meet the famous Slasher. This looks all right. You've spilled something on the vest. I can get it out."

"You don't want to meet the Slasher. Especially if he's raising hell with you."

"What have you done to make him raise hell?"

"A basic difference of opinion."

"Ted, you're not off on one of your tangents?"

Oliver turned on her. "What do you mean 'tangents'? You make me sound like some kind of a nut, you're so quick to jump on a guy."

"No, but you get an idea and no one—"

"Idea! I don't deal in ideas. I deal in facts. Like packing."

"Have you discussed this with Chas and Pete? Sometimes it helps—"

"Oh, sure. Pete's okay but he hasn't been around enough to have developed any—you know."

"Chas has a good head on his shoulders, though, doesn't he? He must be helpful?"

"Oh, yeah. Real helpful."

Chapter 14

Vortices of snow rushed from behind the building corners to attack the office windows of the chief of the South American Division of the CIA, hurling themselves against the glass, dashing a glaze upon it before spinning away on the wind, their remnants building saber curves on the sills, the blasts rattling the glass, transparent puffs of cold infiltrating into the inner space around Oliver's left cheek and ear. It was warm enough in Slasher O'Rourke's office otherwise, but Oliver's feet waited coldly to be summoned to the seventh floor.

"Never mind Claudie Clinkscale," the Slasher was saying. He had clasped his hands behind his head, rumpling his already mussed thick blond hair, straight strands standing on end.

"Look, Slasher, we've got to find out if Claudie knows Debbie took the initiative, asked to see me. Twice."

"Who the hell cares?"

"Would you mind asking him?"

"Yes, I would mind it all to hell. If Claudie doesn't know about you and the girl, why in hell would I tell him? Answer me that."

"If he doesn't know she came to see me that first time, then we can assume she took direction from someone else. Someone other than Claudie. We oughta know who it was. If Claudie already knows all about it, okay, no harm done."

"Sure, no harm done except Claudie might ask what in hell the COS Mexico's doing fooling around with his girl down there, scaring her ass off, she runs home to Mama." O'Rourke grinned, showing the gap between his front teeth.

"Someone else scared her ass off, not I."

"Forget it, Ted."

"Let me ask him then, if you don't feel like it."

"Sssh—" said O'Rourke, shaking his head. "You gotta be —" He raised his arms high and yawned. "You're not making sense, Ted."

"She's back up here and Lord knows what she's telling him."

"Okay, Ted, okay. You got bigger things to worry about."

"In case she gives him some nutty version of what we talked about, you've got my contact reports to fall back on. I sent them up here. It's all there in the record."

"Ted. Who's got the time read all that shit? Ted, you gotta understand. It's not our deal. Not your deal. You don't own Mexico, you know. You can't run the frigging country all by yourself."

Oliver let out his breath, turned his face from O'Rourke toward the violence of the wind and snow roaring silently a few feet from where he sat. The only sound in the room was the soft whir of the heating system.

"She used to work for him, know that, Ted? Here in Washington, even before he went to work for Bondie. Something else. You don't know Congress. Claudie and Bondie find out you going after his girl—you know—what then?"

"What then?"

"Take your average congressman. Doesn't know shit about the agency, know what I mean? Believes any stupid thing some screwball whispers in his ear. You tell Claudie about the girl, he tells Bondie. Right away Bondie starts thinking we running some kinda play around left end behind his back. Understand what I'm saying, Ted? Screw up everything the old man's trying to do—turn it inta piece a shit."

Oliver was silent.

"So now you see how it looks from here, you running around on your own all over the place, some general got himself killed. Bad case of localitis. Couldn'ta picked a worse time throw your monkey wrench, things getting geared up, getting under way."

"Mexicans the ones'll be throwing monkey wrenches, Slasher, once they figure out what's going on. Something else.

The inspector general know about this little arrangement you got?''

"Aw, come on, Ted. Only thing the IG wants to know is if you're playing grab-ass with your secretary. That's all they care about. They wouldn't understand this.''

"That why you haven't told 'em?''

"Okay, smart guy. Inspector general gets this all bass ackwards, I mean the way you see it, all hell breaks loose. Be all over town. That what you want? Wanta get another crusade going? Your ambition personally start that? Agency go through all that again?''

"You answered my question.''

"Damn right I did,'' O'Rourke was saying, grinning again, when the telephone emitted a soft beep. He lifted the instrument, shot a pleased look at Oliver, and jumped up. "Let's go.''

Oliver took a deep breath. "I can find my way up there, Slasher.''

"You think I'm gonna miss this?'' O'Rourke led the way into a passage and stopped before closed elevator doors that showed a keyhole at the side instead of up-and-down buttons. O'Rourke pulled a key ring from his pocket, showed a key to Oliver, winked at him, and put the key in its slot. O'Rourke thus revealed himself as a holder of the highest award in the CIA—the Grand Cross, equal to the Garter in court circles, to the Nobel among commoners—a key to the elevator that terminated its upward run in the director's seventh-floor suite. Ordinarily the Key was awarded to the senior administrators, to those who called the director by his first name, to the briefers who went with the director to Congress or the White House, who held the charts for him, to his budget and fiscal experts, to the bright young careerists who drafted his papers. It was so rare for an operations officer like O'Rourke to have a key that Oliver was impressed. He turned away from O'Rourke lest his face show it.

"What they say he does,'' said O'Rourke as the elevator doors closed on them, "is he rolls up his sleeve and reaches way to hell up inside you and feels around until he gets a good grip from behind on your tongue and then—*whap*! He jerked his forearm down. "Yanks you out through your own asshole and you're hanging there looking from your insides out. No, sir." He shook his head at Oliver, grinning. "This I gotta see."

And he led the way from the elevator into the dimly lit reception area, more starkly impersonal than a dentist's office, as noncommittal in its beige tones as the lobby of an apartment hotel. Oliver sank into the gray-upholstered couch and leaned forward to take a magazine from the coffee table. The rumble of typewriters, the whacking of printers, the ringing of phones came through the door of the room to their right, defining its mission. The same beige carpet was on the floor, but the room was far more brightly lit than where Oliver slumped, turning the pages of the magazine without seeing them. The other room was busy, alive with the movement of people going about their morning tasks, the odd cheerful remark floating into Oliver's hearing. It seemed to him remarkable that they could be so unconcerned, too callous to send even one curious glance in his direction.

O'Rourke was sprightly as he stuck his head around the doorpost to confirm their presence. He came back, grinning, rubbing his hands. "He's on the phone. Won't be long now." Oliver nodded without looking up from his magazine, his mouth dry. " 'Sreally too bad you couldn't listen to me and old Claudie," added O'Rourke.

Oliver grunted. O'Rourke sprawled in an armchair by the couch, legs straight out on the rug in front of him, humming, and Oliver could feel his eyes on him. He looked up to see the director's secretary coming through the door from the other room, wearing the bright smile of a surgical nurse. "He's ready for you now, Mr. Oliver." She was going toward the door that gave directly onto the director's office. Like a dog rushing to be let in, O'Rourke crowded up to the door just ahead of her. Oliver put the magazine down. His hands and feet were cold.

"Excuse me, Mr. O'Rourke." she said, not smiling, pushing by O'Rourke to take the doorknob. She looked past him to Oliver. "This way, Mr. Oliver. Have a seat, Mr. O'Rourke. I'll call you when he wants you."

Slasher O'Rourke looked at her unbelievingly. "But—"

"The director asks that you wait here, Mr. O'Rourke. Go in, Mr. Oliver. Let him—please. Thank you. Sit down, Mr. O'Rourke. I'll call you when he's ready for you." She opened the door and stood back to let Oliver by. Oliver glimpsed the director just to his left, standing behind his desk, still on the phone. He hesitated and looked at her. "Go right ahead," she said as the director hung up the phone. O'Rourke's astonished face was right behind her, a sneer beginning to curl into place.

"Sit down, Mr. Oliver." The director was the same height as Oliver, more spare, wider across the shoulders, narrower in the waist, lightly built but also fragile. The word in the halls was that he wasn't well. When Oliver took his seat in the red cloth-covered armchair across the desk, the director seemed to loom, magnified, over him, as though placed higher. There was no trickery here, Oliver knew, recognizing that what put the director above him was the aura of authority—and no illusion, either.

For a moment their eyes met, the director glancing at Oliver from under untrimmed dark brows while putting some papers aside with long-fingered hands. Oliver ordered his own hands loose on the arms of the chair, refusing to let the fingers grip the rough-textured upholstery as they demanded. His hands were acting as though he had carried them struggling aboard an airplane bouncing down the runway in a fight to leap from rough ground into the cushioning air.

The director's cheeks were the rosy, wrinkled brown of an old apple, the flesh clinging to the vertical lines of the lower face, following the delicate jaw's strong lines, his features attenuated by thought and by diet. A strict diet and the avoidance of stress were what the doctors had prescribed, according to office gossip, implying that the doctors had no sense of humor at all or a severely sardonic one. The director's smoldering eyes would be the prominent feature in the oil portrait that would hang in the hall of the Langley courtyard after he was replaced by a new president, became embarrassing to this one, or withdrew in the next engagement with disease. The eyes seemed independent of the rest of the face, which hardly changed while the eyes went from cool to cold, from burning angrily to an uncontrollable quick flicker of disgust. The features—the mouth, in particular—rarely altered, the facial lines mostly immobile, determinedly set. The look of the eyes alone gave life to what might without them have been ordinary—the eyes alight were plugged into the fiery thoughts within. The rare painter might catch that. The long faces of El Greco's saints came close but the models were much too tame, those soulful derelicts borrowed by the painter from the asylum.

Oliver's hands were under control but it was going to get tense keeping his eyes steady on the director's, which were examining him again. The other man took care of that by turning just enough in his chair to look up toward the large steel engraving of Lincoln that hung alone on the wall behind him. "There is a man whose motives were widely misinterpreted in his time. President Lincoln was badly misunderstood—is still, Mr. Oliver." He turned to put the eyes back on his guest. "Why did he take up the challenge, fight through to the end?"

"To preserve the Union."

"Ah, then, why is it, with that perceptiveness, your going immediately to the heart of the matter, that we seem to have this small difference of opinion, Mr. Oliver?" The director's expression changed little, but the eyes showed warm amusement. The interview was not starting down the path Oliver was expecting. Except for brief visits to the seventh-floor office most of his past dealings with the director had been through intermediaries, Slasher O'Rourke the most recent and appearing now to be the least reliable.

"Behind the chatter, the gossip, the jockeying for position, for privilege, for rights, Mr. Oliver, behind the frantic competition of the publicists for our attention, to sell us their views of the world, behind all that, there is still the quiet struggle to keep alive what Lincoln stood for in his time. Oh, it doesn't wear the same garb, I grant you. Among other differences, the field of conflict is international. But I don't need to tell you that Lincoln's hardest battles were with his own people, not with those in rebellion. He had to struggle with the first in order to put down the second. That feature hasn't changed, Mr. Oliver. Not a whit. It is my belief, despite the widening of the field of battle, that vital decisions will be made—or will be avoided—in the same city that was the scene of Lincoln's tragedy." He looked down at the the hands clasped across his stomach, opened his mouth to take a breath of air.

"Tragedy! A word used even to describe an auto accident these days. The tragedy of Lincoln was not his assassination at the day of victory. Actually that spared him from seeing, as Henry Adams did, sitting in his house on the corner of the park across from the White House, the disgraceful behavior of the politicians who betrayed Lincoln's vision. No, Mr. Oliver, the tragedy that wore Lincoln down was the constant struggle with his own people to keep the Union together, as you so acutely noted."

Here Oliver, becoming even more tense as he could see the path along which the director led, turning now to beckon him to follow, was surprised by a sudden, wider smile on the director's face, taken at the same time by the sadness of it.

"The Spaniards, Mr. Oliver, are our half-brothers, the same father by a different mother." He sat back in his chair and put his hands on the arms, his tie hanging smooth but his shirt bunched over gaunt ribs. "Or better, what? Cousins, the metaphor deserving more attention than I care to give it at the moment. The Mexicans are cousins many more times than once removed from the family, Mr. Oliver, as are the other distant relatives to the south, generally." He held up his narrow hand. "I will admit the exceptions you no doubt have in mind without the need for you to cite them, Mr. Oliver, so let us not part company on that score.

"You see the Congress and you know of the struggle between the Congress and anyone sitting in this chair. Your ordinary congressman—and oh, how ordinary some of them are, all too representative, Oliver—has small attention for anything beyond electoral tactics, parliamentary maneuver, the sharp practices at which many of them are, indeed, expert. Matters of substance may be left to their legislative assistants. Unhampered by intellectual modesty, their aides on the intelligence committees have the leisure to picture themselves sitting in this chair with all authority but—need I say it?—no responsibility. Your years in intelligence work, Mr. Oliver, would count for nothing with them, not useful, more likely disqualifying you for objective judgment. In short,'' and he smiled briefly, ''and I have indeed gone on long about it, they choose the terrain on which we must engage them.

''To go further with the military analogy, I must concentrate on defending vital positions and allow the inconsequential ones to be occupied by the enemy. And this brings us back to the subject with which I might have begun—Mexico, Mr. Oliver, important to you because you are there, because it is the scene of past triumphs.'' Here the eyes went dustily reptilian for half a second. ''Mexico must seek its proper level. Mexico may learn the importance of behaving as a good neighbor, controlling migration, drugs, not constantly carping at our foreign-policy initiatives. Otherwise, Mexico doesn't matter in the great scheme of things, Mr. Oliver. Look at the great changes in Europe and the prospects of chaos that come with the reversion to old bigotries and you'll understand that well enough. We must see to it that your talents are put to use in that wider arena rather than left to molder in a backwater. While I can't be more specific at the moment, there are to be several key spots opening up soon, any one of which I think you would find more than agreeable. We'll be in touch with you on that.''

The director's glance was quickly appraising. Oliver refused to shift in his seat, as his body requested, made particularly uncomfortable by the last suggestion. The confidences that preceded had led straight to that temptation. A pit in the trail was hidden by a mat of grasses, the sharpened stakes waiting below. The director coughed quietly, balling up his fist at his mouth, coughing again, for a moment showing his body's frailty.

''Congressman Bondie Birdsong has sat in the chair where you are. I have never nor would I ever speak to him as I have to you of President Lincoln. Lincoln? A cliché, a birthday, joined with that of the Father of Our Country for the benefit of the shopping malls in Texas in which Birdsong has a keen interest. Nor would I speak thus to Claude Clinkscale, although I suspect he might have a keener view of Lincoln than does his congressman. Congressman Birdsong is a voice, a crude but influential voice on the House Select Committee on Intelligence. I need Congressman Birdsong, Mr. Oliver, and I need him bad. The people in our office of estimates—when they think I'm in too much of a hurry for one of their papers—are fond of saying if I need something bad, that's how I'll get it. I must take that chance.

"You see, Oliver, the non-Hispanic members—I here do my best to conform to contemporary barbaric usage—of Congressman Birdsong's district might not be pleased by his flirtation with a group of people in Mexico they would regard as distasteful, if not threatening. His opponents might exploit that to the disadvantage of the congressman. The congressman asks only that we say nothing of his involvement, that of his people, in our official reporting channels—just for the time being. And if Birdsong must play on the emotions of the gullible among his constituency—note my avoidance of the word *demagogue*—the portion he refers to as Hispanic, and if he asks us—you, too, Oliver—to turn a benign eye away from the minor mischief of México Irredenta for some brief time, we lose nothing by accommodating him. Rather the agency stands to gain a great deal. And that's all I ask of you." He rocked slightly in his chair, spread his hands, and regarded Oliver intently. "I don't know how to make it any clearer."

"Why is it so important that we not report on an apparently new and growing political faction in Mexico?"

"Ah, well, I didn't think we'd need go into that—an officer of your experience." The director lifted his hands to express his surprise at the low intellectual level of the question. "We leave the conventional political reporting to the embassy, do we not? Leaving us free to do what we're charged with doing, what we're expert at."

"We had a cable saying the National Security Council wanted us to report on México Irredenta because of the lack of reporting from the embassy."

The director might have been quoting Oliver's own words to Lankester about the cable relaying the NSC request. "We can't waste our resources on making up for the deficiencies of an embassy. If the NSC is disappointed by embassy reporting, that is for the State Department to rectify, not us."

"Who will see to it that the embassy responds to the NSC request?"

The flesh at the director's cheekbones was red, two spots of anger burning not far below the surface. "The cable you received was sent in error and the error will not be repeated to the embassy, I can assure you. The NSC has lost whatever interest it had in the Movement." Another person might have permitted himself a sly look at that remark, but the director was too annoyed for that. "Were it not for that foolish cable slipping out over the holidays, we would not be having this conversation."

"General Robles, the one who was killed the other day, a decent man, much respected, was already asking questions about the Movement. The Mexicans know that and they'll be following up on his questions."

One hand went up. "I told you I would allow your exceptions to my Latin American rule. I accept that General Robles would be one, although, frankly, your bringing him into the discussion at this juncture I consider grossly sentimental."

"The Mexican government may think it sees a CIA hand behind the camouflage."

The director's voice was perceptibly a pitch higher. "Mr. Oliver, you seriously misread your job description if you think you are called upon to represent the interests of the Mexican government before me."

"Right now I'm representing to you the dangers of a scheme that the Mexican government will interpret as intervention in their affairs."

"The CIA is the object of constant false accusations of such activity, as you must know." The reptilian look was in his eyes again and it did not go away. "The government, the PRI, would use such an accusation as a pretext for stamping out the Movement, is that what you mean? Not this time, Mr. Oliver, not this time. The Movement soon will have built so much international support for itself that the government of Mexico will hesitate before exercising its accustomed tactics of repression against opposition." The director glanced at his watch without bothering to conceal that movement and raised his eyebrows. He had invested a good deal of valuable time in Oliver. "Have you any further questions?"

"The Mexican government will be asking the questions, I'm afraid."

"Do you imply by that your devotion to Mexico will tempt you to help them find the answers?"

Oliver was stunned by that.

Before he could think of what to say, the director was going on. "I'll give you two things to think about. And then I have important business to attend to. One is this. Neither you nor the Mexicans can prove a thing. For example, this woman of Clinkscale's who seems to fascinate you. There's nothing wrong with her being there. The Mexicans can't object. Political parties in Latin American are regularly importing consultants from here to help them in their campaigns. Secondly, did you succeed somehow in revealing the arrangement between the agency and Birdsong, the principal effect would be another scandal, another investigation of your beloved agency. Before you act in a precipitate and disloyal manner, think about that."

Oliver wanted to tell the director that he had thought of that—had talked to Lankester about it. As quickly as a snake strikes, the director's hand darted out to press a button and he spoke at the machine. "Bring Mr. O'Rourke in with you. We're through here." He looked at Oliver. "You have disappointed me, Mr. Oliver."

He picked up a document and began to read it as though Oliver were not there. O'Rourke was squeezing past the director's secretary and she stepped back, glaring at him, but letting him go first. O'Rourke stood before the director's desk, shooting covert glances at Oliver.

"Excuse me, Mr. O'Rourke," said the secretary as she came to sit down in the chair by Oliver.

The director glanced at O'Rourke. "Mr. Oliver and I have reached an understanding."

"Yes, sir," said O'Rourke. He was staring at the steel

engraving of Lincoln. Then he turned his head to look at the wall on either side of the engraving, then back at it.

"May I have your attention, Mr. O'Rourke?"

"Yes, sir!"

"By 'understanding,' I don't pretend that we agree." The director looked at Oliver. "However, I rely on Mr. Oliver's sense of discipline and his regard for the welfare of the clandestine service to, uh, to, uh, put to one side the differences between us on this one matter. Is there anything you want to say, Mr. Oliver?"

Oliver shook his head.

"You two heard what I said and Mr. Oliver's evident concurrence with it. Thank you. That will be all."

They were dismissed. When O'Rourke and Oliver stood up, the secretary got up also and went around behind the director. "They put this too high. If you decide to keep it there, I'll get them back to hang it lower down." She tilted her head, one hand on the frame of the Lincoln portrait.

The director's eyes darted over to see Oliver's reaction. Oliver smiled.

"Don't you think so?" said the woman.

"Never mind that," said the director, his face flushing red. "Thank you, gentlemen." He went back to his papers, not looking at them, his ears now a flaming red.

O'Rourke jerked his head at Oliver, who ignored him. "I have been under some strain with all this, the shooting, all that. If you concur, I might just take some time off. Leave Lankester in charge."

The director did not look up. "As you wish." He waved them out with a quick gesture.

As they went to the elevator doors O'Rourke spoke in a loud whisper. "What happened?"

"You heard him," said Oliver, holding his arms out on either side. His shirt was wet in the armpits. "Ever see that picture of Lincoln before?"

"No." O'Rourke was frowning. "That photograph of him sitting with the president is usually there. So what?"

Oliver looked at O'Rourke, blew his breath out, closed

his eyes, opened them, shook his head, and said, "An unusual man."

"Who? Lincoln?"

"Diane? Diane's in Steamboat Springs."

"What's she doing there?"

"In Steamboat Springs? Skiing, I daresay. That's what
you do in Steamboat Springs. Anything I can do?"

"Skiing! I hope she breaks her neck."

"Really, Mr.—"

"Oliver. Ted Oliver."

"Oh, okay. Gosh, she'll be sorry she missed you."

"When she getting back?"

"Monday morning. Unless she breaks her neck, that is."

"Look, this is important." Oliver looked at Diane's
empty desk and her typewriter. "Can I give you a note to
her?"

"Sure. Make yourself at home. I have to run up the hall.
I'll be back in a few minutes."

Dear Painted Lady [Oliver typed]
1. I need traces on Saturnino Mora, and on his political
   group, México Irredenta, with logical variations of the
   latter. Current hot stuff only without the doctoral dissertation footnotes so dear to your heart. Secondly on
   Debbie (Deborah?) Kraus. Tricky. She is U.S. citizen
   and don't check outside agency. Worked in congressional offices with one Claude Clinkscale last few
   years. Clinkscale currently working with Congressman
   Bondie Birdsong (D, Texas). Birdsong is on our committee.

   Carlos Robles, retired general shot and killed in
   Guanajuato a few days ago.

   Chato Escobar, FNU Mexican friend of Kraus and
   employed Relaciones Exteriores.
2. Talk to Marge at this number: 2-11-0073 which is safe
   apartment where I'll ask her to be M-W-F 1130 Mexico City time. (I know inconvenient time for you but

hard for Marge be there other times. Children. Or work out better time between you.) If no answer try again very next day same time. She will also try to get you at home here weekday evenings if she has a message from me.

3. If too much or too sensitive for phone, send data to Marge at home address, Avda. Castillo de Chapultepec, 27, not to embassy. No return address, no identifying data inside. Draw one of your James McNeill Whistler butterflies on the outside of the envelope.

4. In your role of senior member of the agency gossip tree, it may come to your attention I am in v. bad odor at present, or still, should I say, as result of what you and Marge have referred to in past as quixotic behavior. Anything you do of above nature on my behalf may get you into bad jam with a senior political appointee to this agency.

5. Final thought. If you hear anything funny going on about Mexico, pass that on, too, and much obliged.

6. Am going into wilderness to contemplate someone else's navel.

Your admiring,
Aztec Eagle

Oliver fished about in the drawers until he found an envelope, sealed the note inside it, and wrote Diane's name on it. He put another piece of paper in the machine, rapidly typed three single-spaced paragraphs, and sealed it in another envelope. He wrote an address in France on the face of it, scrawling "Air Mail" on it in red capitals. When he had done that, he stared at a poster of a church on the wall until he noticed that it showed the yellow towers of the basilica in Guanajuato. He turned in the chair to face a calendar. He was sitting there with his eyes closed when the young woman who shared Diane's cubicle returned.

"You work with Diane on Mexico?"

She shook her head. "Guatemala. We fill in for each other when one of us is away."

"You a skier?" Oliver handed her the envelope. "Look, thanks a lot. You got Diane's home number?"

"Somewhere here. Just a minute. She'll really be sorry she missed you."

"She may be sorry she ever met me. Wonder how long it takes for an airmail letter to get to France."

"Gee, I have no idea."

"Guess I'd better phone. Look, thanks for everything."

Chapter 15

"The Cañon de Cobre, by the way, is four times the size of the Grand Canyon and quite a bit deeper," said Oliver, concluding his announcement.

"Goodness! How do we reach you?" asked Mrs. Pott. She, Lankester, and Sanders were sitting in front of Oliver's desk.

"I don't think you do. I fly up to Chihuahua and take a train from there. It's about a five-hundred-mile train trip. Of course, if I see a telephone booth in the canyon, I could hop off and run over and call home. However, seeing as how I'm on leave—"

"Marge and the children going?" asked Sanders.

"No. School. Besides, Marge has shown little interest in dusty train trips, one reason I'm going now. Well, you two give Chas here a hand the next couple of weeks."

"I would like to know what it is that would take you to Chihuahua and that canyon," said Lankester, frowning at Oliver.

"Well, Chas. You know, it's not the sort of place I'd ever take the time to go to in the normal course of events. I'll give you all a lively trip report with color slides and synchronized commentary, if you insist on it, when I get back. Nothing elaborate, maybe an hour or two."

"I see on Mrs. Pott's desk a request to withdraw five thousand dollars in operational funds," said Lankester. "I'll have to know exactly what that is for before I can consider authorizing it."

"Don't worry, Chas. That's not a request. It's a receipt and I've already drawn the money. I have a revolving fund, as I guess you know, and I'll account for it at the end of the month as usual. You'll need to set up one of your own."

"Mrs. Pott, I must ask you to recover those funds from Mr. Oliver and return them to official funds."

"Oh, dear, how do I go about—"

"Why do you ask her? I'm the one who has the money."

"Then I must ask you to return it. What need have you for operational funds while on leave in Chihuahua?"

"Well, you never know who you might run into, a place like that."

Lankester said, "That's not a satisfactory answer. As of now you have ceased being in charge of the station. You have no authority. Mrs. Pott, again I must—"

"Hey, Chas. Leave Mrs. Pott out of it. She's just a middle-man. Middleperson."

"I resent your flippancy. Return those funds, then, until I can consult headquarters and get guidance on this."

"Oh, dear, what's happening to us?" asked Mrs. Pott.

"You'd look silly going to headquarters on something like that, Chas, the minute you take over."

"I think he's right about that, Chas," said Sanders.

"See here, Sanders. I'll ask for your opinion when I want it."

"I can't believe this!" said Sanders, reddening.

"All right, Pete," said Oliver. "Cool it."

"I hereby order you to return the five thousand dollars in official funds you have taken illegally and without proper authority."

"Oh, really!" Mrs. Pott stood up. "May I be excused?"

"Me too," said Sanders, standing.

"Mrs. Pott. Mr. Sanders. Remain here, both of you. I require you to witness his answer."

Oliver stood up too.

"Adios, folks, I'm off to Chihuahua."

Lankester stood up to face Oliver. "The cable from headquarters authorizing you to take leave said nothing about your drawing operational funds. Therefore I see no choice but to report to headquarters your refusal to return the funds."

"You surprise me, Chas. The cable didn't say anything about my going to Chihuahua, either, did it?"

Lankester's eyes widened. "No, but—"

"Think about it. Really, you'd look foolish going to head-quarters on this. It's not only Slasher O'Rourke who'd assume the responsibility was too much for you—what would the director think?"

Something over a thousand miles southeast of the Cañon de Cobre—about as far as one can go in that direction and still be in Mexico—on the southern side of the city of Tuxtla Gutiérrez, capital of the state of Chiapas, Oliver and Inocencio Brown were together on a piece of forested high ground known as El Zapotal for the *zapote* trees on its slopes. They were standing on a concrete walk, looking over a low wall into a pond some feet below and beyond them. Oliver was doing the looking actually, and doing that through a pair of binoculars. The glasses were not needed for the ducks swimming in the foreground. But the back of the pond was overgrown, and through the trunks and behind the green leaves on the far bank, shy water birds could be seen standing in shallow water or stalking silently about the shadows in the black mud.

Brown was holding a clipboard on which he had been copying down names Oliver had called off to him. "That's about the last of them, Inocencio," said Oliver. "The *garzita azul*, there, is our own little blue heron. No need to put him down."

"The best zoo in Latin America," said Inocencio.

"So they say."

"And you one a those bird-watchers. I didn't know that."

"Birders. We like to be called birders. You say bird-watcher, we think you're making fun of us."

"Birders. Okay. For my part, I like those jaguars."

"Yeah. I think I'm through." Oliver took the clipboard. "Thanks." They moved on along the path. "I'm not a serious birder, Inocencio. Just light cover for the trip."

"Gonna use an alias this time?"

"I'm afraid I'd look silly. I got the hotel room in true name. Showed my license at the airport to rent the car. It gets complicated. Hard to sustain an alias over time when there's a chance you'll run into someone who knows you."

"That's the truth. Feel like a damn fool. Myself, I'm looking for my roots."

"Really?"

"No, not really. All day yesterday I'm trying to think some reason go to Chiapas anyway. Almost in Guatemala. Doesn't make sense to go there. So I got me an ancestor for cover, the way you got your birds in this zoo here."

"Who's your ancestor?"

"Well, you pick a priest, Bartolomé de las Casas, it looks disrespectful. I kinda like this Diego de Mazariegos. I read about him. I tell you, those conquistadores one buncha tough cookies. One hell of a name, too, de Mazariegos. Beats Brown any day. Founded San Cristóbal, only he called it Villa Real de la Chiapa."

They walked out to the road. "Want me to drive, Inocencio?"

"Sure," said Brown, handing Oliver the car keys. "I do cities. Give you the mountains. Watch the reverse on this Jetta. It sticks. You gotta press down real hard."

The road wound up the slopes to where a lip of cliff was always hanging over them on the one side, the land falling away in a scarp on the other. Few trees remained on the sides of the mountains to interrupt the views from the highway. The lonely fields were steep and the wind rustled through the dry stalks of corn to traverse space a thousand feet above the valley below.

After they had been climbing for half an hour, the views across the mountains of Chiapas became so imposing that Oliver pulled over once he saw a rare patch of stopping place at the cliff edge. The two of them got out to look over silent space. Far below their feet a ribbon of stream, picked out by dots of bordering trees, worked its way across the valley bottom.

The next mountain across the valley rose nearly to the height at which they stood; green and yellow patches were the high fields, pines marched blue along the sharp ridges, grew in patches down the tawny hillsides like hair on a bison. On the next mountain beyond that the fields faded to russet, brown, and red. Beyond that the mountainsides were purple, then a dark blue, rank after rank hazed until cloud and the final ridge were one.

The wind was soft, just rattling the cornstalks on the lip of the field suspended above the road behind them. "Makes you feel real small," said Brown.

The sententious remark irritated Oliver because it touched his own thoughts so closely. He was not at that moment amused by the delight the natural world seemed to take in reminding man of his puniness, of the pettiness of his concerns. Contemplating the vastness of the landscape forced Oliver to ask himself whether it mattered at all if they discovered who killed General Robles and whether Bondie Birdsong's fraud was exposed. The scene in the director's office just a couple of days ago was so remote that he found it hard to persuade his mind to retrieve the words of their conversation.

Men had stood here before Oliver's time and would stand here when he had gone. The mountains would remain when no more men came to stand and look at them. That was their message: Do what you want. Whatever you do won't matter.

"Well, we are small, Inocencio. But that's no excuse to give up on what we're doing. It's not a question of self-importance. We can't be persuaded by standing here, be so affected by space or by time, the idea of infinity, that we forget why we came. All that has its own meanings, defined in other terms than ours," Oliver insisted. "I mean, we're always signing contracts. It's not that we're important in ourselves. In human proportions what matters is living up to the terms of the contract."

"I don't know what you mean, signing contracts."

Oliver would not have been so shaken by the rebuke of the mountains had he been more sure that his errand in San Cristóbal made sense. No point blaming Inocencio. "I mean like our coming over here. Our setting out on this project. Seeing it through."

"Keeping our promises, you mean."

"Anyway, those mountains," said Oliver, giving them another look before getting back in the car. "They only say whatever it is you want them to say to you."

Inocencio said nothing to that.

An hour after that stop they were still twisting and turning on the mountain road but coming out of the clouds that swept over the road at the highest point. Inocencio Brown had exclaimed gloomily at the sight of sandaled Indian men in their pink jerkins as they came down to the highway through mist and tall brown grass on muddy paths. "There some more of them," he would say, pointing at a group sitting on the side of the road. "Waiting for that *colectivo* you pass back there. Going to San Cristóbal." The women wore black, some had blue shawls wrapped around their heads to cushion the loads they carried. "See how the women working? I tell you, getting close to the end of the world. Chiapas!"

Inocencio had been quite good about Oliver's driving. The braking with his feet when a sputtering bus hurtled at them from around a narrow curve, his clutching at the dashboard when Oliver passed a chugging soft-drink truck, his cursing when a tailgating Volkswagen sped ahead of them on a blind curve, were involuntary responses. Oliver was not offended.

Then, at a steep curve, Oliver caught a glimpse of the city in the valley of Jovel some hundreds of feet below. A hundred yards farther there was just enough space on the side of the road for Oliver to swerve off, a white Volkswagen bug whining at his rear bumper, and brake to a stop on the shoulder. As he braked, Inocencio glared after the Volkswagen grinding out of sight around a curve.

The place where they stopped was carpeted with brown pine needles. As the Volkswagen took its noise with it, around them was only the sound of dripping from the heavy branches that drooped low from the pine trees above the road, bending with beads of condensation on the green needles, large drops plopping on the top of the car. Ragged patches of soaking mist moved gray through the tops of the trees.

"Get a good look from here at the city your new ancestor founded."

Inocencio laughed. "Founded a city. That's something. How many people ever found a city? Never thought about it before." They stood together looking down into the valley. "Well, not so bad. Just like a lotta places in Mexico. Mountains all around, city down in the valley."

"What's different are the clouds, the mist."

"That's right. And this the dry season too."

On the way up Oliver talked to Inocencio about sitting at the table on the balcony at Guanajuato when Robles was shot. He told him of inquiring about México Irredenta of Gobernación— just Gobernación, he did not mention Diego by name. He told Inocencio how Debbie Kraus had gotten in touch with him and why he was interested in her. He told him about Saturnino Mora and how, almost in desperation—he used that word with himself, not with Inocencio—he was coming now to San Cristóbal de las Casas to try to find out, once and for all, why Mora or his movement, México Irredenta, had found it necessary to kill General Carlos Robles.

"You sure they did?"

"Well, 'sure.' I don't know. What else we got to go on?"

"Huh. Gobernación in on this?"

"No." Actually Oliver had called Diego to tell him he was taking leave, going to vacation in San Cristóbal for a few days— strange to be telling Diego the truth he had not seen fit to tell the group at the office. He had felt low ever since the incident— Diego would understand. Diego had been sympathetic but allowed himself to tease Oliver at the same time. Why go to San Cristóbal for a vacation? Nothing there, nothing in Chiapas, he had said. Except Palenque, he had gone on to say. Of course, Oliver was going to visit the Mayan ruins at Palenque. Oliver had hastily agreed, saying good-bye then, but not before he heard Diego go on to comment: Most people go by Villahermosa to reach Palenque. Why, he was asking, would Oliver go out of the way to San Cristóbal? Again Oliver had said good-bye and hung up.

"No, Gobernación doesn't figure in it."

"Just wondered." Inoncencio laughed. "So, just the two of us against San Cristóbal. That's okay by me. We can handle that."

"No, three of us. I've asked someone else to come. Harley Drew. He's a retired ops officer. Retired to the south of France. Last post was in Mexico. Good Spanish. So that makes three of us. But there's something I ought to tell you that's been bothering me. You got in this because of Lester, Inocencio."

"That's right. Too bad Lester can't be here. Maybe just as

well. Lester here, he'd try to take over." Inocencio smiled. "Lester, he was something, the old days—"

"Inocencio. Excuse me but there's something I've got to make clear."

"Something else about San Cristóbal. Look there, the city, tight, not all spread out everywhere, what you call it, uh—"

"Sprawl. What I want—"

"Sprawl, that's it. Take Mexico City, take those towns up in California, used-car lots, signs, shopping malls, junkyards, all along outside."

"Right," agreed Oliver. "The city has a center, the plaza down there, and everything leads to it rather than away from it."

"That church on the edge of the plaza, that'd be the cathedral, the other church towers standing up all over town, some up on those hills, no high buildings."

"Right. Low roofs, red-tiled roofs. The streets are straight, patches of green trees, there."

"And those mountains all around. I'm prouda my ancestor. Come to look at it, he lay out quite a town here."

"Listen a minute, Inocencio, what I want to say," said Oliver, returning from their paean to the city to what he felt he owed Inocencio. "Point is, I'm doing this on my own, Inocencio. What I mean is, headquarters isn't in it either. I'm on leave, to tell the truth."

"They don't care who killed Robles?"

"No. What's more—"

"Well, up there, sitting in Washington. One man gets killed. What's that to them? Nothing. Only matter to us."

"Well, even more than that, they don't like my spending time on this, on México Irredenta. Rather I stayed away from it."

"They not always right. Anyway, we know what we're doing."

Oliver let out a breath. "Well, there you are. This isn't an agency job, Inocencio, strictly speaking."

"Okay by me."

"Good, good, Inocencio. I wasn't sure how you'd feel about it, headquarters not behind us in this."

"I say, screw 'em. What we need them for? I always like working on my own."

Oliver smiled at Inocencio and, in an excess of relief and to Inocencio's mild suprise, he took his hand and shook it.

Chapter 16

Oliver came down the stairs from his hotel room to the door of the dining room, a long room whose windows on one side gave onto the eighteenth-century courtyard. A waiter in a white jacket met Oliver at the door and asked, *"Grupo?"*

"No," said Oliver, after a moment of studying the waiter's question, "I'm alone. Solo."

The waiter stared at him a moment, as though giving him a chance to retreat, then turned on his heel to lead Oliver down an aisle between red-clothed tables, up a few steps to a platform raised like a stage above the tables. There sat four round tables each with eight place settings. At one of these a hollow-cheeked man about Oliver's age and size, hair cut short, sat alone, looking up as the waiter approached.

"Hey, Manuel," the man said in rasping English. "What happened to that scotch? El scotcho." He leaned back in his chair, pulled the sleeves of a heavy gray wool sweater away from his wrists, and bugged his large brown eyes, lower lids drooping, at the waiter.

The waiter rolled his eyes, swayed his head from side to side, and pulled out a chair for Oliver next to the other man. "Bartender, she no here," he said in English.

Oliver remained standing, shaking his head at the waiter, pointing to the tables for four below. The waiter shook his head. The seated man spoke again. "Abandon hope, friend. He wills you to sit here."

It was not at all what Oliver had planned. He intended to sit and wait for his friends—he was early—at a table of his own, one of those tables below that would seat four persons. He asked again to be seated below. The waiter smiled and pulled out the chair a few inches further. "Wait," said Oliver, in Spanish, standing. "I want to speak to the maître d'hôtel."

The waiter bowed and replied in Spanish. "Very early. He is not here yet. Were he here, he himself would ask you to sit at this table."

"Give up, friend. Metterdee, she no here either. Unless you're with a tour group—? Give the man a break, Manuel," said the other, still addressing the waiter in English. "Give me a break, too, Manuel. Trying to save yourself work, I know, but how about room enough to swing an elbow?"

Oliver slowly sat down one space away from the other man. "I'm not with a group. What difference does that make?"

"Don't do much traveling these days, do you? It's all groups now. In the last three days French, German, and Spanish."

"You with a group?"

"Hell, no, but I do happen to be staying here," said the man, obviously a North American. He ground out his words slowly in a throaty voice, giving what he said an extra significance. He so weighted the words that his speech had additionally a sardonic flavor to it. And by keeping his large eyes on Oliver, Oliver was persuaded to pay attention, although he was still thinking of finding a table of his own. "Your groups stop off here. At Villahermosa you stare baffled at the Olmec heads, get on a bus for Palenque. Get off the bus there, wishing you'd read the archaeology books in your bag instead of the whodunits. Climb around till your feet hurt, back on the bus, come here for a day or two, bus takes you out to San Juan Chamula or Zincantán, where they tell you you'll get scalped if you try to take pictures of the Indians, only reason you came in the first place. So you go up the street here to San Jolobil, buy an armload of textiles—you got a choice of Pantelhó, Chamula, San Andrés, Chenalhó, Tenejapa, Bochil, did I miss a coupla tribes? Back on the bus for Tuxtla Gutiérrez—wait'll you ride that bus through the mountains—catch your plane out of Tuxtla, breathe deep, scratch Chiapas off your list." The droop of his lower lids gave him the cynically aware expression of an old hunting dog. "My name's Grogan. Sam Grogan." He put out a hand.

Oliver took it. "Oliver. Ted Oliver."

"Pleased to meet you, Ted. I suppose you could do it all backward, the other way 'round. How do I know? Group of Brits shuffled through the courtyard a little while ago, all gimpy from the bus ride. You probably heard 'em. They'll be up in their rooms now, drinking with great concentration, troop in here soon enough asking in pinched tones for things the chef never heard of. Some artsy-crafties from Seattle come in tomorrow. Then a couple of strings of bird-watchers. Along about here they're quarreling, not speaking, formed into factions, husbands and wives snapping at each other.

"Ah, Manuel, the scotch at last. You took and went to work and did it on your own, didn't you? Well, a big *gracias*, Manuel. Don't really need that bartender, do we? And glory be, you remembered the fizz water. Manuel, you're a paragon! Our new friend here may need a drink, too, Manuel, if you could wait a goddamn minute before rushing off to catch a smoke behind the kitchen door, he just might ask you for something." That was all in English too. "I'm not kidding, if you're not in a group, you have to fight every inch of the way here."

Oliver asked the waiter for a glass of white wine while he thought how he would carry out his plans with this unexpected observer on the scene. Of course, the man might leave before the others arrived. Might as well get that settled right away. "Have you eaten?"

"No, I've fallen into this quaint habit of quaffing my aperitif before I eat, rather than after."

"That was a dumb question, wasn't it?"

"I've heard dumber. So you're fluent in Spanish?"

"Not fluent. Did you say bird-watchers?"

"Yeah. This place processes bird-watchers through the assembly line. They got a good thing going. Face it, Ted, you're what your common run of politician likes to call a minority. Don't cater to the likes of you and me."

"Evidently. I happen to be down here after birds myself, Sam. Group of one."

"That figures, with the white wine."

"Not necessarily."

"Why do people watch birds?"

"Well, I don't know. Something you enjoy."

"What's wrong with drinking beer? Or sports? Playing poker? You must be some kind of communist. I bet you don't watch television."

"I watch some things." The waiter arrived with his wine.

"Yeah, some things. Bird-watching sets you apart. You're superior to us ordinary Americans."

"It's not that way at all. Where'd you get that idea, anyway?"

"Watching bird-watchers. Why else you watch birds?"

"Well, look, uh—"

"Sam."

"Yeah, Sam, I know. Look, bird-watching is one manifestation of an interest in the outdoors, in nature, maybe a dab of science. Some people like to botanize, others like bats. Or work in the garden, for that matter. You can't confine bird-watchers to a singular category—"

"I can and I do. Did you say botanize?"

"Collect plants, I mean, study them, identify them, taxonomy. Sorry about botanize."

"I wasn't correcting your English, I wasn't sure what you meant. I guess if you feel called upon to watch something, birds are marginally less repulsive than bats. Many Hispanic bird-watchers?"

"Gosh, I don't—well, of course every country has its biologists. Mexico has some very competent—"

"I'm not talking about scientists. Answer is no. How about black bird-watchers?"

Oliver shook his head. "What's your point?"

"WASP enterprise, isn't it? Like the environment."

"Well, not exclusively, by any means."

"Fellow I know says people watch birds because they don't like people."

Oliver smiled politely. "Maybe some of them. Look, Sam, it's a distraction for most of us, a means of getting away from—"

"Bird-watchers. Group most likely to include opinion leaders, community activists, advanced degrees." Grogan sipped his scotch. "You're prominent in church affairs, you pester your congressman, you're on the school board, interested in foreign affairs, belong to the League of Women Voters, you read the newspapers, buy the books, go to the concerts, the galleries, lobby for the environment. What else?"

Oliver laughed. "Where'd you get all that?"

"Boring, too, all of it. Unlike many of our countrymen, I don't find bird-watchers cute or funny. More sinister. Like the Germans. Individually all right but in packs repellent, arrogant. The sociological fragment from which I quoted does not originate with me. I'm quoting the experts, the pollsters, census data, your bird-watcher's profile. Certainly a minority, I guess, if you buy the description, and they're probably dying out, taking their loathsome virtues with them. The canaille will triumph in the end. That's the message of history."

"Are you always this cheerful? If you know all that about bird-watchers, you ought to know that they prefer being called birders rather than bird-watchers."

"I know. I happen to like calling them bird-watchers. I'll bet you whatever you want to put up that I have observed more bird-watchers in the past month than you have seen in your whole bird-watching career."

"How so?"

"I'm their assistant shepherd when they come through here. How long you gonna be here?"

"I don't know exactly," said Oliver. "Depends on whether I can fill a few blanks in my life list. Why?"

"Oh, God, one of those." Grogan rested his head on the tablecloth by his whiskey glass.

"I came to Chiapas to try for a resplendent quetzal, hope for some trogons, especially the citreoline."

"Chiapas, bird-watcher's paradise. Well, you're probably not interested but I could use some help from someone who speaks their language, divert their attention briefly from birds to higher things—an assistant, a sheepdog to nip at their heels, keep the flock closed up nice and tight. But, no, you got your bloody life list. I might as well get you a free ticket to our dog and pony show, however, seeing as how you're one of our opinion leaders."

Oliver saw the opportunity for a cover more substantial than filling out his life list. "Well, Sam, what's involved in being assistant to the assistant shepherd?" Oliver began.

"What's the matter?" asked Grogan.

"Someone's joining us." Inocencio Brown was walking up the steps, thanking the waiter, crinkling his eyes at Oliver, turning to speak to Grogan. When Grogan turned to examine the newcomer, Oliver waved his napkin violently behind Grogan, shaking his head. "*Buenas tardes*, señor," said Oliver pointing at the back of Grogan's head, scowling.

Inocencio paused, looked from one of them to the other, "*Buenas tardes*, señores," he said, bringing a cultural shutter down over his eyes. He sat down as the waiter pushed the chair in behind him and asked the waiter for a menu. Oliver smiled at Inocencio approvingly.

"How you doin'?" said Grogan to Inocencio, who seemed not to hear him. Grogan seemed to lose interest in Inocencio after studying him a moment longer.

"*Ein* scotch, Manuel, *bitte*. Okay, you can't help being a bird-watcher. How'd you happen to get into birds?" asked Grogan.

"My work isn't exciting," said Oliver. "It's a living but you need other things."

"Oh? What's your line of work?"

"I do risk analysis, if you know—" Inocencio looked up from his menu at Oliver, putting his head on one side, raising his eyebrows to mimic interest. Oliver looked away from him.

"Oh? Nothing wrong with that. Must be very lucrative during the time of troubles we've been passing through these past few generations. Scare people half to death then offer your services. Done a bit along that line myself. Like to kick it around with you." Oliver's heart sank. "Not risk analysis as such. More the study of probabilities. Not unrelated, am I right?"

"You're right there." Oliver took heart. He had not looked forward to a discussion of risk analysis with a person who knew what it was. Why did I choose that line of work? he was asking himself.

"Probabilities. They're getting back to that again after a criminal and senseless period of neglect. It's all fashion, Ted, even at the higher intellectual levels. I did some playing around with the spacier stuff, you know, up there at the border of the infinite, the eternal. Philosophy, your layman'd call it. Exchanged a few ideas by mail with old man Russell when I was in knee pants. Gave the old fraud a few things to think about before he went all loony. Interesting field, risk analysis. Hope you and I'll have a chance to fiddle around a bit with a few of the more esoteric concepts."

"Fascinating," said Oliver, determined to avoid that, "and are you still a philosopher? If that's the proper occupational title for the field."

"Well, little problem came along about then and I ended up one of those shavetail platoon leaders ended up with his own company in combat. Got paid off in Japan, tried my hand at Zen, ended up a master. Martial arts. Black belt—nothing fancy. Took a Harley-Davidson across the States for kicks. Started with one female on the back, turned her in on a new one in Rockford, Illinois, dumped that one in Ohio, ended up with another lasted all the way to New York. Then a little private work for some rich Chinese in Singapore, cross-border stuff. Things our government wishes to hell it knew how to do. Not your run-of-the-mill citizen, Ted. Never could settle down. My field? You name it. The road not traveled, I guess. Maybe a little something like bird-watching, last few years—enter the Brits."

Oliver turned his head to see a huddle of men and women by the door of the dining room, dazed by the bright lights of the dining room, waiting for their own shepherd to appear.

"Excuse me," said Oliver, getting to his feet.

"You all right?"

"Back in a minute."

The tour guide had arrived and along with the headwaiter was chivvying the British group toward the platform to the tables set for eight, so that Oliver was having to push against a tide of cross and hungry travelers. He was able to seize the arm of an overweight man with long strands of hair brushed across a large pink scalp. He was revolving slowly like a tree trunk in a flood, struggling to be free of the crowd he found himself in. This person wore an impressively wide double-breasted blue jacket, had a paisley scarf at his neck, and a cross look on his face as he was carried along by the movement of the British party.

Oliver squeezed the arm, hissed in his ear, "You've never seen me before."

As the man turned his bulk surprisingly fast, his pettish look became an irritated smile. "Dear God, Ted, what sort of place—"

"Listen. You don't know me. Twenty-one hundred at the Luz del Día, Avenida General Utrilla, up the street from here."

"Ted, if you please—"

"Luz del Día, General Utrilla, nine o'clock."

When Oliver returned from the men's room, the British group had been seated and the man Oliver had spoken to was sitting with them. Nearby a white-haired man stood at one side of the table, glaring at the man in the paisley scarf.

Grogan asked Oliver, "You all right?"

"Little touch of the old belly. I'll be okay."

"They're discharging a surplus Brit," said Grogan, looking toward the table next to them. The British organism had rejected the man Oliver had spoken to and the waiter was leading him to their table.

Oliver spoke quickly. "My name's Oliver."

"How d'ya do," said the other. "Drew."

"Mr. Grogan here," said Oliver. "And señor, uh?"

"*Mucho gusto,*" said Inocencio, looking briefly at Drew before putting his head back down into the plate he had ordered.

"I didn't get the name," said Grogan.

"Drew. Harley Drew. Yes, indeed, waiter, I would like to order."

Drew and Grogan ordered in English, Oliver in Spanish. "You want to split a bottle of wine?" Oliver asked Grogan.

"No. I got this new glass of whiskey. Excuse my plebeian tastes."

"Do you recommend the local wine?" asked Drew.

"I won't be responsible for it," said Oliver. "I was going to try a red."

"I'll take a chance," said Drew.

"You a bird-watcher?" Grogan asked him.

"Certainly not," said Drew.

"You were saying," said Oliver, turning to Grogan, "that philosophy—"

"That was a long time ago." Grogan picked up his new glass of whiskey.

"Mr. Grogan here was a collaborator of Bertrand Russell."

"Indeed," said Drew.

"Not a collaborator, exactly. Just a kid in knee pants."

"Remarkable," said Drew. "You were acquainted, then, with Wittgenstein."

"Oh, yeah, Wittgenstein. Naw, never had any dealings," said Grogan, continuing to address to Oliver his answers to Drew's questions, taking a gulp of whiskey.

"Inscrutable in his way, was he not? I'd be most interested in your assessment of Wittgenstein's change of view, his virtual renunciation of *Tractacus logico-philosophicus*—"

Inocencio looked up from his eating to stare at Drew for a moment before the veil fell across his eyes again.

"I was telling Oliver here, I dropped all that. Finally dawned on me those guys just playing their precious word and number games, a case of flying rapidly in ever-decreasing circles till they disappear up their own asshole. Too remote from the real world for me."

"Ah," said Drew, regarding a bowl of soup with suspicion. "I wonder what this is."

"Soup of the day, according to the menu. I tried to analyze it but found it unidentifiable," said Oliver. "What have you been up to since?" he asked Grogan.

"I've been devoting my time to watching the comrades, Ted. I'm one of those crazy guys feels he owes his country something."

"The comrades."

"The Russkies. Yep. Fidel's boys. Bugs, Jugs, and Polskis.

E-Germs. You name it. The occasional Chicom. Now, with everyone getting all lovey-dovey . . .'' Grogan shrugged.

"Must have been very exciting while it lasted,'' said Oliver. He tasted the wine and told the waiter to pour a glass for Drew.

"Pulled off a job or two for the company. CI sort of thing—counterintelligence, Ted. In and out of the Soviet Union more than once. Black. Made me sign a paper I'd never tell what I saw there. Glasnost. They don't want that kind of thing out in a period of good feeling, know what I mean? It'd fry your goddamn mind, Ted.''

"What company was this you were with?'' asked Drew. Inocencio was eating his dessert, a rubbery-looking flan, head down, but he glanced quickly over at Grogan.

Grogan grinned. "Sorry about that, friend. The agency.''

"The agency?'' asked Oliver.

Grogan grinned. "The CI of A, Ted.''

"You mean you're—I didn't think you were allowed to say—''

Grogan shook his head quickly. "No, sir, Ted. You don't catch this old trooper in the glue factory. Oh, they wanted me to fly a big-ass desk out at Langley. Show the troops how to do it. Not my cup o' tea, thank you, ma'am. Me, sit in an office in a suit comma issue comma blue comma dark? Write papers. Go to meetings. Read other people's papers. Screw your secretary. Go to another meeting.''

Inocencio got to his feet. "*Buen provecho*, señores.''

"Good night, sir,'' said Drew.

"*Buenas noches,*'' said Oliver.

Grogan nodded at Inocencio and turned to Drew. "Where's your group hail from?''

Drew raised his eyebrows, studying the plate the waiter was setting before him. "I am not a group. I travel alone.''

"Oh, I thought—what brings you here?''

"I am a journalist. I am here to do a series of pieces on the Lacandón Indians.''

"Uh, okay, who you write for?''

"It's called the *Journal de Provence*.''

"Oh, sure, the *Journal de Provence*. Any relation to the *Providence Journal*?" Grogan laughed heartily.

Drew frowned. After a taste of meat, he had put his knife and fork down and taken to tearing off pieces of bread, washing them down with wine. "If you know the *Journal*, you will know also that it's widely read in the south of France, a leader in the formation of intellectual opinion. Cultural history is my field." Drew pushed his plate away. The waiter asked him if he wanted dessert and Drew put up a hand, notably delicate with such a large torso, and shook his head. Wiping his mouth with a napkin and brushing crumbs from the front of his jacket, he rose and said, "I bid you good night, gentlemen."

As Drew left, Grogan turned to watch him. Turning back to Oliver, he said, "We gotta talk, Ted. You and I. You look like a good American."

"Well, I hope so," said Oliver, considering the flan the waiter had placed before him.

"Ted, the vultures are moving in." He spoke in a low voice, fast. "I may need your help. That pair of jokers, for instance."

Oliver frowned and shook his head. "Who do you mean?"

"Fat stuff, just waddled out of here, for one. Writing articles on the Lacandón Indians for some French paper. Cultural historian." Grogan snorted. "Tubba lard wouldn't know a Lacandón Indian from Sitting Bull."

"Something not right there?"

"You damn right something ain't right. For one thing he didn't offer to pay his share of the wine. Didn't you notice? Maybe you're in the habit of treating any overweight deadbeat produces a hoity-toity accent like that."

Grogan had picked up a detail that had not occurred to Oliver or to Drew.

Grogan sat back in his chair, bit his lip, and narrowed his eyes at Oliver. "That Mexican barging in on us, sitting there listening to every goddamn word we say. Where'd he come from? I mean, we're no sooner sitting here than some Mexican materializes out of thin air. I mean, what gives?"

"I wonder if it was wise of you to reveal your intelligence background in his hearing."

"They're off checking the old dossier right now, you can bet your ass. If they didn't already know. Good. Okay by me. Get an idea what they're up against."

"You mean—"

"Ted, I'm talking chaos in Mexico. Mexico's getting ready to knock the PRI to hell off its perch."

"PRI?"

"The government party. The Institutional Revolutionary party." Grogan snorted again. "They're dead and they don't know it. Just waiting for someone to push 'em over. This—"

"Who would do that?"

"Guess who, Ted." Grogan grinned, frowning at the same time. "It's up for grabs, Ted, right on our goddamn border. Wrong people get in. A-dee-os! Place is up for grabs, Ted." He put his head closer to the tablecloth and to Oliver at the same time. "What's the fat guy up to?"

"I take it, Sam, you think there's something wrong there. What is it that made you suspicious of those two?"

"I've been around, Ted. There's not time—okay. Just for example. This marine got a good ole buddy blown away the other day. That's the kinda game the other side's playing."

"That's awful. Where—"

Grogan cut Oliver off with a sweep of one hand. "Right in front of my goddamn face, that's where. Like at a table where we're sitting right now. I mean right here in Mexico, just a few days ago. Jesus!" He closed his eyes and shook his head as though shaking water from his hair. He recovered. "Sorry, Ted. But this was an old, old friend, a general, no less. We'd been through things together best described as grueling. Happened in a place called Guanajuato. Was in all the papers. Down here, the Mexican papers. They were after both of us but they got him. Halfway wish it had been me, Ted. Never mind. Forget it. But you see why I've gotta give a little thought to that Mexican. And fatso trying to infiltrate the party of Brits. Even they wouldn't stand for that."

"It's interesting. I wouldn't have guessed—"

"Believe me, Ted. These ringers run to type, and in the business you get so you can spot 'em a mile away. Types I've seen before. The fat one's a phony and he can be neutralized. But the the other? Listen, Ted, what you ought to know: There's a highly select group of very concerned, very dedicated people working on some very interesting concepts. Once you start putting some of the Mexican pieces together, it begins to make sense. A picture starts to form, know what I mean? I can't go into all of it here, not now. Things to do.''

"Sam. Tell me, what are you doing here in San Cristóbal?"

Grogan winked at him. "How do you like, let's see, consulting?" The smile left his face. "I won't kid with you. I'm here on a job, Ted. Alone. And I need your help. How about breakfast? We can talk. I need your help and not only with the damn bird-watchers, either. You with me, Ted?"

"Well—"

As Grogan got up he gave Oliver a one-sided grin, thrust out his hand, and gave Oliver's a hard squeeze. "Okay, tiger." He winked. "See you in the morning."

Chapter 17

It was five minutes before the meeting time of nine. Oliver lingered on the corner of Insurgentes and Calle Adelina Flores, and just as he was about to give up, he saw Grogan come out of the lighted entryway of the hotel into the dark of the street and turn the other way. He was tempted to follow him but turned instead to join Inocencio and Drew at the Luz del Día.

The narrow street he took ran straight to the edge of the city, flanked by attached low buildings, straight to where the mountains sat at the city's end, closing the view. A short way up from Oliver the bulk of the church of Santo Domingo, the walls painted a faded buff, glowed from the shadows that had gathered in the canyon of the street. The clouds had broken and were boiling past the valley of Jovel. They seemed to slow to a stop to hang, moonlit, when they reached the mountain. When the clouds crossed below the moon, the only light came from the sudden glare of a passing car, shining orange on the walls and deepening the shadows in the doorways and the shuttered windows along the narrow street. Oliver stumbled on the flagstone walk, careful of the high curbs above the cobbled street. Walking, he brushed one hand against the walls of the one- and two-story buildings that sat close, used them to steady his way.

The small courtyard of the Luz del Día was immediately inside the high door that gave onto the street. A fountain sat in the center of the courtyard, a large tree in one corner spread its branches over that quarter of the space, pots with ferns sat about the yard. Four of the six round white metal tables had people sitting at them, candles glowing on their faces and on the bottoms of the umbrellas above the tables. The blue-gray walls were dark inside the arcade formed by the arches of white pillars on the four sides. Oliver followed Inocencio's instructions and walked a dozen paces to the middle door on the far side of the courtyard, and there he stood to knock.

Inocencio opened the door. Inside was just room for three leather-topped round tables. Two of them were empty. Seated at the third, barely fitting into a leather bucket chair that squeaked as he turned to regard Oliver, sat Drew, an oil lamp burning in the center of the table, a cup of coffee beside him.

"Well, Ted," said Drew, reaching to take Oliver's hand, making a small pretense at getting up. "Who in the world was the entertainer at dinner?"

"Wasn't that fun? Awfully good of you to come, Harley. How do you like our office?"

"An improvement over what we had in Mexico City."

"Inocencio's work. He seems able to arrange just about anything," said Oliver. "You're looking fit, Harley. The south of France agrees with you."

"Indeed it does. But my question is: What sort of trouble are you in now?"

Oliver sat down. "Sit down, Inocencio, and we'll put our Lacandón expert in the picture."

The tomato-colored walls of the room—their office—were nearly bare, a place carefully kept free of clutter. On one wall, an oval mirror with dried flowers around it, against another, a wooden cupboard, the doors open, with blue and white pots, orange and green plates, the Talavera pottery from Puebla, on the shelves. In a corner spleenwort grew thickly in a terra-cotta jar as fat as a small wine cask. On the wall opposite the door was a faded poster showing a group of *estudiantes* singing on the steep steps of the University of Guanajuato. Guanajuato again. Oliver had no patience with omens. Nevertheless, he had taken the chair at the wall side of the table so that the needless reminder was at his back.

"I really appreciate your coming, Harley. We couldn't do this alone."

"I might concur with the indispensability of my presence were you to tell me what it is that I'm here to do," said Drew.

By ten o'clock Oliver had explained Inocencio to Drew and Drew to Inocencio. He had told Drew about General Robles and México Irredenta and the assumption that the Movement had caused the death of General Robles. He told about his meetings with Debbie Kraus. Inocencio furnished a scathing description of Chato Escobar. Oliver made it clear that he was on leave, carrying out what he termed "a private investigation." He left out of his account his interviews in Washington. He had not told Inocencio of the collusion of the director of the CIA with Bondie Birdsong. His reluctance to speak of that to Inocencio did not stem from any lack of trust of the man, Oliver realized. Rather, he would find it shameful to admit.

"So," Oliver concluded, "there you have it. The three of us on our own. On our own against the world."

"I trust you exaggerate. Although, with your known fondness for the forlorn hope, you do seem to have burned your boats," was Drew's first comment.

"Like Cortés in Veracruz," added Inocencio. "Has to go forward now, on past the volcanoes to Tenochtitlán! Can't turn back. Calls us out of retirement to go with him."

"I really appreciate it, both of you—you, Harley, coming all this way, hardly settled in France."

"You were right, to a severely limited extent, when you warned me, as I was preparing to retire, that I would miss the work. For that reason this excursion promised to be mildly stimulating. A problem to solve without a niggling, higgling headquarters looking over one's shoulder—the essence of the work without nanny's scolding from above in Washington. It's that vexing drawback to the life of an intelligence officer I'm grateful to be rid of. I don't miss that bit at all."

"Me too,' said Inocencio. "Like the army. You don't miss the chickenshit."

"Let's hear it for the *Journal de Provence*," declared Oliver, raising a pottery coffee cup. "The very bellwether of French intellectualism."

"Very well, Ted, what was I to do? You tell me to drop

everything, rush to this obscure corner of Mexico—I had to manufacture something to meet your specification of journalist.''

"No, no. It's good. Perfect. Inocencio has come in search of his roots—''

"I already told him. I'm beginning to think maybe Diego de Mazariegos, he really is my ancestor. Who knows? Bet he left a lot of 'em around.''

"—and as I confessed, under Mr. Sam Grogan's skillful interrogation, I am looking for exotic birds to add to the life list I have never kept.''

"Grogan. Really! Absurd!'' declared Drew.

"What we used to call amateur hour,'' said Inocencio.

"Absolutely! Classic case. The confidence man who tricks himself. The puerile fabricator. The 'company' indeed! In and out of the Soviet Union black.'' Drew was between scorn and amusement. "A delusional neurosis. Mild, one hopes, rather than dangerous. At the table I was waiting for you to inform him that he was addressing chief of station, Mexico City.''

Inocencio laughed. "I like to hear that!''

"Even so, he picked it up immediately that you left without paying your share of the wine.''

"Petty!'' Drew waved his hand in dismissal.

"Of you or of him? If he were to think about it, he might work his way to where it would dawn on him that we're friends.''

"Pshaw!''

"We can't dismiss him, I'm afraid, Harley, even though he's a type we've all seen before. After you two left he claimed he was sitting with Robles when he was killed. Grogan has stolen my nightmare and made it part of his adventure-packed story.''

"How can that be? Did you bring it up?'' asked Drew.

"By no means.'' Oliver repeated what Grogan said.

"Where'd he hear about that?'' asked Inocencio. "The papers?''

"What's more, he's got you two in his story.'' Oliver reported Grogan's remarks about the two of them without repeating the adjectives Grogan had used to describe Drew. "And he has recruited me to help support his fantasy.''

"He's crazy," said Inocencio. "Go around bragging like that, he'll get himself disappeared down some barranca. Could be serious." He shook his head from side to side and stifled a yawn.

"Ties him in to México Irredenta, that's what I get from it. As that may be, it's late, and we're all tired." It was warm in the small, high-ceilinged room, pleasant in the lamplight. Oliver yawned. "How's the Hotel Santa Clara, Harley?"

"Quite all right. Elegant but restrainedly plateresque in style."

"You know, that's a house belonged to my new ancestor, Diego de Mazariegos. Got good taste. I oughta be there insteada next door at the Ciudad Real."

"Harley, Inocencio's going to sniff around tomorrow to see what the locals think of the Irredenta people."

"Right. In the morning I mosey across the plaza to the Palacio Municipal, get what you call it—the indigenous point of view."

"The Movement's headquarters are at a place on the edge of town called the Casa del Futuro. That's where Mora hangs out, and the thing for you, Harley, first thing is to phone over there and set up an interview with his nibs."

"Just call up and run out there for an interview? Nothing to it."

"Inocencio's got a lead on it."

"Fellow from some Chicago newspaper at the hotel asking the desk how to call old Mora, how to get out to the place. They don't understand his English, don't know what he wants, I help out."

"And he got the interview just like that?" asked Drew.

"They give him an appointment right away. Seem pretty interested in talking to the newspaper people. You want, I'll make the call." Inocencio yawned again. "Nothing else, maybe I'll go now, come by your place in the morning."

"And we'll make a call to the Casa del Futuro," said Drew. "Presumptuous name. I don't think I'm going to like Mora."

After Inocencio left, Drew said, "Come on, Ted, out with it. There's more to this than you've said. What are we doing in San Cristóbal?"

"Well, you've got most of it. I've kept the really disturbing part from Inocencio. He's happy to be back in harness, but I've let him go on thinking Robles's death is the reason for our interest.''

"Strikes me you feel the same way.''

"I do. Robles was a rare person, one of those rare birds who keeps on asking questions, the kind of people who brought us civilization by insisting on answers to their questions.''

"Mm, that has a plausible but possibly specious ring to it. I'll have to think about it. But you admire him.''

"I admire the way he persisted until he defined the question and kept right after it, determined to get the answer. We wouldn't be sitting here otherwise.''

"What was his question?''

"I don't know. But, by God, for his sake, we're going to find the answer, Harley.''

"Bold talk, Ted.''

"Yeah? Furthermore, when we get the answer we'll know what his question was.''

"Possibly so. What is it that is too disturbing to tell Inocencio but that you seem quite ready to unload on me? Can't we trust Inocencio?''

"Completely, Harley, it's not that. Inocencio gave a big part of his life to the outfit. It's more that I don't want him, well, disillusioned. I guess that's it.''

"Ted, dear boy, I find you forever suprising. You're quite ready to spoil my illusions, but tell me, what illusions would a former leader of a CIA surveillance team in Mexico have left to him?''

"Listen, Harley. The agency's behind México Irredenta. That's what. The director's sneaked back to waging war on the Mexican government, on the Institutional Revolutionary party, that's what.''

"Oh, come now, Ted. He would have gotten over his grudge against the PRI by now. There are far more important things to engage him.''

"He keeps a lot of balls in the air, Harley.'' Oliver repeated the discussion with Clinkscale. Then he mentioned Slasher O'Rourke.

"O'Rourke! No! Not O'Rourke. He should have moved on by now, to even more impressive roles."

"He's still around. I suppose the director finds him colorful. Anyway, he does what he's told. And if he didn't, the director would put someone in the job who would."

"The excuse of the collaborator. You're far too charitable. If Slasher's involved, I'd believe anything. Well, nearly anything. Not what you allege."

"I brought up the inspector general to Slasher. His first re-action was to pretend that all the IG cares about is minor personal peccadilloes. Then he went to the other extreme, admitting that if the IG knew about the game he and the director are playing, it would blow the thing wide open. See? I'm not imagining things."

"Your childlike faith in the Office of the Inspector General! A creaky bureaucratic deus ex machina, rather than the all-seeing god of the Greeks. A good gray senior civil servant swooping down to intervene in the affairs of us mortals. Really, Ted! You combine deep cunning and guile with your naïveté."

"Listen, Harley. Let me tell you about the picture of Lincoln on the wall behind the director."

When Oliver had finished telling of his interview with the director, Drew was silent for a moment. "Are you sure about the business with the Lincoln picture?"

"No doubt about it. Talk about guile."

"Merely an artifice to bring you around, Ted. I wonder if you haven't read considerably more into all this than is there."

"What do you mean exactly, Harley?"

"From what you tell me you seem to have taken a few more or less disconnected or, it may be, loosely connected facts—occurrences, statements—and woven them into what you conceive to be a conspiracy."

Oliver poured himself coffee. "I'll be up all night. Harley, you know the contempt, the dislike, well—describe it however you prefer—the director has for Mexico. Maybe not Mexico. It's just that he's permanently mad at the Mexican government and at the PRI."

"One can resent Mexican policy in a number of areas without declaring war on her."

"But it's perfect cover, don't you see, Harley? The director uses Birdsong's sordid political maneuver as cover to back his opposition to the PRI. Okay, México Irredenta may not win an election but it would—don't you see?"

"It would what?"

"I imagine the Slasher would say that it would send the PRI a message."

Drew wrinkled his nose at the phrase. "Only if it were to be discovered, Ted."

"Maybe the director doesn't care if it is. Figures he can just deny it. It would be hard to prove anything."

"Ah, you admit that, do you?"

Oliver leaned forward and raised his hands at Drew. "Let me go over it again. The director cuts off all reporting on the Movement, México Irredenta, to prevent word getting out that Bondie Birdsong's using the Movement for his own low motives in Texas. In return, Bondie is helpful to the director on the House Select Committee on Intelligence. Got it?"

"Yes, yes."

"That's how it looks to Bondie and Clinkscale. But for the director it's great cover for another attack on the Mexican government, on the PRI."

"That's where you leave me, Ted."

Oliver shook his head impatiently. "Listen, Harley. Something else. Clinkscale and Debbie—I don't pretend to understand this part—both talk about new techniques, the use of TV, doing it with mirrors, no need for grass roots, all implying that the Movement is hollow, illusory, virtually nonexistent. And listen to this, Harley, the audience for all this is not Mexico itself but in the States. How do you like that?"

"I find it distasteful, but Ted, surely you're aware of the hired campaign consultants, the use of TV in politics at home. This sounds like more of the same."

"You agree with me, then."

"Not at all. I'm simply saying that you seem to have run onto an international elaboration of the same."

"But Harley! Doesn't it bother you that it's so dishonest? So false? It's a sham. Mexico shouldn't be treated like this, just to satisfy the low ambition of someone like Birdsong."

"Ted, you are old-fashioned! Tell me, is there no such movement? Is there no México Irredenta?"

"Well, sure there is. Some members, no one knows how many. It's hard to tell. That may be an additional reason why we're not allowed to investigate it. We'd reveal the sham. In the meantime, they sell it abroad as a real, thriving political party."

Drew sighed. "I think we both need some sleep."

"All right, Harley. I admit I'm going on hunches, not proof. Just stick with me for a while on this one, Harley."

"I can't evaluate your hunches. Of course I'll stick with you. But to be quite honest with you, Ted, rather than your pursuing a private investigation, as I think you said, I worry that you've embarked again on your private feud with the director of the Central Intelligence Agency."

At breakfast time Oliver was pacing in the courtyard of the hotel, looking for Grogan. Neither had phones in their rooms, so it was a matter of waiting in a central place. Oliver did not look forward to having breakfast with Grogan. It was duty that required it. The sound of high-pitched voices made him turn to see the British group issuing from the dining room. Grogan must have been with them, although Oliver had not noticed him when he looked into the dining room. Grogan was talking to a young woman with a briefcase, probably the tour leader, he supposed.

Grogan saw Oliver and came over to him to speak in a low voice. "Switched signals on me, Ted. Sorry. Can't talk now. Try to keep an eye on those two jokers for me. Well, see you later."

Oliver stood in the door to the hotel, watched Grogan climb on one of the buses that sat in Calle Adelina Flores, its fumes pouring into the space between the low buildings. He stayed there until the buses left. He started for the dining room but turned to go to the hotel desk. He waited until a man behind the desk got off the phone, then asked the man where the tour group was going. The man raised his eyebrows, shrugged his shoulders, and turned to speak to a woman with heavy glasses who appeared to be making up a bill, shuffling through a sheaf of chits.

"Oh," she said, turning to peer at Oliver, "San Juan Chamula, I suppose. To the cathedral and the *zócalo*. And they go to the Casa del Futuro for Don Saturnino Mora's lecture." The man was listening to them and he said something to her. "Oh, how do I know?" She looked back at the papers on the desk. "He says they don't go there for the lectures now. They use the auditorium at the museum."

"Who is Mora?"

"Oh, he's some very old man who lives here. He's quite famous, I think. I don't know much about him. Look, I've just come here from Mexico City. He's some sort of figure from the past."

"But why, I mean, what does he talk about to the tourists?"

She was clearly impatient, wanted to get rid of him. "How do I know?"

"Thanks very much. One more thing. The museum where the auditorium is. Where's that?"

"Oh, up behind the church of Santo Domingo. Please, señor. I'm extremely busy."

Chapter 18

"Nancy has a sore throat. As usual, the moment you leave they get sick. I only hope it's not strep and that Tom doesn't get it."

"Or you."

"Well, we all miss you. Let's see, what's been happening? Chas Lankester called yesterday with a rather peculiar question, I thought, considering."

"Oh?"

"Said he wondered whether you had really gone to the Cañon de Cobre. Said he was worried. Didn't I think that was abnormal behavior. Poor Chas! I said I agreed completely, but we'd been married a long time and I was used to it."

"If poor Chas calls again, tell him the last you heard I'd spent all my money on drink and loose women and was seen sleeping on a bench in the railway station in Los Mochis."

"How are you?"

"Fine. I miss you too."

"Oh, and your letter came. Drawing of a butterfly on the envelope. I hope it makes sense to you."

"Good. What's she say?"

"Should I read the whole thing?"

"Well, unless you can gist it."

"I'll try."

Oliver was sitting in one of the rooms at the front of the hotel, just off the street. A thin, vexed-looking woman at one of the desks, one red fingernail stabbing at a long column of figures, had gone back to her computing. After looking Oliver over carefully and questioning him, she had agreed cheerlessly that he could use the phone for a long-distance call. At the desk nearest Oliver sat a man with slick black hair, toying with his mustache, his eyes wandering around the room as Oliver listened to Marge's voice. The man seemed to have no function beyond holding in front of his face a magazine that he had given up reading for eavesdropping on Oliver's end of the conversation, English Comprehension 101.

"It's to 'Scaly-throated Leaf Scraper'—ugh—'from Eastern Pigmy Blue,' " Marge began. " 'One. Only current repeat current record of the names you left here, excluding footnotes useful for a doctoral dissertation, is to effect your general and Lester the Lizard knew each other a few years ago. You probably knew that. See end of this letter on some other names.' That's paragraph one. You get that?"

"Yeah. Not much, then."

"Oh, no, there's quite a bit. I'll have to read this part:

'While I was off skiing (and you'll be pleased to know I broke a finger although not my neck) Senior Horse's Ass gave Snookums—' Does that make sense to you?"

"Yeah, that blond secretary of Slasher's—go on."

" '—gave Snookums a job to do and she came to ask the girl filling in for me, the one you talked to the other day, if she could handle something on Mexico, like an expedited name check and stuff, as she put it. My substitute took a look at the name on the paper she was shown and advised Sweetie Pie that since subject was U.S. citizen she was unable do search without written authorization. Oh, said Honeybunch, blushing with girlish confusion, what do you mean? What am I supposed to tell our Leading Sports Fan, he won't like it, he needs this, like, right away?' " Marge paused.

"Okay, I'm with you. Go on."

" 'Within two minutes she came tapping back on her spike heels to snatch back paper with name, this time blushing with anger probably because His Vulgarness had informed her he considered her stupid. Forget what I said, she said, and forget that name and forget that I ever asked you about it. Well! Colleague did not forget! Name is Leslie Rose Grogan on which elegant name I have done some quietly insubordinate if not highly illegal research.' "

"Leslie Rose?" exclaimed Oliver.

"Turns out to be a boy's name," said Marge. "Poor thing."

"Go on."

"Ted, think about your phone bill. I'm only doing the main points from here on."

"Okay."

The man at the desk cleared his throat and turned in his chair to put his back to Oliver. He had not turned a page in the magazine since Oliver had begun talking on the phone. Oliver moved a foot or two farther away from him.

"This person, Grogan, volunteered to a Miami lawyer in 1983 he in close touch with high officials Cuban government. Lawyer wrote the agency who sent someone to interview Grogan. Grogan evasive, implying he could not trust agency.

"Next report 1985 from Hong Kong saying Grogan approached station, said he in touch senior Chinese Communist official who had come in disguise to Hong Kong, seeking to defect. Station got Grogan's agreement to surveil meeting and found so-called official was Wang Shu-ming with numerous aliases, well-known intelligence fabricator."

"Wow!"

"What did you say?"

"Just, wow!"

"Oh. In Tokyo—this is a week later—Grogan told U.S. military attaché Tokyo he had passed hot lead—quoting again—on top Chinese Communist official seeking to defect and CIA station Hong Kong had shown no interest. Says he thinks CIA views Chicoms with favor, that CIA people bunch of cookie-pushing pantywaists. He's certainly right about that," added Marge.

"Shut up and go on."

"On Maupin tour of Leningrad, Moscow, and Kiev, 1987, tour member who roomed with Grogan wrote letter to agency saying Grogan told him several times he on classified CIA mission and he afraid KGB was onto him and told him to inform CIA if anything happened to him. Once in Leningrad asked the roommate to cover him while he picked up material on nuclear triggers—are there such things?"

"I guess so. Go on."

"Material on nuclear triggers from dead drop outside Hermitage. Roommate refused to become involved and told Grogan he foolish to be engaged in espionage, recklessly endangering other members of tour group. Roommate reported matter in letter to director suggesting CIA train its people to be more discreet.

"Senator Stone of Florida passed letter—this is undated—from Grogan in which Grogan volunteered go Iran, free hostages, alternatively, lead troops in Nicaragua. In letter Grogan doubted resolve of CIA and would collaborate with agency only if ordered to and absolutely necessary to accomplish mission. Preferred to operate as singleton directly under appropriate White House authority. CIA legislative counsel thanked Stone for letter."

Marge took a breath. "*Soldier of Fortune* magazine printed letter signed Sam Grogan, describing himself as expert in unconventional warfare, calling for abolishing CIA with its record of failures stretching from Bay of Pigs to Iran and calling for completely new organization made up of volunteers with the brains and guts the CIA lacks.

"Here's the final item. Pigmy Blue says Grogan is employed on the Hill, where he's worked for several different congressmen in field of constituent services. This is the last item. 'A pretext phone call to the office of the congressman you mentioned reveals that Grogan is on his staff working in constituent services as is one Deborah Kraus. Hope this helps. A question: What in the world are you up to now?' Good question, that," added Marge. "When are you coming home?"

"Look. Call her, would you? At that number I gave you. Uh, and give her this message. 'From Eye-ringed Flatbill to Hop Merchant. Exceedingly helpful. Please let us know something of the level of mention or discussion in U.S. or foreign media of the leading personage named in my note to you or his political party.' What I'm looking for, Marge—some kind of publicity or propaganda campaign seems to be getting off the ground here aimed at foreign opinion. I need to find out if it's showing up in press or TV up there.''

The man at the desk jumped up and smiled when Oliver thanked him for the use of the phone. It was the woman with the adding machine who looked up from her work to ask Oliver to repeat his room number.

Chapter 19

The name Casa del Futuro did not seem particularly fitting for the gloomy bulk of the large house on the outskirts of San Cristóbal. Dark pines hung over the high wall, trees that would have been improved with pruning to let sun into the dark compound behind the wall. Written in black spray paint on the stucco wall by the door were the large sprawling letters: *Repudio De La Opresion Yanqui Al Pueblo Mexicano.*

"Oh!" Drew exclaimed. "What a warm welcome! Repudiate Yankee oppression, do they? You wonder how they'll receive a pair of Yankee visitors coming to kowtow to the Great Chacmool."

Drew had been just as peevish in the taxi coming out. Despite the fine day—that morning the clouds drifting above the sunny streets of the city were the conventional cottonwool sort—Drew had refused to consider Oliver's suggestion they walk to the Casa del Futuro. "Furthermore, I very much resent being accompanied by a dragoman," he said, "particularly by one whose Spanish is, if I may say so, much inferior to mine."

"Harley, that is not the point. I need to get in there. Believe me, if I could think of any other way to do it—"

"They granted the interview immediately. So much for all of your dark suspicions!"

"Oh, well. Perhaps it's the worldwide reputation of your paper. Inocencio's theory is they run the Casa del Futuro like a dentist's office. If a patient cancels, they run you in. 'This one's from the *Journal de Provence*. Pull his front teeth out.' "

"And once this interview is over, what am I supposed to do?"

"Write it up and win a Pulitzer."

A wide wooden door had a smaller door let into it, and over the worm holes on the smaller door was posted a note printed neatly with a marker advising passersby of the presence of a dangerous dog within.

When Oliver knocked on the door, they could hear bolts being drawn and locks being turned. The small door opened inward some three inches and a hostile eye appeared darkly in that space. Scrabbling and scratching sounds accompanied the eye, which bobbed out of sight a moment before coming back to its aperture. Oliver spoke in Spanish. "Mr. Harley Drew, correspondent of the French newspaper *La Journal de Provence*, is here for his appointment with Don Saturnino Mora."

The door opened enough to allow the eye to take in both of them and then slammed shut.

"It's *Le Journal*, not *La*." Drew was still grumpy.

"Oh, well, what the hell, Harley."

The door opened and the man told them they could enter. As he spoke Oliver caught the full force of the man's garlic breath. He was breathing heavily as though exercising vigorously. That and the scratching noises were immediately explained. Held by a short lead in the doorkeeper's hand a Doberman pinscher was gasping at its collar, pawing the air with its forelegs, grinning with spitty eagerness to get at the two visitors. The doorkeeper was slashing the dog about the head with the end of the leash.

"Great God almighty!" roared Drew, skipping past the dog to collide with a stocky person dressed in a black suit like that of the dog's handler. He had a thin dark mustache and a skeptical expression. Separating himself from Drew, he politely enough introduced himself as chief of administration.

Oliver explained: "I am interpreter for the famous journalist Señor Harley Drew, foreign correspondent for *Le Journal de Provence*, the influential French newspaper. And this is Señor Drew."

The chief of administration seemed fully as suspicious as his colleagues, the guard at the door, and the dog. "Well, we have quite adequate facilities for translation—it is English, is it not? Not French?"

"Both," said Oliver quickly. "And speaking frankly, Señor Drew prefers my services. We have worked often together." He pretended to explain this to Drew, addressing him in English. "I told him you insist on having me as your interpreter."

"What a dreadful animal!" With or despite Drew's remark the chief of administration nodded and Oliver hoped he had been accepted as interpreter. He led them into a sunny courtyard astonishingly ill kept, the plants appearing dead or dying, the tree at one corner bearing starkly bare branches. There, a tall man in a white *guayabera* shirt and neatly creased black trousers, younger than the others, stood obviously awaiting them.

"I wish to present you," said the chief of administration to the tall young man, looking at the piece of paper he held in his hand, "Señor 'Arley Dreff"—he pronounced, still looking at a the paper—"of the—" He paused to frown at what was written on the paper.

"Le Journal de Provence," Oliver supplied.

The other man was looking from one to the other of them. He spoke in good English. "A cordial welcome, Mr. Drew." Drew emitted an identifying monosyllable. "I act as secretary to Don Saturnino," he explained urbanely. "The interview will take place in the library. Do you speak Spanish, Mr. Drew?"

"No, he doesn't," said Oliver quickly. "Just a few words." Drew grunted.

The chief of administration was finishing his interrupted introductions. "—present to you, Don Victor, son of Don Saturnino Mora." The chief of administration, indicating Oliver by thrusting heavy black eyebrows in his direction, announced that Drew wanted to use his own interpreter.

"Oh, is that so?" said the son, looking again at Oliver, studying him, the lids low over his eyes. Oliver studied him back. Don Victor had wavy brown hair, the narrowed eyes a dark brown, active, shifting from Drew to Oliver and back. The nose was surprisingly—to Oliver—small, poorly designed, didn't fit the jutting chin beneath the wide mouth. The son made a decision, although he did not seem happy with it, giving Oliver a cold look as he said, "Of course, Mr. Drew. If that is what you want. It is nevertheless my custom to sit in on the interviews."

"Yes, certainly." Drew had been maneuvering to put Oliver between him and the dog, still pawing at the flagstones at the entryway, straining at its collar, whining and choking.

"Señor Drew says that is convenient," repeated Oliver in Spanish, eager to show his agility as a translator. Don Victor gave Oliver another cold look.

The library was a long dark room. Oliver stumbled over a corner of the rug on entering. Drew tripped on a footstool and caromed into an unexpected refectory table, knocking over a globe of the world, which Don Victor helped Oliver put back on its pedestal.

As their eyes recovered they became aware of a figure seated under a large Mexican flag draped on the wall at the far end of the room. Don Saturnino wore a white farmer's shirt over his thin chest, black trousers, his feet bare in leather huaraches. The main features of Don Saturnino's face were heavy brows above dark blue round glasses that not only hid his eyes but reinforced an impression of ill health. His hair was still dark but skimpy, damp on his skull. The nose was narrow from the front but hawklike, angry, in the paper-thin, paper-white skin of the shrunken face. The mouth was thin-lipped, a wavy pale line across the lower part of his face, the jaw moving even when he was not speaking. Blue-veined hands rested on either arm of his chair, a chair of a regal sort with a high back. A wide-brimmed sombrero with a high crown lay at his feet. Whether or not calculated to do so, the pose reminded Oliver of a familiar photograph of Emiliano Zapata.

Don Victor presented Drew to Don Saturnino but did not refer to Oliver. The two of them stood uncertainly together in dusk before the throne. Don Victor pointed out two straight chairs behind them and they sat down. He took another chair and sat down himself, a few feet to their left. This was followed by a silence during which Don Saturnino cleared his throat several times but did not otherwise acknowledge the introduction. Don Victor spoke again. "Señor Drew has come from France for the interview with you, Father. He is interested in the Movement, in your views of Mexico."

Drew started to speak in Spanish. Oliver elbowed him and

interrupted, speaking loudly: "Señor Drew wishes to ask for your views of the problems of Mexico, Don Saturnino."

The only sound in the silence was a noise from Drew's stomach. After a minute Oliver whispered, "How about another question, Harley? In English," he added, in a still lower tone.

"Francia!" exclaimed Don Saturnino suddenly, and then was quiet again. Oliver found himself tensely leaning forward to listen. Don Saturnino took a few sharp breaths and began talking in a low, quavery Spanish. "Did you French ever comprehend that the promise of the Mexican revolution died when the election was stolen from Don José Vasconcelos through the machinations of the fascist thug, Plutarco Elías Calles, and the oligarchs whom he served?" Mora lifted one hand from his lap and waved it as though shooing a fly. "That occurred in the year of Our Lord, 1929."

He paused and Oliver translated. Drew grunted an acknowledgment, assuming the question to be rhetorical. He had a pad on his knee and he scratched briefly on it with a ballpoint pen. They peered at Mora in the dimness and waited.

"You, the French, were again misled by the hopes revived by the election of General Lázaro Cárdenas, the governor of Michoacán, to the post of president. False hopes. In truth, he did well by Mexico in expropriating the holdings of the arrogant British and American oil companies. That was in the year of Our Lord—" He paused.

"The year 1938, it was, Father," supplied his son in a loud voice.

"I know that, I know that." The old man was cross. "That's what I said. In the year 1938." There was silence, again. Don Saturnino shifted in his chair and seemed to be saying something. Oliver, forgetting the pretense of translation, glanced over at Don Victor. "Don Lázaro listened to the dishonest advisers who surrounded him," Mora resumed. "And from that time on—" said Don Saturnino. He paused again. His mouth was working. Words slipped out but died before reaching across the space to the two of them.

"Well, translate, then!" That was Drew.

"I can't hear him," whispered Oliver. He spoke loudly.

"Your views of Mexico today, Don Saturnino, a question of great interest to our readers."

Mora stopped his mumbling but did not answer.

"Your views," the son was almost shouting. "Views of Mexico, Father."

"No!" said Mora suddenly. "Impostor!" he shouted, his voice breaking. "No more. Enough. Go, impostor!"

Don Victor stood up. "I'm sorry, gentlemen," he said. He looked embarrassed, angry. Oliver was on his feet, too, only too ready to leave before Mora came out with another such blast. Don Victor put his arms out and turned them toward the door. "My father had an exceedingly full day yesterday. Other interviews. He becomes overstimulated, and as a result he did not sleep well last night. He's very tired. We'll schedule another appointment." All these suave words, Oliver noted, were delivered in a smooth English, but Don Victor's lips were twisted with anger, his eyes narrowed to slits, darting from Drew to Oliver and back, and he seemed in a hurry to get rid of them.

"Out this way, please. I'm afraid he's not well. He didn't mean what he said. Think nothing of it. Today is not a good day."

Oliver murmured regrets as they went to the courtyard, pushing Drew along in front of him. "Señor Drew is at the Hotel Santa Clara," he said.

"Yes, yes, we'll see about that."

The dog leaped out of a nap to begin gargling again on their approach to the door. The dog handler kicked at the animal. Drew hesitated then scurried past the dog and down the steps.

"He's gaga, isn't he?" That was Drew's remark when Oliver followed him out and the door slammed behind them.

"Shh." Oliver held up his hand. Voices were raised behind the closed door. He could not make out the words. The dog whined.

As they climbed back into their waiting taxi Oliver said, "Gaga or not, he saw through us quick enough. Impostors. How in hell did he know?"

"Impostor singular, by which he meant you rather than me. My cover held up all right. It was the silliness of your interpreting for me. He saw through that immediately, gaga or not. Good. We can forget the interview now, can't we? Haven't you learned whatever it is you want to know? That place gives me the creeps. I'm not going back there.''

Oliver was thinking about something else. "Out," he said, and repeated it. And after that: "About."

The taxi let them out in the *zócalo* at the corner by Drew's hotel. Thick rolling clouds had begun boiling above the tops of the trees in the plaza. The touch of the sun gilded the purple borders of the clouds, but the breeze impelling them swept down through the streets. The air was distinctly cooler. "Look," said Drew, shivering, "isn't that Inocencio?"

Inocencio Brown was sitting on a wrought-iron bench on one of the paths cutting diagonally across the Plaza Mayor. Hat low over his forehead, he had been reading a newspaper. He put it down on his lap when he saw them. Oliver and Drew walked over to greet him.

"Something else about the city your ancestor founded," said Oliver. "Catch that smell of wood smoke in the air?"

"Siddown a minute. I've been thinking."

"Good," said Oliver. They sat down on either side of Inocencio. "Guess where we've been—conducting an interview with a subject deep in twilight sleep."

"Do you think he was drugged?" asked Drew.

"Twilight sleep—just a metaphor."

"Interesting thought, however."

When Drew finished describing their visit to the Casa del Futuro, Oliver commented. "A reasonable account, allowing for the usual journalistic inaccuracy."

"Such as?" said Drew.

"Well," said Oliver, "the Doberman was not the size of a small horse. And you left out the most important thing." He told Inocencio of Mora's accusation.

"How'd he know you're impostors?" asked Inocencio.

"He meant Ted, not me. Ted credits Mora with second sight. The poor old soul's gone around the bend, that's all," said Drew, adding, "Shall we get coffee?"

"Wait a minute," said Inocencio. "I got something to tell you. The gigolo. I know where I saw him now." He paused while Oliver reminded Drew that the gigolo was Chato Escobar, the companion of Debbie Kraus. "Maybe tie into something," Inocencio went on to say. "We're on a case, Cuban case, the Dirección General de Inteligencia, back in those days. This Cuban officer was working on the local employees and the clericals in the embassy."

"Our embassy."

"Right. Maybe that's why I think gigolo when I see that Escobar. The DGI fellow, he's picking up Mexicans and running them at the single women in our embassy. Wives too. We spent, I guess, maybe a coupla months on the case off and on. Get pulled off for priority jobs, then get back on it, try to identify the contacts, people he's using. Anyway, that's where I see that Chato. We catch him at one meeting. But we never figure out who he is. Now I remember him."

"Well," said Drew. "After all, a person in External Relations has every reason to meet with an official of the Cuban embassy."

"Naw, this wasn't no social get-together," said Inocencio. "They in clandestine contact, that DGI fellow, that Escobar. No doubt about that."

"Working in External Relations, Harley, he's in a perfect spot to mix with embassy people and other foreigners. And here's our Debbie, his girlfriend."

"Not exactly hard evidence, is it?" asked Drew.

"Just a gigolo, Inocencio?"

"No," said Inocencio. "I say take a look at that girl, Debbie, maybe doing a job for the Cubans."

"Inocencio. If we're right about that—" Oliver did not complete the thought.

"Yes?" asked Drew. "If we're right? Or if we're wrong?" He shivered. "Either way I am freezing. Fickle weather! Shall we get some coffee?"

"Naw, I better stick around here. I got a project," said Inocencio.

* * *

Over a soup of *crema de espinaca,* large helpings of a lasagna delicate enough to earn a compliment from Drew, and a bottle of red wine, they held a staff meeting that night in the light of the oil lamp on the round-topped table in the office, their private room at the Luz del Día. Oliver reviewed Diane's message about Grogan and Kraus. "Slasher was name-tracing Grogan for Claudie Clinkscale, I bet you anything. If Grogan talks to others the way he did to us, Clinkscale might have wondered if Grogan had been planted on him by the agency." Oliver shook his head.

"But getting back to the outlandish business with Mora," said Drew, "how can one take this matter seriously? Surely, with Mora in the condition so evident to us, there's not the slightest hope of his being the charismatic leader of any sort of movement. Frankly, Ted, I think this trail has gone cold. If ever it was warm."

Inocencio said, "You could think maybe it's some kinda scam. They just pretend about this thing long enough to fool the voters. Then, after the election in Texas, they don't need it and they drop the old man. But you still got the gigolo. What about him?" He shook his head. "Anyway, this morning," he began, "after you go for coffee, I walk around down there to look at the statue of Bartolomé de las Casas, he was the bishop here. They name the place after him. Then I go on down Avenida Benito Juárez. I see this white Jeep Cherokee come past with a fat sergeant in it, looking over at me. Benito Juárez, it's one-way that way so I turn around walk back up, cut over past the Pemex station on the corner and go back to the *zócalo* where I was, and sit on one of those white iron benches, only this time along the street, the one that goes in front our two hotels. I decide I'll wait and see what happens, and if nothing happens, I'll mosey over there to the Palacio Municipal, that pink building at the bottom of the plaza—"

"More of a peach color, I'd say," said Drew.

"Yeah, maybe peach. That's the *casa de gobierno,* government house, there. Behind the pillars along the walk there you got all the offices, over at the right, *turismo,* the one's always closed, then radio communications, Agua Potable y Alcantarillado, traffic, Hacienda, and then Dirección General de Seguridad Pública del Estado. There, where you see those police standing around inside the door, talking, that's the one for me. Then the white Jeep Cherokee pulls up and parks across where I'm sitting. The fat sergeant—you know they all wear those dark blue uniforms with the boots halfway up here—is pissed off he had to go all the way down before he could turn around, come back up Insurgentes. Then drive in all the traffic back around the plaza, the *zócalo*. He sees me when he pulls up and he gets out of the Cherokee, not looking at me now. I think this is a small town and maybe I don't look too much like a tourist. You know, the raincoat, the hat, tourists going around dressed like anything. Well, he goes into Seguridad there.

"A bowl a this spinach soup a meal in itself. After a while I mosey over to Seguridad, where you see the sentry slinging that automatic weapon. 'What's a good place to check records in this town?' I ask. 'What kinda records?' he asks, a young fellow. 'Better ask the sergeant.' He calls him and the sergeant comes out, he's hitching his pants, looking me over. I give him the roots line and I thought maybe he buys it, now he knows what I claim I'm doing here. 'The churches,' he said. 'Try the baptismal records.' This sergeant, he's not so dumb as he looks. That's a right answer."

Inocencio shook his head. "Can't do it. Anyone like my lasagna?"

Drew said, "If you can't finish it. We can do with another bottle of wine, I think." He looked at the label as he got up to go outside to ask for another bottle. "Baja California. Really, not at all bad."

"Then I say," continued Inocencio when Drew returned, " 'that's a good idea. By the way, who's your local historian?' Sergeant says 'How about the *licenciado*? He's into that.' Now we go through the passage in the middle of the building, got the sign, 'Juzgado Muncipal,' where you can see the gardens behind. We go up the stairs. This *licenciado* turns out to be a young fellow, maybe forty or so, blue suit, gold-rimmed glasses, maybe about my height—he doesn't get up—mustache, a lot of hair he works on to get it to go across the top to his ears where it's thin on top and also getting gray. He's at a desk in this bare office with maybe a filing cabinet, tile floor, and a coat rack. Picture of Benito Juárez. He doesn't get up but he asks me to sit down. The sergeant comes in and stands in the door with his arms behind him, listening. The *licenciado* looks over at the sergeant and back at me and he doesn't say anything either. So I explain how I'm there looking up my roots and we sit like that for maybe half a minute. The *licenciado* is a *subsecretario del estado*, so he's right up there, and I'm wondering what they think they got on me.

"He starts right in, polite enough, what am I doing over here in San Cristóbal just as though I'd said nothing a minute ago. I'm polite right back. 'Tourism,' I said. 'I'm a tourist but not like the others. Looking for my roots, as I said.' The sergeant lets some air out but I ignore that. 'Who are the men with you?' the subsecretary says."

"Aha!" said Oliver.

" 'Men? I come by myself. By the way,' I say. 'I'm an American citizen.' 'Is that so?' says the *licenciado*. He doesn't believe me, see? The sergeant pipes up. 'You got identification?' Well, have I got identification!"

"Hope you didn't show them those expired Gobernación credentials."

Inocencio smiled. "You not going to forget that. I show my passport. I sit there easy, got nothing to hide. They look at it and the *licenciado* and the sergeant taking little looks at each other as though they read something special into that. Then, still polite, who those two men with you? He's right back to that. I don't play around too long: 'Oh, them, you mean. I go to the Posada to eat and they put four of us at a same table.' This place handles groups, I start to tell them, and they say, yeah, they know all about those groups. Well, two of these people real nice Americans I run into over here again in the *zócalo*. You said there were four of you. Yeah. I don't know, the other he said he's some kinda philosopher, name Reagan, something like that. Back to you. Well, that one, he's one of those people come to Mexico to look at birds, write 'em all down. They look at each other again. Then I act natural. You know, hey, what is this? Something wrong those guys? Seem nice enough to me.

"Who's the other one? Some kind a newspaper, magazine writer. Works for a French outfit but I think he's an American, down here to do some writing about those people. What people? Those Indians. Which Indians? You know. If you say the name, I'll know. Never mind. What you talking about at dinner? Let's see, birds, all sorts of things, philosophy, oh, yeah, risk analysis. The bird one is into risk analysis. They don't ask about that, maybe the *licenciado* doesn't want the sergeant to know he's not exactly sure what kinda analysis that is. And vice versa. How about politics? Politics? That's right, Mexican politics. They don't know Mexican politics, I say, just tourists. How about there in the *zócalo* today? You talking philosophy? That's the sergeant. I show I don't like that kind of remark and don't answer right away, and the *licenciado* clears his throat and gives the sergeant a dirty look. The French one or American, whatever he is, was going on, laughing, he was interviewing someone who went to sleep while he's talking to him. I don't know. Someone named Mora. He woke up and called them an impostor and they get right out of there."

Inocencio poured coffee from the pot the waitress had brought. "Now right here it starts getting interesting. *Licenciado* tells the sergeant to get someone, I didn't catch the name. We sit there not saying anything. I hum a little tune wondering what comes next."

"We shouldn't have talked to you in the plaza," said Oliver.

Inocencio nodded. "That's all right. I'm picking up things. Pretty soon the sergeant comes back with a fellow, younger than the *licenciado*, maybe thirty something, one of those short fellows, light build, small but neat looking, wears a brown leather jacket, a brown shawl hung around his neck, brown trousers, brown shoes, a very snappy dresser. Serious looking with brown, maybe more dark red hair he combs straight back, little bit of wave in it. Stands up straight and puts his hands on his hips and looks me over. Then he takes the shawl and pulls the ends tight and holds it like that and walks around the room looking at his feet. *Licenciado* sitting up straight in his chair now, so this new one is somebody. This one takes me around again and I give the same story. He's not from around here."

"How do you know?"

"Just the way he acts. Not like a local. Looks like Distrito Federal to me. *Licenciado* careful the way he talks to him. This one asks where you two staying. I tell him I think you in the Posada, other in the Santa Clara, they went across the street there for coffee. Ask me to come. Thanks but I want to finish the newspaper. Asks for names. I shake my head. I'm not too good at names. Just met you that once, then again today in the *zócalo*, here. Now, listen to this part. He asks me if I know Saturnino Mora. He asks if I heard about México Irredenta. Have I ever heard of El Movimiento, the Movement. He asks me what I think of Grogan—see, he's already got the name. Oh, he's that one, in my opinion he's a little bit eccentric, I said, *muy raro*, and a big talker. Then he asks me if I know the *americana*, name of Kraus—"

Oliver whistled. "He knows Debbie!"

"That's right. This one wants to see my passport. He gives it back and tells me not to say anything to you about what they talk about with me. It would help a lot if I could find out what you two doing here. And I don't mean birds, he said. Tell you, feels pretty good having that passport. They don't know what to do. They look at me, I'm Mexican but turns out I've got this passport. Sure, I'm glad to help, but tell you the truth, I don't think those two fellas doing anything here. Listen, the leather jacket, he's going to check around and pretty soon they'll turn me up, sure as hell, reveal a record. And he goes to the hotels, gets your names. I don't know what they're gonna reveal."

"Same as yours, depending on where they check. Look, Inocencio. Keeping their eyes out for strangers this way and they did a pretty quick job of separating us out from the regular tourists—what do you think? They trying to keep people away from Mora, keep us from seeing through whatever it is that's going on here?"

"Well, sure looks like they don't want us poking around."

Chapter 20

"I'm not going to be able to get you on a bus," said Grogan, " 'cause we got a couple of real snotty tour leaders." It was late the following morning. "But you gotta hear this guy. Talks like you wouldn't believe, Ted. We're taking the bird-watchers up the street a little way, up to the Santo Domingo church. All you do, Ted, is walk on up until you come to a cross street, Escuadrón 201. Go kitty-corner left, past the front of the church and on to where you see the little statue of Diego de Mazariegos, and turn right. You can't miss it there at the end of a bunch of arches where there's a smaller building with a dome and a sign says *biblioteca*—means library, right?—building looks like a teapot and the museum's right there, the hall we use's inside. The bus parks down below on the Twentieth of November— that's a street. Once we finish up there, I jam the bird-watchers back on their buses, turn 'em loose to spend the afternoon all lined up with their binoculars, arguing about some damn bird, what in hell kind it is. See you up there, catch a late lunch at the Posada afterward. How about it?"

The Indian women knitted, talking loudly among themselves beside the blue cloths on which they had spread trinkets and textiles, sitting on cobbles and on the beaten earth of the church grounds. As Oliver passed them by they looked up to call out to him in Spanish, hardly interrupting their talk with each other.

Grogan's bird-watchers—two bus loads of them—were filing obediently through a room with a display of artifacts. Beyond and to the right, half a dozen steps led up into a small auditorium. Grogan stood inside, waving people in. "On down front," he was calling out. When he saw Oliver he bugged his eyes at him. "How you like my troops? See you after this at the Posada. Go on down front."

People with binoculars and cameras strung around their necks rested their hands or placed their jackets on the empty spaces beside them, shaking their heads to show they were saving a seat for someone else. Oliver found space at last between a young woman and an older man. The man leaned across to say to the woman, "I'm telling you again—you haven't the remotest chance of catching even a glimpse of one of those."

"Oh, how can you be so sure, Harry?" She looked at Oliver then and at the binoculars he had put around his neck when he had given some thought to fitting in. "What do you think? We're talking about the chances of seeing a great curassow."

"Oh, quite good, I think."

"Rubbish," Harry growled.

"Oh, pay no attention to him," she said. "Have you ever seen one?"

"Yes, near Tuxtla Gutiérrez."

"Male or female?" grumped the man, examining Oliver.

"Both," said Oliver.

"When'd you go there?" Harry asked, scowling as he looked Oliver up and down.

"You're with the other group, aren't you?" asked the woman.

"This was on another trip," said Oliver, improvising. "Maine Audubon."

"Oh, when were they here?" the man persisted, still scowling.

Oliver was saved by Grogan. He was on the stage, calling out, "Now folks." He clapped his hands and shouted, "Hey, everybody." The people standing turned to find their seats and began to sit down, gradually leaving off calling back and forth to each other.

"Welcome, everyone. My name's Sam Grogan. Guess you expected to see a different kind of bird up here"—mild murmur of amusement—"and instead you get the old jungle fighter, Sam Grogan." He cleared his throat. "Several of you asked about the slight deviation in the program you saw on the notice board over at the hotel this morning. Let me tell you something. A lot of intelligent, concerned people just like you have come through here on your nature or your archaeology tours, seen all the sights and visited the sites—right?—in spite of all the marvelous things they've seen here they've left with a profound and painful—no, not Montezuma's revenge—" Another more restrained murmur of amusement. Wrong crowd for that remark, thought Oliver.

"No, a frustration at not getting a clear look at today's Mexico. How come, some of them have asked, how come we're not getting a look at the most exciting new thing in Mexico today, with its headquarters right here in Chiapas? They want to know why this is being kept away from Americans who come down here. How come this conspiracy of silence?

"Yes, people come here, just like you, interested in birds, the native peoples, the fabulous scenery, the fantastic mountains, the archaeological sites, shopping for textiles, people who like you are keenly interested in current events, thinking people like you, and they've gone home feeling cheated because the truth about today's Mexico is being withheld and concealed from them. They hear the tired old propaganda from the same old gang that's been running Mexico into the ground for their personal gain all these years.

"And that's why we've arranged this ever-so-brief little deviation in your schedule, designed, with the cooperation of your tour leaders, to give you what you've been asking for."

"I don't remember asking for it, did you?" grumped Harry on Oliver's right, bending to look at the young woman on the other side of Oliver. She shook her head and shrugged her shoulders, her eyes going back to Grogan.

"Like I said, not the same old propaganda, but an exciting look at what the future of Mexico can be if we bring our influence to bear. Our belief in freedom and human rights instead of intervening to prop up a repressive regime, backing the wrong side as we always seem to do. And on that point let me add just this one more thing and then I'll stop talking. And this is really important. What you hear today is going to blow your mind, I guarantee it. When you get home, share the news, tell your friends about it, what you heard down here today. Tell them about the exciting changes going on down here. Tell them it's our obligation—yours and mine—as good neighbors, to spread the word about the new Mexico, about the new faces coming on the scene, the courageous people who are working to make it all happen, and demand of our government, especially your congressman, to give our sympathy and our support''—Grogan was slowing down, separating his words for emphasis—''instead of propping up the tired old party in power. Let's change U.S. policy to one of backing freedom and prosperity in Mexico.''

Solemn pause. Then, quickly: ''And now I give you—'' And here Grogan, perspiring, put an arm out toward Victor Mora, who was striding confidently down the aisle to the platform. Mora was hopping up the steps to the stage, holding up his arms and directing a wide smile at the people seated on the benches. ''I give you Mexico's rising new political star, Victor Mora. Let's give him a hand!''

The birders were clapping politely, interested half smiles on their faces, as Mora smiled at Sam Grogan, thanked him for the introduction. Grogan was standing so as to face Mora, applauding him, grinning out at the crowd, now letting the applause die away.

''Thank you.'' As Mora looked out at the crowd his smile faded. ''Yes, I am Victor Mora, son of Don Saturnino Mora, the founder and the leader of the new movement destined to sweep Mexico clean, to polish the tarnished luster of the Mexican revolution''—here Mora tossed his head and looked sternly at the crowd—''a revolution, we must admit with shame, that has been betrayed—betrayed with your help!''

That made them sit up. Mora was mild again. ''My father, Don Saturnino, would have wanted you to be his guests, to visit him at the Casa del Futuro here in San Cristóbal de las Casas.'' Here he let his voice fall quiet so that the crowd went still, sitting erect to hear the next words. ''My father is not well, and for that reason I have come here today to give you his message. Don Saturnino has dictated to me his political will that begins with these words: 'No one man is important. No, it is the people who matter.'

"No, our good American friends. For me, for all of us, my father's loyal followers, it is the Movement he founded that matters—the Movement that will bring a new prosperity to all, not just a few, of the Mexican people. He demands of us, his devoted followers, only that we carry on his lifelong struggle for a better Mexico. A struggle that has left him worn-out but still determined to bring about change in his beloved Mexico.

"Why should you be interested in what happens to your neighbor? For a number of reasons, familiar, I am sure, to people as sophisticated as you are. But the chief reason is that your complacency empowers oppression in Mexico. Yes, and we Mexicans ask you: What chance do we have for change in Mexico as long as you support the enemies of the Mexican people?"

The words themselves were worn, Oliver thought. Worn with overuse, like the stub of a pencil. He could let them pass through his mind, hear them without needing to consider them. The emotional content of the message and Mora's delivery were what he noticed. Mora had a public manner more attractive than his private one—true of many politicians, many actors. The manner was far more impressive than the banalities he uttered. Mora's English was clear, colloquial—Oliver was listening for a peculiarity of pronunciation. There! He was pleased at the confirmation of what he remembered.

Mora had his audience with him. Oliver could see, as he looked around, that judgment had been suspended. Even the grouchy fellow on his right had stuck his lips out to nod and frown his approval of Mora's demand for change in Washington, ready to offer the sympathy Mora demanded of the United States. For Mora spent far less time on Mexico proper than on the role of the United States in Mexico, scolding the birders for the actions of their government, and they seemed to be enjoying it. The themes were those that Debbie Kraus had less skillfully delivered to Oliver: imperialism, intervention, investment. Prescription: back México Irredenta, disinvestment. When Mora wound up his short, dynamic talk—nicely timed for a North American audience—the birders greeted him with heavy applause.

Grogan was standing, calling out as the applause died down. "How about that? Get that story to your congressman when you get home. Tell him how others see us. Let's alert America!" He turned toward Mora and revived the applause by clapping again and the audience joined in, coming to their feet.

Oliver was not applauding but thinking. The bird groups were neither Texans nor Hispanics. The appeal was being made to a wider group than Bondie Birdsong's constituents. When the clapping stopped, exhilarated talk bounced off the low ceiling and reverberated from wall to wall.

"Fascinating!" said the woman next to Oliver. "You get a whole new slant on Mexico."

"You certainly did," said Oliver. "Enjoyed meeting you. Good luck with the great curassow. You'd do well to try the zoo in Tuxtla Gutiérrez. I did. But don't tell Harry."

"Shame on you." She laughed. "Good-bye."

At the door in the back of the hall Grogan was handing out leaflets to the people shuffling out, he himself going on out the door with the first ones. Near the door the chief of administration at the Casa del Futuro was gazing about with a tough expression on his face—hard to tell from where Oliver stood if the look was one of detachment or of contempt for the members of the audience as they filed past him. The skeptical look of the day before looked harshly cynical in the light of the auditorium.

At the edge of the stage a flock of birders was listening to young Mora, asking questions. Mora was putting himself out to be attractive, his eyes wide rather than narrowed, his lips turned into a smile, accepting compliments on his talk, nodding to indicate he understood a question, frowning sternly as he answered it. Oliver could hear a snatch of his answer: "—not the people of the United States at all but your government that's always backing the wrong—"

Charisma: Claudie Clinkscale suddenly appeared in Oliver's head, sipping a gin martini. Unlike the woman on his left during the talk or gruff Harry on his right—unlike what appeared to be the majority of the listeners—Oliver had found no charm in Don Victor Mora. But he recognized that Mora had the indispensable ingredient that Clinkscale had defined: the ability to inspire indignation if not fear. Perhaps the content of his speech didn't matter, the easy clichés of antigovernment propaganda.

Mora had persuaded this open-minded crowd of educated North Americans to feel guilty about conditions in Mexico—not a personal guilt but an annoyance with their government in Washington. Mora, the demagogue, had made them cross at Washington, and a good percentage of them would go home to do something about it.

Oliver did not want the chief of administration to see him, so he put his head down and joined a clutch of birders on their way up the steps to the rear. He was able to get past the chief of administration without being noticed. As he reached the door to start down the steps he heard a gasp and a voice say; "Oh, my God!"

It was Debbie Kraus. Oliver did not speak, hurrying off, taking flight past coveys of birders, out the museum door into the open, onto the flagstones of the porch of the church of Santo Domingo. At the end of the cloister he glanced back to see Debbie at the door, shielding her eyes from the sun, confirming her sighting.

Chapter 21

Oliver sat at one of the round tables in the Posada, elbows on the red tablecloth, Debbie nervously on his mind. She would be quick to let Clinkscale know he was in San Cristóbal. And she would identify him to Grogan. That was the more immediately ticklish worry, however minor compared with the eruption of anger as the news flashed from Clinkscale to Birdsong to the director. At the moment Oliver was preparing himself for nothing worse than prickly embarrassment, an unpleasant scene with Grogan undeceived if Debbie had informed Grogan before he turned his bird-watchers over to the tour leaders. There, now— Grogan had come into the dining room. Oliver put his hands in his lap, bracing himself.

Needlessly so. Grogan came up to the table, held up a hand of greeting. "How!" He pulled out a chair, turning to look around before sitting in it: "Where in hell's Manuel gotten to? If ever I needed a drink." He sat down, still looking around the room.

"That was quite an introduction, Sam."

"Oh, shucks, Ted" said Grogan, grinning. "What'd you think of our boy?"

"Impressive. Tell me, where's he from?"

"Where's he from? Manuel! I thought you'd gone AWOL, buddy. *L'écossais, s'il vous plaît,* Manuel. Okay, a scotch, then. Have it your way." Grogan turned to Oliver. "From Mexico, that's where."

"He's certainly speaks good English."

"Well, you have to. Your latest surveys show that Americans

are latently biased against foreign political leaders unless they speak colloquial English. Exceptions are cute French or amusing German accents. Vaudeville in the rose garden. That prejudice is equally shared by your overeducated bird-watchers.''

"Oh, I wonder about that.''

"I'm quoting the experts, Ted. It's an unconscious bias, they say. Being out of the mainstream, you forget that it's all TV these days. Victor can look 'em right in the little red eye while fluent English pours out of him. Never mind that it's all bullshit. You're impressed. Say, this guy Victor Mora, he's like one of us. My kinda guy.''

"Something I noticed, Sam. He says 'out' and 'about' like a Virginian.''

"Yeah, you caught that. You're right, Ted, but it's not Virginia—Canada. Same kinda accent. Victor was born up there. That's where he got his English.''

Oliver closed his eyes, almost involuntarily, for a short prayer of gratitude. He had no idea what the information meant. The shock came from its fitting General Robles's last words—famous last words—about Canada.

He opened his eyes to see Grogan looking curiously at him. Oliver clasped his hands around his stomach. "Bit of a pang just then. Guess I'm hungry. Skipped breakfast.''

"Sorry I had to run off like that. Neither one of those two witches would let you on their bus.''

It made it worse that Grogan was so friendly. "It worked out all right, Sam.''

"You can see how I'm running my ass off around here. They keep telling me help is on the way. 'Bear with us, Grogan. Help is on the way,' And now you turn up, a real-life bird-watcher. I'm gonna check with the powers that be, see about taking you on as assistant shepherd. How about it?''

Powers that be meaning Clinkscale. "Sam, I appreciate it, but I really doubt I'm going to be around that much longer.''

"You never know. I'll ask anyway. I need to goose 'em again.''

"Yeah. Tell me about Mora.''

"Old or young?''

"Well, young, to start with."

"Ted, tell you the truth, but don't go 'round quoting me. Victor's an SOB."

"Really? He had the crowd at his feet."

"Oh, hell. Bird-watchers! Nothing personal, Ted, but whadda you expect? Manuel, you've been upped two grades. I find you in every respect fit for command of a gastronomic brigade."

That brought Clinkscale back again. Oliver wondered if Clinkscale and Grogan sat around drinking together in Washington, gin martinis for one and scotch for the other, whether Bondie Birdsong ever joined them, what fables Grogan would spin for his employers. "Yes, the *filete de res,* Manuel. Iced tea. Well, he had quite a message, didn't he, about our policy, the way we're involved in Mexico, supporting the government?"

"That's only his bullshit, Ted."

"But they ate it up, Sam. Is the idea to get the bird-watchers lobbying Congress in favor of the Movement? Against the Mexican government? Down with the PRI?"

"Right. Not only bird-watchers. All the groups that come through. Europeans too. Especially the holier ones, like your Swedes. Get the world talking. People get bored and they need new subjects for their indignation."

"Uh-huh. Where was Mora born in Canada?"

"I dunno. Understand, no one says much about that."

"How come?"

"Well, Ted, it's not so good, your great patriotic Mexican antiforeign rabble-rouser being born some funny place like Canada."

"How'd it happen?"

"Well, Ted." Grogan looked around the room, crooked a finger at Oliver to draw him closer, and whispered, "I heard his mother happened to be up there at the time."

Oliver shook his head while Grogan laughed. When he stopped laughing Grogan said, "Sorry about that, Ted. Listen! Serious business. What you got, tiger, on our two phonies?"

"Well, Sam. I saw the fat one and it turns out he had an interview with Mora elder—"

"No kidding. He think Mora's a Lacandón Indian chief? Interviewed the old boy, hey? Let's give some thought to that."

"Well, he works for that newspaper, the journal whatever, after all. I think he's harmless enough."

"Ted, excuse me, but a sheltered life has not prepared you to spot the phonies."

Inwardly, Oliver sighed, thinking how soon Grogan would regret that remark and a number of others like it. How to prevent Grogan's making a worse fool of himself? "He went out to a house on the edge of town. He said Mora is very old. And that he, Mora *padre*, that is, is a bit peculiar. Before he could get anything out of the interview Victor broke it off."

"He would, the son of a bitch. He's pretty damned peculiar himself. Jealous of Daddy."

"Is he? He also said that Mora, Victor, I mean, doesn't seem to resemble the old man."

"No, that's right. It irritates the hell out of Victor baby too. They say he looks like his mother."

"Who was she?"

"Well, the word is she was a Canadian studying down here, a lefty. Mora was quite a swordsman in his time, they say. Hard to believe. But he heard about baby boy up in the tundra somewhere and dragged him down here and made him heir apparent. Getting more and more apparent."

"She still around?"

"No, the story is that on her deathbed she got in touch with Saturnino about the kid. First he'd heard. Very romantic but also cloaked in mystery."

"Why?"

"Well, Ted, would you go around bragging about how you're illegitimate?"

"I suppose not."

Grogan shrugged. "He may look more like his mother but Victor's got all of pater's annoying mannerisms. And opinions. Resembles him there, all right. What about the other one, the Mexican ringer they ran at us?"

"I don't think there's much there, Sam. I ran into him down in the *zócalo*. He claims to be a descendant of Diego de Mazariegos, one of the conquistadores that defeated the Mayans here-abouts. Frankly—"

"Claims to be, yeah, right. Tell you what he is. He's a cop."

"Really? How'd you learn that?"

Grogan winked at Oliver. "Frankly what?"

"Oh, just that I find other people's ancestors boring."

"He does that on purpose. See? He bores you to distraction and you don't give him another thought."

"Getting back to Mora elder. The French one got the impression that he's quite unwell."

"Right. He's not only way over the hill but, as you put it, quite unwell. Meaning sick, I take it."

"Mentally?"

"Mixed up, more. Let you on in a secret. That crew'll keep him going as long as they need him as a symbol. Sedated. When they don't need him anymore, when sonny boy can stand on his own two feet and dear Father gets to be too much of a burden, they pull the plug on the elder statesman."

"Pretty cold-blooded."

"Oh, didn't I say? It's not just that Victor is an SOB—they're all SOBs."

"When's this going to happen?"

"Well, I tell you, Ted. I'm predicting pretty soon now. I heard no more interviews with the old boy. Too unreliable. Says nutty things that make our noble cause look ridiculous. Maybe your fat friend had one of the last interviews. Everything's in the auditorium from now on. Junior gets to shine."

"Does the old man live out there, stay in that house?"

"What's all the interest in the old guy all of a sudden, Ted?"

Oliver would have to be careful. "It strikes me as sad, that's all. Like to have seen the old fellow in operation before he goes. From what you say he must be an interesting person."

"Naw. Sad the way they treat him, sure. Interesting? I suppose. But the old man was a point-five-oh-caliber SOB himself in his prime. Anyway, he's out in left field now with the heir coming up to bat. You heard Victor. The old man's line was the same, straight anti-American stuff. They always stick something in about how they're just crazy about the American people. You buy that, I got a bridge I'd like to show you."

"What I don't understand is your connection with the group, Sam. Where do you fit in?"

Grogan winked at him. "Well, Ted. I'm not down here for my health, I can tell you that. Give you three guesses."

Before Oliver could think of his first guess, he heard Debbie's voice again, as though she were sounding chimes next to his ear: "Oh, my God!" *Re sol do*.

"Well, if it isn't cutie pie! At last. I hope you're ready to pick up a little of the work around here," said Grogan to Debbie. "I've been running—"

Debbie ignored him, standing above Oliver, hands on her hips. "I just called Washington, Mr. Smart-ass Oliver. Claudie Clinkscale's on your case now. You better believe—"

"Hey, you two know each other?"

Debbie turned to Grogan. "Sam Grogan, I can't believe—you're so incredibly stupid, sitting here talking to him. I just talked to Claudie. He goes, 'Oh, no! I don't believe it!' He's gone ballistic. You know who you're sitting around getting drunk with, don't you? This is fantastic! Wait'll Claudie—"

Grogan was staring at her and then at Oliver, who was getting to his feet. "Well, Sam. Nice knowing you."

Twenty minutes later Oliver was seated at one of the leather-topped tables, a pad at his right hand and a glass of iced tea in front of him. Inocencio Brown was sitting across from him, head back, eyes on the ceiling, thinking. "Okay, Harley," said Oliver. "You've made your point—it's a forlorn hope. But right now we're running out of time."

"The problem with you, Ted"—Drew was sitting hunched in a chair at another of the tables, frowning heavily at Oliver—"is that you don't know when to stop."

"We've got to have a little fun before we're through, Harley, that's all. We owe it to ourselves. Let's go over your shopping list, Inocencio."

"Fun! Ted, you know as well as I do—at this stage it's sheer desperation on your part. Surely they'll be putting in motion the machinery to shut us down here. What can you possibly do? Inocencio, try to talk some sense into his head.''

''Sense? Inocencio? He's shopping for fifty kilograms of plastic explosive, a hundred feet of fuse, ten detonators. Inocencio's going to blow the road between here and Tuxtla.''

''Psssh!'' said Drew, waving both hands at Oliver in disgust.

Inocencio leaned both arms on the tabletop and winked at Oliver.

''All right, Inocencio, take a look.''

''Two flashlights,'' read Inocencio. ''Batteries for ditto. Two heavy blankets. Blankets?''

''There may be glass along the top.''

''That's a good idea. Pliers, screwdriver, yeah. I'm putting down a *como se llama*—crowbar,'' said Inocencio. ''There's a *ferretería* on the corner across from the dry-goods.''

''Okay. I'd better get over to the hotel and check out. I'm bringing my gear back over here.''

''I don't know how they feel,'' said Inocencio, ''you living here. How you going to shave, take a shower?''

''From now on I've got to stay out of sight. I'll sneak down the street after dark to your room or Harley's, take a shower.''

Oliver was folding the last of his clothes on the bed of his small third-floor room at the Posada. He had picked up his laundry at the desk, paid his bill, showered, and changed. He had told the woman at the desk he was going to Tuxtla Gutiérrez to catch the morning plane for Mexico City. Let her pass that on when they come looking for him.

It was too late to reach Marge at the safe house. He would call from somewhere in the morning to see whether Slasher O'Rourke had found out he was in San Cristóbal. Hell to pay and no pitch hot, Oliver muttered as he closed the bag. He took a last look around the room and picked up the bag.

There was a knock on the door.

Oliver put one foot down to keep the door from opening more than an inch or so and leaned his shoulder into it—like the dog handler at the Casa del Futuro.

Grogan was outside. "Hi, Ted." He spoke quietly. He looked subdued. "Like to talk, if you got a minute."

"You alone?"

"You mean Debbie?" He had a lopsided grin. "Yeah, I'm alone."

Oliver opened the door and backed into the room. Grogan came in and looked around. "So this is the new part of the Posada. Not bad. I got one of the old rooms, size of your waiting room in a bus station."

"Sit down." Oliver pointed to the sole chair and sat on one of the two beds.

Grogan sat down. "Don't pay any attention to Debbie. She gets excited, she can be a real pain in the ass."

"Yeah, well—"

"Well, Ted, I just thought I'd come by to say that, uh, some of the things I said." He clasped his hands and looked down at them. "Guess it made you wonder, didn't it?"

Oliver was considerably more uncomfortable than he would have been if Grogan had been angry with him. He looked away from Grogan and wondered what to say next. Sorry you're such a storyteller. Thing is, Grogan meant no ill by it. He'd done no harm. "I could use some help, Sam," was what Oliver was inspired to say. "What with your background."

Grogan raised his eyes and looked at him, searching for a sign that he was being mocked. "Like what?"

"I'm worried about the old man. The way they're treating him."

"Yeah? What's that got to do with you? I mean, Debbie told me who you are. She said Claudie came down to Mexico and gave you a briefing on the whole deal. And right away, as soon as he left, you made a big play for her."

"Debbie—how shall I put it? The first part of that is accurate. The second part is the opposite of accurate."

"I think I get the distinction."

"I made no play for her." Oliver shook his head. "Being a friend of Debbie's, you may want to believe her."

"I'm no friend of Debbie's. It's mutual. She's Claudie's friend, if that's the term for it. Debbie describes events as she wants them to be. She wouldn't know the truth if it walked up—'' Grogan laughed and turned red.

Oliver pretended not to notice. "You know Chato Escobar?''

Grogan shook his head. "No, should I?''

"No. Another friend of Debbie's, if that's the term for it. Where does Don Saturnino stay, Sam?''

Grogan didn't answer right away. He looked down at his hands and clasped them and unclasped them several times. "Want to tell me why you need to know that?''

"Anything I tell you would only get you in trouble.''

"I'm in trouble already. Debbie's calling Claude to say she saw me with you. I don't give a shit. Okay. The house, the big house, what they call the House of the Future, where they meet the public, in the library there. They don't let him stay there anymore. Kept everyone up all night. Gets worked up and starts shouting all sorts of crazy things about the rest of them, especially Victor. Thing is he's down on Victor and sonny boy finds that embarrassing. Father's been relegated to a house up behind the main house. Living room with a bedroom and bath, sort of a guest cottage. Why? Do you really want to see Mora?''

Oliver shrugged.

"They'll never let you in. Debbie's running all over town, passing the word about you.''

"That the only other house, outbuilding?''

Grogan looked at Oliver and blinked. "No. To get to the guest house you go around to the left of the main house and take a path up a slope. Wait. You know there's a wall around the whole place, don't you, in addition to the wall around the main house?''

Oliver nodded.

"Take that path, first you get to a red-painted gardener's shed with no gardener. You go by that and then there's a vegetable garden the cook's wife scratches around in and then a sort of a summerhouse—you know.''

"A pergola?''

"I guess so.'' Grogan looked at Oliver's bag. "You going somewhere?''

"Back to Mexico.''

"Before or after you drop your card on the old man?" Grogan grinned. "How's it go—*pour prendre congé*?"

Oliver smiled back. "How many people live there beside Victor and his father?"

"The chief of administration. You may have seen him up there at the auditorium today. Hollywood version of a Mexican bandit."

"What's administration mean in this case?"

"Security. There's his assistant, the dog amah, gets dragged around the joint by a drooling Doberman with a red tongue and long white teeth. There are two other bodyguard types—they all pack Colt Forty-fives, the automatic pistols. Whether they know how to use them, I don't know. A fat cook in a gray skivvy shirt with soup stains in front and a dirty apron that presumably once was white—he keeps a forty-five hung over the cutting board next to the dish towels. Not exactly your Quaker meetinghouse. The cook's wife or whatever is the cleaning woman. I don't think she got issued a pistol. She looks scared witless all the time. The dog handler walks around after her to see she doesn't steal any state secrets. That's the entire ship's company plus Victor and the old man, of course. A few note takers and horse holders come in and stand around during the day. They button the place up at night like it was Tet and the Viet Cong racing up and down the street outside."

"What are they afraid of?"

Grogan shrugged. "Beats me. Maybe a visit from the Mexican government. Maybe you."

"What time they button up?"

"Maybe ten. I've never been there later than that."

"Who looks in on Mora at the house?"

"The cook's wife takes Mora a bowl of slop, some kinda gruel they give him, a couple of times a day. The dog and the dog wallah escort her on this mission. He unlocks the door and stands around while she spoons something into Mora when he's not up to feeding himself, which I guess is getting to be more often the case than not. She collects the old dishes and then the convoy returns to base. I've seen her make the food run by herself, when the chief of administration's not watching, the dog officer feeling the escort duties to be infra dig and also because he is a lazy ass."

"You keep your eyes open, Sam."

Grogan grinned sheepishly. "A couple of hours ago I would have given you a pretty nifty riposte to that opening."

Oliver smiled. "They keep the guest house locked all the time, then."

"As far as I know. The old man's alone there at night and they don't want him lurching around the grounds, ranting and raving."

"And no one else sleeps there?"

"I doubt it. I think he hollers a lot. What you ought to know is that Bruto—that's what they call the Doberman—they let Bruto out at night to run loose on the grounds. You may find that point worth noting."

Oliver nodded. "I do." He picked up his bag with his left hand and put out his right. "Well, Sam—"

They shook hands. Grogan grinned. "I figured you weren't down here after any crenellated citronella."

"Citreoline trogon? Too bad we didn't have a chance to kick a few more concepts around."

"Nice knowing you, Ted."

Oliver had let it go too late. When he walked out of the Posada onto Calle Adelina Flores, he saw the white Jeep Cherokee parked at the curb. He turned quickly left and found the fat sergeant blocking the way.

"Get in," said the sergeant. "You're under arrest."

Chapter 22

An automatic weapon lay across the lap of the young policeman seated in the back with Oliver. As he would neither answer the question nor look at him, Oliver leaned forward to repeat it to the sergeant. "Where are we going?" The sergeant ignored him, hands busy with the wheel, his eyes on the street ahead, and he did not answer. Oliver thought of announcing that he had an American passport, as had Inocencio, but was relatively sure that the sergeant would know that. They were lurching right onto Real de Guadalupe, the sergeant honking and racing his engine to intimidate the cars in front of him, their drivers paying no attention to him. The Jeep was going slowly enough for bystanders and the afternoon strollers to enjoy a glimpse of the prisoner, a challenge to aplomb, being paraded through town in the late-twentieth-century version of a tumbril.

Almost immediately the sergeant jammed the brake pedal down in front of the Palacio Municipal. Oliver climbed out of the car and at his invitation accompanied the sergeant beneath the sign saying *Juzgado Municipal*. With the other policeman clumping along behind, weapon at the port, Oliver was escorted up the stairs Inocencio had described climbing the day before. The office and the two men sitting in it were much as Inocencio had described, a blue-suited *licenciado* and a thirtyish man in a brown leather jacket. They looked at Oliver without speaking. He expected to be told to sit down. Instead the man in the brown jacket got to his feet and instructed Oliver to follow him. He led him back downstairs and turned into the garden behind the build-

213

ing, where he put one foot on a stone bench, assuming this Napoleonic stance in order to say:

"My name is Gomez, Major Alfonso Gomez. I am an officer of the Mexican army assigned to the presidential guard at this moment on temporary duty with the office of the secretary of government." From an inside pocket of his jacket he took a sealed white envelope, handed it to Oliver. "This letter came today. Read it."

Oliver tore the envelope open and read the note inside.

The bearer, Major Alfonso Gomez, was dispatched to San Cristóbal de las Casas with these instructions:

a) He is to investigate rumors of backing of the so-called Movement for México Irredenta by a friendly foreign power;

b) He is empowered to call on the local authorities for cooperation should he need it;

c) In view of your inquiries of me concerning this movement and in view of your informing me that you were yourself traveling to San Cristóbal de las Casas, I have informed him he is authorized to put himself in contact with you to solicit whatever knowledge you may have of the above-mentioned movement, in particular the details of backing by a friendly foreign power. I need not to tell you how seriously my government would view such intervention in Mexican affairs. I trust you will cooperate in every way with Major Gomez by furnishing him with whatever information you have on this matter. You may deal with Major Gomez as though dealing directly with me. He represents me personally in this manner.

The signature scrawled at the end was that of Diego.

"Well," said Oliver, "would you like to read this, Major?"

"No."

"Perhaps you had better keep it, anyway." Oliver handed the envelope back to him. "That's clear enough. What can I do for you?"

"You can answer the question," said Major Gomez, showing himself not given to wasting time on formalities.

"Which is?"

"See here, Mr. Oliver." Major Gomez took his foot off the bench. He took either end of the narrow brown shawl that hung around his neck and adjusted them until they hung evenly below the belt line of his brown trousers. As Inocencio had said, the major was small in stature, neat. The jacket and the matching brown clothing were as close as he could get to being in uniform and still wear civilian clothes. "Don't waste my time. There are at least five of you Americans in San Cristóbal in one way or another connected with the political element at Casa del Futuro.

"Today, a leader of that same political element addressed a number of Americans in the auditorium of the church of Santo Domingo. You were there. This is not the first group to be so addressed in that auditorium in the past ten days. Foreign newspaper people have conducted interviews at Casa del Futuro, and we have learned that two television crews are coming from the United States, as well as one all the way from Spain, to film interviews as well. A Congressman Beerson in the state of Texas the night before last gave an interview on television in Corpus Christi praising this movement, this so-called México Irredenta. The question I put to you—and I know the letter I gave you instructs you to give me every assistance in this matter—the question is this and only this: Is a presumably friendly foreign power lending support to this movement?"

"Yes, Major Gomez. I think it is."

The major was surprised, as if by merely touching Oliver he had caused him to fall over. It took him a moment to recover. "You think it is. What does that mean? Either you know or you don't."

"I need to gather evidence to confirm what I think. With any luck I'll have it tomorrow."

"Never mind luck and never mind tomorrow. We're going back upstairs now, and the *licenciado* will depose you. Come along."

"Wait, Major. I'm not the person to give the deposition. Furthermore, I suggest that we do not conduct such a sensitive interview in front of the *licenciado*.''

"Don't come on me like that, coming to Mexico and telling us how to conduct our affairs. See here—I say the word and the men of Seguridad Pública will go out and haul the whole lot of you in."

"Exactly! Like sending the sergeant to arrest me. Hardly the method the secretary of government himself would use did he want to ask me a question."

"It is not correct to allege that the sergeant arrested you. But if he had, I am sure the secretary of government would agree that you would have deserved it. Come along."

Oliver put his own foot up on the bench, resting one forearm on his knee, leaving the other arm free to be raised to emphasize his point. "Hear me, Major. The secretary of government will be extremely interested in the answer to the question of interference by a friendly foreign power. He will need to consider the implications of that answer carefully. He will want to consult with others. The president himself, I daresay. He will need to decide how to deal with those responsible, those here and those elsewhere. I am sure he trusts you and depends on your discretion, am I correct in that?"

Major Gomez nodded, frowning with impatience.

"Thus he would not want the *licenciado*, the sergeant, the policeman, their wives, their children, their friends spreading the contents of a deposition all about San Cristóbal, on the streets, in the cafés, in the—"

"All right, all right, Señor Oliver. What is your point?"

"Talking to foreign reporters, to television crews, to Mexican reporters, so that the secretary himself would hear the news first on the television, then read it."

The major had whirled about and gone further into the garden. Oliver watched him walking in a small circle, his arms folded, frowning at the ground. He came back to where Oliver still stood with one leg on the the bench, looking as though he would like to assert a prior claim to the podium as well as to the pose, stroked his chin with one hand, and said, "And if that were correct, what would you suggest?"

"Let me leave and I'll report to you in the morning."

"Impossible!"

"I will give you my parole, my oath as an officer."

Major Gomez curled his lip at Oliver. "You are not an officer. You are a civilian."

Oliver nodded at the major. "I see. You don't have the authority. If that is the case—perhaps you do not want to take the responsibility—call the secretary and ask him for instructions."

Gomez reached to take his chin in one hand, looked at his feet again, and then at Oliver.

"What time tomorrow?"

"You can forget about a fishnet," Inocencio Brown said to Oliver. "Closest fishnet, that's down at Puerto Madero, maybe Puerto Aristo."

"I was afraid you'd come up with some objection or other. So what we need now is a pair of heavy-duty scissors—better make that shears. Here," said Oliver, "let's do another list." He wrote. "And let's see now, cord, two of those balls, stout stuff. Clothesline, preferably not plastic, one of those loops say about twenty feet. Wire cutters."

"Wire cutters?" Inocencio shrugged. "Everything else is in the car. I'll honk the horn out front, I get back."

"What I want to know," said Drew, who was opening a cold bottle of white wine, "is what you think you'll come up with for the major in the morning." He chuckled. "I wager the jail here is something to behold."

"If I don't come up with something in the morning, I wager you'll behold it."

Drew shook his head. "It's a mistake to trust Grogan. He knows exactly what you're up to."

"Oh, Harley. Don't be such a fusspot."

"What am I supposed to do? Sit here forever, waiting for you?"

"Go look at Santo Domingo. It's very well done. A good baroque facade. Or go down the other way to El Carmen and look at the tower. Unusual."

"And be pounced on by Major Gomez while admiring these monuments? Thank you very much."

They were silent for a time, Drew reading a book and occasionally sipping wine. Oliver drawing on the pad, looking over at Drew from time to time. Finally Oliver said, "Don't you want to come along, Harley?"

Drew was sighting the wine carefully as he refilled his glass. "The Boy Scout aspects of our work have never interested me, as you may remember, Ted. Go earn another merit badge."

When he heard the horn outside, Oliver turned with his hand on the door to the courtyard of the Luz del Día. "We'll be back for dinner."

"I doubt it."

When Oliver got in the car Inocencio grinned. "I was thinking. One long time since I'm out on a black-bag job."

"Got your black bag?"

"What I need I got in my pocket. All that stuff, what you wanted, that's ina back there. Where we going?"

"Drive up to the *periférico*. We're on reconnaissance."

"You think we oughta drive by it's still daylight?"

"No. We're after something else."

"Oh. Too bad Harley feels that way. We could use another body," Inocencio observed.

"Yeah. Harley prefers to stand on the battlements, shining his powerful intellect on the problem, leave the rough stuff to his intellectual inferiors."

"Rough stuff takes some intellect, too, someone ought to tell Harley."

"He knows that. He's in a sulk now because deep down inside he would like to go along. Trouble is he's too heavy to be easily maneuverable."

They were at the corner of Ejercito Nacional when Oliver shouted to Inocencio, "Stop!" Oliver was rolling his window down.

"I got cars behind me."

Oliver stuck his head out the window and shouted to a young man standing on the corner. "Pete! Hurry up! Jump in back." When Sanders was in the car Brown sped on up General Utrilla, leaving the church of Santo Domingo on their left. His eyes went to the rearview mirror to look at Pete Sanders. "Inocencio, this is Pete Sanders. Pete, this is Inocencio Brown." Sanders shut his mouth, which had been hanging open, and acknowledged the introduction. "Pete's come to apprehend me. Right?"

"This is amazing. I just left the Posada. They said you were staying there, but the desk said you'd gone to Tuxtla Gutiérrez. I was, like, what do I do now?"

Oliver laughed. He turned to talk to Sanders in the back of the car. "Move that stuff over. What's the latest news?"

"Lankester wouldn't show me the message from headquarters. It came flash precedence. Chas was bouncing off the walls. 'Get down there to San Cristobal'—mispronouncing it—'and get Oliver back here. I mean right now, Sanders!' "

"You sure as hell got here fast."

"Chartered a plane to Tuxtla. Rented a car there. Not even a toothbrush."

Oliver laughed. "Chas explain how you get me back to Mexico City? Why didn't he come himself?"

Sanders grinned. "You know Chas. He really thought you had gone up to the Cañon del Cobre."

"I went there once," said Brown.

"Didn't you believe me?"

Sanders shook his head. "Mrs. Pott and I knew better. She said you were leading everyone down the garden path."

"How's Mrs. Pott bearing up?"

"Thank God for Mrs. Pott. We've been getting together in corners. She giggles a lot. Lankester comes storming in, telling us to get back to work."

"I feel I've been away for years. What work?"

"Nothing. He sat there frowning at me. I suspect he was trying to decide if he should send me up to Cañon de Cobre. I was about ready to go, too, anything to get away from there."

"You see Marge?"

"Called her from the airport before I left. Told her I was coming here. She knew you were here. Said to give you her love."

"Telephone operator must have told her. I didn't want Lankester bothering her."

"He did anyway. Not very nice, Chas, when he gets nervous. What are we doing?"

"Pete, Inocencio and I have something lined up. Best thing for you, I think, is to hop out along here and we'll see how things look in the morning. Where you staying?"

"Nowhere. Why can't I come along?"

"Hey, Pete here, he's one of ours, isn't he?" said Inocencio.

"I sure am."

"We could use another body."

"Oh, hell, Pete, okay," said Oliver. "Here's the story."

Some ten minutes later Oliver spoke excitedly. "Look! There! Exactly what we're after."

Inocencio slowed down. "That's some kinda school there. In back of a church. That's not so good."

"Forget what the priests told you. This is one of those ends that justify the means, Inocencio," said Oliver.

"You must be a Jesuit."

"Better keep moving. It'll be dark enough soon."

They were driving past the stark rear of a yellow-painted building with a fenced-in cement tennis court at the corner. Beyond was a soccer field. "What is it you're looking for, a dog?" asked Sanders.

"Dog?" exclaimed Oliver and Brown at the same time.

They came back at dusk, twenty minutes later. Inocencio stopped the car. "Who would keep a dog on a tennis court, anyway?" asked Oliver.

"Maybe they think someone crazy come along try to steal their net," said Inocencio. "I don't think it's such a good idea, taking it from a church. Bad luck, maybe. What the kids gonna do?"

"You know any good-luck tennis courts in town? I bet the priests don't let the kids play on their court, anyway, Inocencio." Oliver got out and walked across the street to the gate at the tennis court. "Nice boy," he said to the dog.

The dog was a high-legged, long-haired black mongrel, half

black Labrador, half Irish wolfhound by Oliver's analysis. He came to the fence and sniffed at Oliver, wagging his tail. Oliver regarded him for a moment, opened the gate, and stood back. The dog contemplated the opening and trotted out to sniff at Oliver's trouser leg. "Good boy," said Oliver, not touching the dog. The dog turned to look down the street, walked a few steps, broke into a trot, his gait picking up as he went out of sight around the corner.

"Some kid leaves him in there." Brown was standing by Oliver. "You really want—? Okay, better just go ahead quick now if we're going to do it, not stand around talking all night. Here the wire cutters."

"Pete, keep an eye up and down the street, will you?"

Oliver and Brown were panting, partly from exertion and partly from nervousness. "Good thing we bring these damn cutters," said Brown. "Take this knife and cut those cords at the bottom."

"Okay. I got 'em."

"Get the wire outta the top. Mary, mother of Jesus, stealing from a church! Hold while I pull."

"Okay. Let's roll her up and get the hell outta here."

"Cut in half is twenty-one feet. That's no good," said Oliver.

"Three into forty-two is fourteen, still pretty big," said Inocencio Brown.

"Yeah. Four into forty-two is ten plus," said Oliver. "Still hard to handle."

"Look," said Sanders. "Cut it into six pieces and tie two pieces together. That makes a net each for us and they're almost square."

"How fortunate you dropped by, Mr. Sanders," observed Drew. "We would have been stumbling over the arithmetic of that complex problem all night. I'd give a bottle of wine to know what the people outside were saying when you were dragging that net through the courtyard."

"Oh, Harley. We didn't drag it and nobody—where are those shears?"

"Still bothers me taking it away from kids at a church like that."

"Oh, come on, Inocencio. We'll put an apology in the poor box and enough for a new net. Really!"

"Wonder how much one of these sets you back," continued Inocencio gloomily.

"You don't want them bringing the dinner in here, do you, with your swag spread all over the floor? Mr. Sanders, be good enough to come along and we'll fetch your plates. I have already eaten. I could not wait any longer."

"Thank you, Harley," said Oliver, over his shoulder from where he squatted by Brown on the floor. "See, Inocencio? He wishes us well. It's just that he'd die rather than admit it."

Chapter 23

"Neither do I," whispered Oliver. "Wonder where he is." He and Brown were sitting quietly on a blanket they had flung on the top of the wall enclosing the grounds of the Casa del Futuro. Although there were no shards of glass embedded in the top of the wall, the blanket made the cold stone capping more bearable. Oliver's legs dangled on the inside of the wall. Inocencio straddled it. They had parked the car among the pine trees that flanked the wall on the road running past the left side of the compound. The dark mass of the main house within its own walls could be seen fifty yards off to their right.

"See anything?" That was Sanders below them on the road side of the wall.

"No. Not a sign yet," said Oliver. "I don't know what's the best thing to do—sure as hell once we get down in there he'd show up."

"Maybe make some noise," Sanders called up to them.

"He gets ahold of us, we make some noise, all right." Inocencio was blinking, peering about the gloom of the grounds.

"I'd get down if there were a tree anywhere close enough to the wall to get back out again."

"Better not do that," Inocencio whispered, adding, as though to himself, "Bad luck can come, taking that net the way we did. Wait! Over there. What's that?"

"That's him," said Oliver.

"Who?" asked Sanders.

"Bruto," said Oliver. There was moon enough to show Bruto padding along the path that ran up the slope to the left toward the gardener's shed. The animal snuffled with his nose close to the ground, pacing with hindquarters high. "Sst!" said Oliver. Bruto stopped immediately, holding his narrow head high, moving it slightly from one side to the other, searching. "Sst!"

Bruto was trotting, head up and shoulders high, over the uneven ground through the pines toward them. The twists of his cropped ears stood like horns on his head.

"We used to say, dog inside, stay outside."

"Well, Inocencio, this's the only chance we got." Oliver was watching the dog with something a good deal like fear stirring deep inside him.

"I know. I just remember that."

Bruto emitted a low sound between a grunt and a growl. He had seen them and he began coursing about beneath them, sniffing the ground, from time to time stopping, raising his head to look at them. Trotting off to one side, he lay down beneath the pines, paws in front of him, hind legs cocked under him, watching them, ears alert.

"Ugly animal!" said Oliver. "What a nice mutt that was, back there at the tennis court. We draw this stupid beast, flopped down on his belly like a toad. How we ever going to get a net over him?"

"Where'd he go?" That was Sanders. The two of them reached down to give Sanders a hand, pulling him up to hang on, legs off the ground, chest across the top of the wall. "Do we know for sure he's vicious?"

"You volunteering to find out?" asked Oliver.

"Not so stupid, anyway. Pretty smart," said Inocencio. "He figures he let us make the next move. Shoulda brought Bruto a nice piece a steak," said Inocencio. "He go off somewhere and eat it."

"Then come back and eat us. Okay, fellows. Our strategy is perfect. Tactics seem to be the problem at the moment."

Bruto yawned, relaxing his hindquarters and putting his head down between his paws. "Bruto, he's got all night," said Inocencio. "He got nowhere to go."

"Well, we've got to do something. Pete. See that pine over there with the double trunk? Okay. Let's get down, Inocencio.

On this side, I mean.'' Sanders slid down and the other two jumped to stand beside him. They could hear Bruto whining on the other side of the wall. "Where's that clothesline? Thanks." Oliver tied a bowline with a small loop and pulled the knot tight. "Think that'll hold all right. That slippery plastic stuff might not. Wish I'd thought of gloves." He passed the end of the line through the loop made by the bowline. "There. That runs free enough." Oliver explained the plan and asked: "Any suggestions? Okay, then. Pete, you go with Inocencio down about a hundred feet that way, give Inocencio a leg up on the wall. Then you come back here. Inocencio, you get Bruto's attention, get him down there. When you've got him interested, give me a whistle. Like this." Oliver gave a low whistle and Inocencio repeated it.

When Sanders came back he and Oliver waited behind the wall. Oliver's heart was beating hard and he was short of breath. He relieved the tension in his hands by coiling and recoiling the line tight around his left hand, loop in his fist, telling Sanders to get ready to give him a leg up. Sanders bent and laced his fingers together at knee level and Oliver rested his left foot in Sanders's hands, right side against the wall. "When I say go give me all you've got. When Inocencio runs back you get on top and stand by."

"I know, I know."

"Good! Glad to hear it." You can't do these stupid things, Oliver thought, unless you're all hopped up.

They could hear Inocencio hissing at the dog. In another moment Inocencio whistled and Oliver said, "Go!" in a hoarse whisper. Sanders heaved Oliver so hard he nearly went headfirst over the wall. Oliver swung to slither down the wall on the inside, turned, searched the shadows for what seemed to be a disastrous stretch of time, baffled by the different perspective at ground level. His head was jerking about until he found his tree, then he was running for it as hard as he could across pine needles soft on the ground, not daring to take the time to look through the shadows and the trunks of the pines toward where Inocencio was hissing and grunting, slapping his hands on the wall.

Oliver reached the tree and leaped to grab with his right hand a broken stub that stuck out on the lower part of the pine. He stuck a foot on a lower stub and pulled himself up, being jerked to a stop when his pocket caught on still another of the sharp stubs. He heaved to rip the cloth, his other foot scraping at the trunk to find a hold to boost him into the U-shaped cleft where the trunk parted. Something seized that foot hard and Oliver kicked back at it, feeling the shoe go off. Somehow he pulled himself, gasping for air, into the cleft. He turned to see Bruto, growling, shake the shoe and toss it to one side. Snarling, the dog leaped in the air, standing then on hind legs, holding one foot against the trunk of the tree, pawing at the bark with the other forepaw, gaping at Oliver. "Good boy," said Oliver as he slipped the loop over the dog's neck. He yanked at it, throwing the free end over the limb beside him. "Pete!"

Sanders came running through the moonlight holding a rolled net in both hands out in front of him, as though running an obstacle race at an office picnic. Bruto was thrashing from side to side to free himself of the noose, gargling, backing away, front legs just brushing the ground, as Oliver looped the line around the limb again and again. Sanders and the dog were struggling. "One—net's—not—" Sanders grunting, the dog snarling. Oliver put two half hitches in the line with clumsy fingers and climbed down, falling on his knees to help Sanders hold the thrashing animal. "Get another net!" Sanders gasped.

Oliver looked hopelessly at the wall, Inocencio and the nets on the other side. Then he saw a net flop up on the wall followed by Inocencio's head as he clambered up the net as though up the side of a ship, throwing another net ahead of himself as he reached the top of the wall.

The three of them subdued the dog and tied the nets into a package with the rest of the clothesline. The dog was whining now somewhere within the bundle. "The hell's my shoe?" asked Oliver. "Maybe—I think maybe—I'm getting too old—this sort of thing."

"Me too," said Sanders.

"Let's get the tools, Pete," said Brown.

The door to the guest house had a padlock on a hasp outside. "Good," whispered Oliver. "Means no one's in there with him."

"Also means I can't get through that kinda padlock." Inocencio played the light on it. "I think I can take off those screws."

"They'll know we've been here. But go ahead," said Oliver. "Don't be too finicky. We're in a hurry."

"Glad I brought the *como se llama*, what you call it, crowbar, they call it goat foot in Spanish."

"Crowbar, the continuation of lock picking by other means," whispered Sanders.

"No. Wait! You were right the first time, Inocencio. Take out one set of screws."

When Inocencio pushed the door open they waited quietly a moment. A gust of foul air curled out from inside.

"Ough!" said Sanders.

The sitting room was small, dark, empty. The three of them stood quiet. A sound of rough breathing came from the room beyond. "Gimme that flashlight, Pete. Wait here. Keep an eye out. Inocencio, you'd better come with me."

After five minutes Oliver and Inocencio came back, whispering to each other.

"What's up?" asked Sanders from the door.

"Pete, we've got to protect the old man until Gomez gets here."

"Who's Gomez?"

"Inocencio'll explain. Inocencio, screw the hasp back on with the lock on it the way it was. Lock me in here. And let me have that crowbar. Anyone tries to get in, I'll give 'em a taste of *como se llama*."

The three were crouching in the darkness at the door while Inocencio started to put the screws back in. "Damn! Where'd that one go?" Inocencio was fumbling about on the ground. "Pete. Give me light."

"Then get to the Palacio Municipal. Gomez said he'd be waiting there. Old Mora needs a doctor, too, but don't wait around for that. Bring Gomez to our position at the wall and throw him over.''

"Gotcha.''

"Pete, get up on the wall and wait for Inocencio and Gomez to come back—and check Bruto to be sure he's still tied up good. Go sit on the wall. Don't let anyone see you.''

Oliver went in behind the closed door and waited. When the other two left, he took a chair in by Don Saturnino's bed and sat in the stench, listening to the rattle of the old man's breathing, trying himself to breath as little of the foul air as he could.

At the Palacio Municipal Major Gomez had ordered the drowsy blue-clad duty squad of Seguridad Pública del Estado into line. Concealing his feelings, as a good leader must even though he doubts the material he has to work with is up to the challenge, Gomez was inspecting each man's state of readiness for combat. He was determined that the mission would not fail because of any professional lapse on his own part. An agitated Inocencio Brown was again insistently whispering in Gomez's ear that they leave for the Casa del Futuro.

At that moment Oliver was standing behind the door of the guest house, crowbar in hand, breathing with his mouth open, listening to the sounds of stealthy breathing on the other side of the door. As determined as Major Gomez not to fail in his part, he was ready to use the crowbar for serious work, should the person on the outside try to come in.

Crouching on the wall, obeying the order not to let himself be seen, Sanders was squinting at the guest house, where he could make out the figure standing to listen at the door. The only sound was an occasional snore from Bruto, asleep in his tennis-net cocoon.

The assault on the Casa del Futuro was a disappointment to Major Gomez because of the manner in which the enemy garrison fell. This came about because the task of feeding Bruto had over time been delegated by the dog handler to Pilar, the cook's wife. Bruto had come to respect her not only for the feeding but for the affection she showed him, a notable contrast with the cruel manner of his handler. Along with this, Bruto had become Pilar's only confidant among the inhabitants of the Casa del Futuro. Her husband, the cook, was no more sympathetic than the others in that house. In Bruto she had found someone who would listen to her.

It was Bruto's custom, late in his night patrols when he felt that he had been outside long enough, to scratch and whine at the back gate of the house. This usually happened around four in the morning. Thus the dog handler had also delegated to Pilar the additional duty of letting Bruto in and tying him up.

When Bruto did not turn up this winter morning, after she had several times opened the gate to look for him, Pilar dressed and went outside to find him.

Major Gomez and Inocencio Brown arrived at the wall to find Sanders absent from his post. They could hear voices on the other side. Sanders had disobeyed his orders when he saw the dark figure leave the guest house to approach Bruto's bundle and kneel by it to utter a distressed cry. The person had begun to fumble with the lashings about the nets when Sanders dropped softly to the ground and ran to hurl himself on that shape.

The voices Gomez and Inocencio heard were those of Sanders and Pilar assuring each other of their good intentions, Sanders embarrassed at having tackled a tiny middle-aged woman and Pilar reciting over and over to Sanders that her sole concern was the well-being of the dog.

Thus the sleeping garrison was betrayed by Pilar's leading Major Gomez and his command through the back door—only after she had been promised that she could return to liberate Bruto when her task was accomplished.

On Inocencio's advice, Gomez ordered the squad to segregate their prisoners in various rooms of the house and keep them isolated for questioning. The only casualty during the assault was the dog handler, bitten on the lower leg when Pilar led Bruto in to visit him in the room where the dog handler sat cold, hungry, legs manacled and arms tied around the back of a hard chair. Bruto yielded immediately to the impulse the situation suggested.

The unexpected attack inflamed the dog handler's sense of grievance to the point that he confessed, when questioned right afterward by Inocencio and the *licenciado*, to his part in the murder of General Robles. He accused the chief of administration of the killing and Chato Escobar of the planning on the ground in Guanajuato. The murder of Robles had been ordered by Victor Mora. Robles was killed for the impertinence of asking questions about Mora's birth in Canada, said the dog handler, and because Mora feared that old Robles was going to gossip about that to others.

"Hardly grounds for murder, that," observed the *licenciado*, staring at the dog handler with distaste.

The dog handler managed a shrug, bound as he was. "I've seen men killed for less," he observed. "Anyone got a cigarette?"

Another disappointment to Major Gomez was the failure of an inventory of the prisoners to show Victor Mora among them. Gomez was walking back and forth in the courtyard in the first cold gray light, a hand on either end of his brown shawl, sawing it back and forth around his neck. The lack of resistance at the Casa del Futuro had robbed him of the chance to distinguish himself in combat. To compensate for being robbed of this minor glory, the deposition the *licenciado* was taking from the dog handler promised to bring immense credit to Major Gomez in army circles. It was no small victory to have found the murderers of General Robles. On the other hand, Victor Mora, the real leader of this despicable México Irredenta faction, had escaped, thereby diminishing the major's accomplishments.

"You must come with me, Major, and hear what Don Saturnino has to say. He is an important witness."

"Yes, in a moment, Oliver. When the *licenciado* has finished with the other. I must think."

Oliver was sitting on a bench against the wall—he could have fallen asleep were it not for the chill damp of the air—in the misty courtyard of the Casa del Futuro at first light, watching the major pace back and forth. Pedro Sanders had passed a groggy ten minutes picking somberly at the tears in his suit, the only clothes he had with him, before getting up to swing his arms to keep warm. Inocencio Brown had sat down on the bench beside Oliver two minutes before and gone to sleep immediately, the old campaigner, neck twisted back against the wall, mouth open. Oliver stretched to search for comfort as he watched Major Gomez pace. He put his own tired legs out to rest on a terra-cotta pot. He stared dully at the huge green leaves of the *quequeshte* plant growing in the pot, dully irritated by the regular crunching of Gomez's shoes as they went back and forth on the flagstones.

Major Gomez suddenly stopped and looked over at Oliver. "Yes," he said. Oliver put his feet on the ground. "One moment," said Gomez, and called to the fat sergeant. Instead of going with Oliver to the guest house, he began issuing a series of orders to the sergeant. "Call the police in Tuxtla Gutiérrez. Have a watch set at the airport to prevent Mora's leaving."

"Yes, sir."

"Send a detachment to the bus depot. He may be heading for Guatemala. Inform the police at Tapachula and at, at—"

"Ciudad Cuauhtémoc, sir."

"At Ciudad Cuauhtémoc, Sergeant."

"Yes, sir."

"The buses to Palenque and to Villahermosa. What else?"

"The airport at Villahermosa, sir."

Oliver walked to the kitchen. There sat the cook, bound sullen on his chair. Through the small pig eyes in his fat face he glared redly at Oliver. Pilar stood scrawny at the stove in a brown dress, a black rebozo around her shoulders, stirring something in a pot. "Pilar," said Oliver. "What about Don Saturnino?"

"I'm heating this for him," she said, turning her eyes, deep in dark hollows in the thin face, to regard Oliver.

"Good. Let me take it to him."

"The door is locked," she said. "I have the key. I'll

go with you," she said, pouring a thick brown gruel from the pot. Oliver started to pick up the bowl but exclaimed at the heat of it.

"Give the gentleman some cloths," the cook ordered Pilar from his chair. "How do you expect the gentleman to carry it?" He curled his lip, showing his yellow teeth at the two of them.

"Poor Don Saturnino," said Pilar as they went toward the gate.

"What do you think of Victor, the son?"

She stopped to turn and stare solemnly at Oliver. "I tell you the truth," she said. "I believe him to be the evil one." She crossed herself and stared a moment more at Oliver, sending a shiver to running on his spine.

Pilar led the way to the gate, where Bruto scrambled to his feet, wagging his bobbed tail at Pilar, his whole hind end dancing, assuming the bowl of gruel to be his. He stopped moving, went still, when he saw Oliver. He growled.

"Well, Brutito, little beast. For shame. Don't bother the gentleman." Pilar handed Oliver the bowl, now insulated by dirty dish towels, and untied Bruto, who came toward Oliver, sniffing at the scent of the gruel. "Careful, not so close," she said, tugging at his leash. "This way, señor. Come, little beast."

She led the way around the back to the guest house, Bruto pulling her along, Oliver well back, walking with small steps, both hands holding the full bowl of steaming gruel, balancing the lid on top of it.

"Look!" Pilar exclaimed. "The window."

It was the window to the sitting room that Oliver had opened to climb through when Sanders had tapped on it to let him know that Gomez had arrived. He explained that to Pilar. She shook her head. "It's against the rules to open the windows, señor." Bruto growled as though to emphasize the need to observe house regulations. Pilar pulled him close to her as she unlocked the padlock.

"Leave it unlocked," said Oliver as he brushed by her to enter the guest house.

"That's against the rules too," she said.

"Please," said Oliver. "I'll shut the window. And please tell Major Gomez I'll wait for him here."

Despite his asking, Oliver heard Pilar snap the padlock shut as she left. So he set the bowl down and pulled the window wide open.

Don Saturnino was lying on his back, the rumpled bedclothes lying almost flat on his emaciated figure. In the blue of the misty morning light his face was a yellow green, eyes sunken in his head, frightened, searching Oliver's face, lips black, the mouth open and gasping. He mouthed something at Oliver and tossed his head back and forth on the bed.

Oliver put the bowl on the bedside table and noticed the pillow lying on the floor. As he picked it up and leaned to raise Don Saturnino's head the old man cried out: "No! No!"

Oliver smiled to reassure him and reached to lift the old man's head. Don Saturnino moved his head from side to side. "No!" he said again, turning his face to avoid the pillow. Oliver had to lift the old head and force the pillow under it. At that Don Saturnino quieted down, still gasping. As Oliver found himself gagging in the close air of the small room, even more fetid than he had found it before, he unlocked a window by the bed and strained to yank it open, beating it with the palm of his hand, forcing it open wide, hoping for a cross draft to sweep out the air.

As he brought the bowl of steaming gruel to the bedside table he saw he had no spoon. Although the gruel was still far too hot to feed the old man, Oliver began to look for one, pulling open a drawer in the table, finding there only a set of false teeth. He got up to crawl out the window to go to the kitchen for a spoon. Noticing a door to a small closet he had not seen in the dark of his previous visit, he decided to look in there.

He turned the knob to open the closet door. It burst open and Oliver staggered back against the bed, spinning about and losing his balance, grabbing at the wall, falling to the floor. Victor Mora stood at the closet door, the crowbar raised in the hand above his head.

Chapter 24

"Stay where you are," said Victor. In his left hand was a Colt automatic, the slide drawn back, ready to fire. "Not a sound." He was panting, nervous, showing the whites of his eyes like an unreliable horse. The eyes rolled over to where Don Saturnino lay staring back at him from the cavity beneath his brows.

"Impostor," croaked Don Saturnino.

"Shut up!" said Victor.

"Murderer!" said the old man.

"Fool," replied Victor, his eyes turning back to Oliver.

"No, he's not," said Oliver, using English.

"You're the CIA one, aren't you? The one who calls himself Oliver. What's your real name?" Victor sneered.

Oliver kept his eyes on him, meanwhile carefully trying to get his feet into a less helpless position, sprawled as he was, half on his back—difficult to feel any confidence like that. Victor was stooping to let the crowbar carefully down to the floor behind him, quickly switching the pistol to his right hand. "Keep still!" His voice was low but shrill, unsteady. "Don't move again like that. I can use this, you know." His eyes narrowed then rolled again toward the window, to the old man, back to Oliver. "I don't mind killing both of you. Not at all. Everyone. Who else is there?"

"Listen, Victor. I was looking for you. We've got to talk, you and I. Enough killing. If you hadn't killed General Robles, I wouldn't be here."

"Another old fool, sticking his nose in where it didn't belong.

Like you. I asked you—" He jerked the pistol at Oliver. "Who is here? Where are they?"

"The police are all over the place. You can't get away. Put the gun away, Victor. It's too late for that."

"You'd better do as I tell you. You're going to get me out of here. Have you a car?"

"No way you can get to a car, Victor."

"You had better pray we find a way. You're going where I go. Wherever that may be. Understand?"

Oliver started to say, "That's crazy," but Victor looked so crazy, his eyes bulging, that he turned it into, "That's—unnecessary. There's nothing to worry about. The Mexicans won't want a scandal. They'll let you go back to Cuba."

"So! Robles knew. I was right. He had to die! But he told you. Too bad for you."

"No, he didn't have time to tell me. He did mention Canada. That got me thinking. That's such a standard gambit, after all. Papering an illegal in a third country, I mean." Oliver was trying to get Victor to discuss his case, his future, rationally. "The baptismal record in the church, the birth certificate in the vital-records department of some Canadian municipality, in some name or other. Victor Smith, Victor Jones. The date would be there to back up your identity. Well, it almost worked, Victor. Now, what you want to do is—"

"You talk like a file clerk." Victor showed his contempt. "Is that your only interest? Those dusty records? What do they matter now?" His eyes narrowed and he smiled, looking less crazy but quite evil with that. "Ah, of course. Counterespionage. The counterespionage clerk naked without his files. You're in a different world now, Oliver. The real world. Stand up!"

Oliver nodded, pulling himself stiffly to a sitting position. "Sure thing," he said. "But you see, when Don Saturnino called you an impostor during our interview the other day—"

"You old fool!" That was in Spanish to old Mora, starting him off again.

"Impostor!"

"Shut up!"

"Look, Victor. The Mexicans know all about you now. That

you're from the Dirección General de Inteligencia. That's okay. Really. The Mexicans don't mind that sort of thing. I mean, nowadays, who cares—''

"Shut up! And get up, clerk," said Victor. Oliver began to rise, holding on to the bedside table. "Now, stay right there and listen to me carefully." Oliver, standing next to the bedside table, could feel the waves of heat from the bowl of gruel. Don Saturnino gave a deep groan. "Stand right there. You go out that window, first. Stop! Not until I tell you. I'll have this pistol on you. And the two of us walk to the house, you in front of me, close. I'll be happy to kill you if you try any tricks, clerk." He snatched the pillow from under Don Saturnino's head. The old man was struggling to get his arms out from under the blanket. A feeble cawing came from his wattled throat.

There was a noise from outside, someone fumbling with the padlock. "No spoon!" It was Pilar cackling and laughing. "What a thing! We forgot the spoon."

Victor slammed the pillow on the old man's face with his free hand. "That cretin of a woman!" His lips were drawn back from his teeth.

Oliver snatched the lid from the bowl, sailing it toward Victor without looking where it went, seized the bowl, hardly feeling the heat on his hands, hurled it toward Victor's face, not pausing to see the effect, and dived out the open window, rolling over and over as he hit the ground.

When he stopped rolling to a haven behind a pine tree, he brushed pine needles and dirt from his eyes and mouth and peered toward the corner of the guest house. At the other side of the house, standing next to Pilar and at a distance from Bruto, stood Major Gomez, looking back at Oliver, surprised. Oliver shouted, "Look out, Gomez!" Victor, his hair and the front of his white *guayabera* a mess of gruel, was climbing out the same window by which Oliver had left, the arm with the pistol held in front of him. He fired once in Oliver's direction, running around the corner of the house, caught sight of Gomez, fired at him, turned then to run for the wall, where the nets by which Sanders and Inocencio had entered were still hanging.

Oliver heard Gomez call out to Pilar and she knelt to unleash

Bruto, who sprang running after Victor. "Wait!" Oliver shouted at Gomez, who had taken two steps forward with his pistol in his right hand. Oliver came to his feet just as Gomez stuck out a stiff arm and fired once, twice, and a third time. Oliver saw Victor fling his arms wide as his feet stopped running and his torso plunged into the carpet of pine needles. Bruto danced up to the body, pounced on it with his forefeet, drew back, sniffed at it, paced about it, head down, whined, and sat down, mouth open as though grinning, looking back toward Pilar.

"Why?" Oliver asked Gomez.

Gomez pressed the button to release the magazine from the pistol. He brought the slide back and dropped the extra round on the ground. "He was trying to escape. You could see that, couldn't you?"

Oliver shook his head.

"Just as well, don't you think?" Gomez bent to pick up his unexploded round from the ground. "He failed. His presence is no longer convenient. Not to us. Certainly not to the Cubans. I think he would agree." He blew the round clean of dirt. "Why? Did you Americans want to preserve him for some reason?"

"*Pájaro vaquero*, the cowbird," Oliver was saying as they sat in the courtyard of the Casa del Futuro a half hour later. Major Gomez had convened them there, feeling the need to bring the morning's work to a conclusion with ceremony. Out of courtesy he asked Oliver to speak first. "The female lays her eggs in the nests of other birds. The foster parents are forced unwittingly to nurture the intruder. And thus, by analogy with—" He paused. Translation of the term *brood parisitism* into Spanish was beyond his present powers. He began again. "And so Fidel Castro repaid Mexico for her long-standing friendship for Cuba by placing Victor Mora, whatever his true name may have been, that—"

"Viper," Major Gomez supplied, spoiling Oliver's metaphor. "That viper in our nest."

"Yes, Major." Oliver was diplomatic.

"Indeed a viper," the *licenciado* quickly agreed, "and very nearly a patricide as well. A near thing. Don Saturnino says that

Victor was trying to smother him with a pillow," he added. At Oliver's urging he had taken a quick deposition from Don Saturnino.

"Patricide only if we accept the Cuban legend," said Oliver.

The *licenciado* looked puzzled, glancing from Oliver to Inocencio and then to Sanders, as though wondering which one of them he might depose next.

"I think you'll find a birth certificate, *licenciado*, some such document, among Victor's papers. The legend of his illegitimacy was a pretext to avoid discussion of his Canadian origins. The false proof of birth could always be produced if it came to that. Victor was formally adopted by Don Saturnino when he took the Mora name. The document would show him to be the son of a Canadian woman who had indeed studied in Mexico. The Cubans would have done the research for the legend—a likely mother, a likely name—for their illegal officer in Mexico."

"But Don Saturnino said nothing of that!" exclaimed the *licenciado*.

"Probably he would not," said Oliver. "But Don Saturnino was well aware of the Cuban role."

"To think he could do such a thing!" asked Major Gomez. "So un-Mexican!"

"I suppose Don Saturnino thought that the Cubans would help to bring him the political success he thought he deserved," said Oliver. "You and I are not politicians, Major. We set limits to our ambitions."

"A pact with the devil," said Gomez. But he did not cross himself as Pilar had done.

"We knew only that a Cuban illegal had been sent here on a political mission," continued Oliver, "an ingenious variation on Castro's methods of export of revolution. No matter what happened in Cuba, you see, Castro thought he could ensure the immortality of the Cuban revolution by capturing Don Saturnino's movement and turning it into a political movement in Mexico that would, one way or another, take power."

"Impossible!" said Major Gomez. "Never." He cleared his throat. "I have a confession. When I first talked to you,

Señor Oliver, and you, too, Señor Brown, I had fallen into the error, an excusable error for which I now apologize, of thinking that you were helping México Irredenta—all of you Americans here—and that the 'friendly foreign power' mentioned by the secretary of government was none other than the United States.''

"I'm surprised at you, Major," said Inocencio Brown. "You think we came all the way to the edge of the world here, Chiapas, to help out on a Cuban intelligence operation?"

"Well," said the major, frowning at Inocencio. "I never thought that, exactly. A question," he went on to say, "Señor Oliver. In how many other nests did the cowbird, Castro, lay his eggs?"

"Be a good fellow, Compañero Sanders, and ask them to bring in two bottles of white wine," said Harley Drew. "Champagne would be more suitable, but a decent bottle may be unobtainable in these remote parts—well chilled, mind you."

"What's the occasion, Harley? Giving yourself a *despedida* for the voyage back to France?"

"No, Ted. We are going to have a merit-badge ceremony. How many does that make? And which one is it? Would it be Flagrant Insubordination?"

"Dog Roping," said Inocencio immediately.

Oliver grinned at Drew. "How about Forlorn Hoping?"

Sanders returned, followed by the girl from the bar, with a tray of cold glasses and the wine. He helped her put them on a leather-topped table.

"You are a fine young man, Pedro Sanders. You listen carefully to instructions," said Drew, "and carry them out faithfully. Not the usual thing these days. May you go far!" He raised a glass to Sanders.

"I should have given Jack Winters some credit with Gomez," said Oliver. "He started all this by giving us the lead to Robles."

"I know Jack," said Inocencio Brown. "Wait'll I tell Lester. He knows Jack."

"Everyone knows Jack. A friend of the station." That was Sanders. "And I thought he was just an old blowhard."

"Confess, young man. It's said to be good for the soul. You think us all to be old blowhards," said Drew.

"No, sir! Not at all," said Sanders, his face becoming quite red.

"I know it's made it simpler for the Mexicans, but I can't quite get past the way Gomez shot Victor down," said Oliver.

"Come, come," said Drew. "Your naïveté is showing, Ted. What did you expect to find at the end of your quest? An undiluted happy ending?"

"Orders from Gobernación, I bet you," said Inocencio. "Gomez doesn't do that on his own. Woulda shot him in the legs or let Bruto chew Victor for a while."

Sanders whistled.

"I agree," said Drew. "Your friend Diego did not achieve high office, Ted, by giving in weakly to sentiment."

They were quiet for a moment. "I wonder how Carlos Robles would feel about it," said Oliver.

"General Robles, he's feeling pretty good right now," said Inocencio. "He's glad you pulled it off."

"We pulled it off. No, I mean about history. None of this will come out. It won't make the papers and it won't be in the history books."

"You'll be writing it up, won't you, Ted? It'll lie there in the agency files, won't it?" asked Drew. "It'll lie there until one day it comes out."

"After no one is left to care."

"Oh, some Robles will be there waiting for it, I wager. We have enough to do without trying to arrange the future, I daresay."

Oliver got up and walked over to pour wine into the glasses. "Yes, the present is full enough for us, Harley. One thing, Pete, I wish you'd get back to Mexico City and persuade Lankester to get on home before I get back. We have nothing more to say to each other. Be sure you tell him that we found your imaginary, nonexistent Cuban illegal at the head of the Movement. He may wish to pause on his way out of the agency to contemplate whatever lesson he may find in that.'' Sanders looked pleased. ''You may be able to expedite his leaving by letting it slip that I'm thinking of bringing a Doberman pinscher back to Mexico as station mascot.''

''With pleasure,'' said Sanders. ''I'll tell him to go out and get a tennis net and cut it up in pieces.''

''Be sure it's from a church,'' said Drew.

''Stolen from a church,'' added Oliver, handing out the glasses of wine.

Inocencio shook his head. ''You make a joke out of it, but I tell you we're lucky it didn't turn out any worse.''

''Anything else?'' Sanders asked Oliver.

''No, I called Marge. I'll take care of the other matter when I get back. When I was in Washington, the director told me that he had several jobs coming open that I might be interested in.'' Oliver raised his glass. ''Well, friends, don't think it hasn't been fun.''

Inocencio raised his glass. ''We got a pretty good team right here in Chiapas!''

''How thoughtful of the director!'' said Drew. ''Did he mention anything desirable? Ulan Bator? Punta Arenas? An expedition to the Zambesi?''

''No, he didn't. But I've got an idea. It's not what I want. And it's certainly not what he wants, either. It's what he needs, though. And the agency needs it bad.''

''What would that be?''

''A new inspector general.''

''I thought maybe you already some kinda inspector general,'' said Inocencio, ''you going around trying so hard to protect the outfit, keep those Mexicans from finding out how the agency's mixed up in this México Irredenta scam.''

Oliver stared at Inocencio Brown, astonished, and a smile came slowly onto his face. ''Inocencio! You knew that all along?''

''Knew what?'' said Sanders, looking from one to the

other of them. "What was it you said just now?" he asked Inocencio.

"Look, Pete—" Oliver began.

Drew interrupted. "If I may, Ted. You were tender about Inocencio's illusions. That it now appears that he had none is no reason to destroy them in others. Gentlemen." He raised his glass. "To our illusions!"

About the Author

John Horton grew up on the north shore of Chicago and attended Indiana University before joining the U.S. Navy in 1940. From 1946 to 1948 he studied at the University of Chicago, earning a master's degree in International Relations. He served as an operations officer in the Central Intelligence Agency at posts in the Far East, in Latin America, and in Washington, from 1948 to 1975. He returned to government service in 1983-84 as the National Intelligence Officer for Latin America. He and Grace Calhoun, married for forty years, live on the Patuxent River in St. Mary's County, Maryland. They have four children and five grandchildren.